'I can't give up the case, Mrs Dedrick. I'm busy trying to find out who kidnapped your husband.'

'There's another way of taking care of you,' she said, 'but I'll give you one more chance. Two hundred thousand dollars!'

'Get out,' I said, and threw open the door.

She put her hand on the front of her dress and ripped it down. Then she dug her nails into her shoulder and clawed into her white flesh, leaving four angry red marks on her skin. As she began to disarrange the furniture I reached for the telephone and dialled.

'I'm in trouble, Paula. In five minutes I'll be on a charge of criminal assault. Mrs Dedrick is setting the stage now. Collect Francon and get down to police headquarters, as fast as you can . . .

Also by James Hadley Chase

and published by Corgi Books

James Hadley Chase

Figure it out for Yourself

CORGI BOOKS
A DIVISION OF TRANSWORLD PUBLISHERS LTD

FIGURE IT OUT FOR YOURSELF

A CORGI BOOK 0 552 10716 6

First publication in Great Britain

PRINTING HISTORY
Corgi edition published 1978

Corgi Books are published by
Transworld Publishers Ltd,
Century House, 61–63 Uxbridge Road,
Ealing, London W5 5SA
Made and printed in Great Britain by
Cox & Wyman Ltd, London, Reading and Fakenham

Figure it out
for Yourself

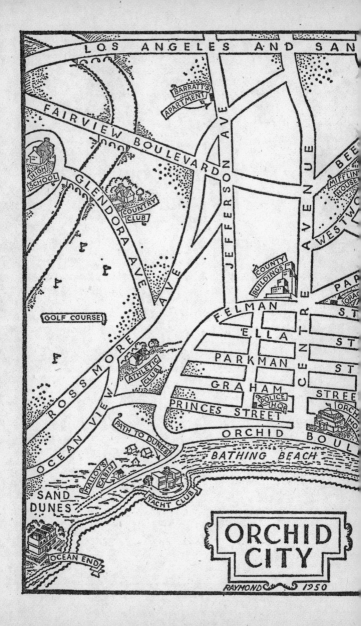

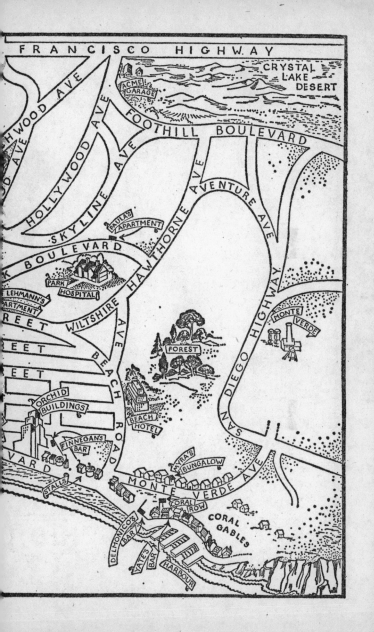

CHAPTER ONE

I

ONE hot June afternoon I was sitting in my office at peace with the world, and conscious that the world was, for a change, at peace with me, when Paula put her dark, lovely head around the door to shatter my pipe-dream.

'You have the Wingrove job to do,' she said.

There are times when I regret having thought up Universal Services. (No matter how tough the job: we'll do it.) As a money-maker it was sound enough, and as somebody else's brainwave it was brilliant, but when I get stuck with something like the Wingrove assignment, then I begin to wonder if I shouldn't have my head examined for putting myself out on such a limb.

The Wingrove assignment was a job I wouldn't have touched with an eighty-foot pole if I had been consulted, but it had sneaked into the office, together with a five-hundred-dollar retainer, when I was in bed with a hangover, and Paula had accepted the money and sent off a receipt.

The daughter of Martin Wingrove, one of Orchid City's most affluent citizens, had reverted to type, and he wanted me to persuade her to return home.

I hadn't much of a proposition to offer her. Wingrove was fat and old and nasty. He kept one of Ralph Bannister's taxi-dancers in a pent-house in Felman Street: a big, brassy blonde whose mode of life would have horrified a monkey. He was grasping, domineering and selfish. His wife had run away with his chauffeur, who was half her age, but hungry for money, and his son was sweating out a drug cure in a private home. Not much of a home background to persuade a girl to return to, but then I hadn't seen her. For all I knew, she was tarred with the same brush. It would be a lot easier for me if she was, and it seemed likely. From Paula's notes on the case, the girl was living with Jeff Barratt, a notoriously vicious playboy who was about as rotten as they come.

I had been offered a free hand. The girl was under age, and

9

Wingrove was within his rights to force her to return home. But Barratt wasn't likely to part with her easily, and she was certain to resist. On the face of it, it looked as if I would be in for quite a time. Obviously, it was a job for the police, but Wingrove had a horror of that kind of publicity. He knew if the police fetched her back, the story would hit the headlines, so he did what so many people have done in the past when they have a particularly dirty job on their hands, he unloaded it on me.

I had been side-stepping the job for the past three days, and had begun to hope that Paula had forgotten about it. I should have known better.

'Eh?' I opened one eye and looked at her reproachfully.

'The Wingrove job,' she said firmly, coming into the office. I sat up.

'How many more times do I have to tell you I don't want that job? Send the money back, and say I'm too busy.'

'You're not suggesting we should refuse five hundred dollars, are you?'

'I don't want the job.'

'What's wrong with it?' she asked patiently. 'It won't take you more than an hour. Why, it would be tempting Providence not to do it.'

'If Providence can be tempted that easy, then I'll tempt it. Now, don't bother me. Get on to Wingrove and tell him we're far too busy to handle the job.'

'I sometimes wonder why we're in business at all,' Paula said acidly. 'I hope you realize there're bills to be paid at the end of the month. I hope you haven't forgotten this desk you insisted on having hasn't yet been paid for.'

I knew she'd go on in this vein all the afternoon if I didn't stop her.

'Well, all right. Send Kerman. Why shouldn't he do a little work for a change? Why should all the dirty jobs have my name on them? You'd think I didn't own this joint the way I'm treated. Give the job to Kerman.'

'He's teaching Miss Ritter to drive.'

'What, again! He's always teaching Miss Ritter to drive! What's the matter with her? No one can take two solid months, six hours a day, to learn to drive a car. There's no one alive who can be that dumb.'

'She thinks Kerman is cute,' Paula said, suppressing a smile. 'I guess it's a matter of taste, but she tells me to sit beside Kerman in a car is an experience all women should have once in a lifetime. I'm not sure if I know what she means. I hope I'm not being unkind, but I think she's neurotic. Anyway, what does it matter? She pays very well.'

'That's all you think about – money! So because Miss Ritter is neurotic and Kerman's cute, I have to do all the dirty work, is that it?'

'You can always engage another assistant,' Paula pointed out.

'Now who's throwing our profits away? Well, all right, but understand from tomorrow Kerman gets down to a job of work. I'll teach Miss Ritter to drive. If she thinks Kerman is an experience, she's in for a surprise.'

'The address is 247 Jefferson Avenue ...' Paula began.

'I know! Don't tell me again. When I die, and you cut me open, you'll find it engraved on my spleen. For the past five days, that's all I've heard.'

I grabbed up my hat and made for the door.

II

247 Jefferson Avenue was an apartment house at the Fairview end of the avenue: a big, square-shaped concrete building with green shutters at the windows and a gaudy canopy over the main entrance.

The lobby of the apartment house was dim and soothing. There were no murals or statues or violent colours to give the homecoming drunks a fright. The carpet was laid over rubber blocks and gave under my feet as I crossed to the automatic elevator.

Hidden behind a screen of tropical palms in brass pots were the desk and switchboard. A girl with a telephone harness hitched to her chest was reading the funnies. She was either too bored to bother or didn't hear me come in, for she didn't look up, and that's unusual in a joint like this. As a rule they head you off from the elevator until they have called whoever you're visiting to make sure you're wanted.

But as I slid back the elevator door, a man in a shabby dark suit and a bowler hat set straight and square on his head appeared from behind a pillar and plodded over to me.

'Going some place or just taking the ride for the hell of it?' he growled.

His face was round and fat, and covered with a web of fine veins. His eyes were deepset and cold. His moustache hid a mouth that was probably thin and unpleasant. He looked what he was: a retired cop, supplementing his pension by bouncing the unwanteds.

'I'm making a call,' I said, and gave him a smile; but he didn't seem impressed by my charms.

'We like callers to check in at the desk. Who do you want to see?' He sounded no tougher than any other cop in Orchid City, but tough enough to have hair on his chest.

I didn't want Barratt to know I was about to call on him. It would be quite bad enough without him being on his guard. I took out my bill-fold and hoisted up a five-dollar bill. The fat bouncer's eyes fastened on it, and a tongue like the toe of an old boot searched amongst the jungle of his moustache. I pushed the bill at him.

Fat, nicotine-stained fingers closed over it: a reflex action born of years of experience.

'I'll just take the ride,' I said, and showed him more of my teeth: those capped in gold.

'Don't take too long about it,' he growled, 'and don't think this buys you anything. I just haven't seen you.'

He plodded back to his pillar again, then paused to scowl at the girl behind the desk, who had stopped reading the funnies and was watching him with a set smile on her foxy little face. As I closed the elevator door he was on his way over to her, probably to share the swag.

I rode up to the fourth floor and walked down a long passage studded with doors. Barratt's apartment was No. 4B15. I found it around the corner: an isolated door at the end of a dim cul-de-sac. The radio was blaring, and as I raised my hand to ring the bell, there came a sudden crash of breaking glass.

I dug my thumb into the bell push and waited. Strident jazz howled at me through the door panels, but no one bothered to answer the door. I sank my thumb into the bell-push again and leaned my weight against it. I could hear the bell ringing above the shrill notes of a clarinet. Then suddenly someone snapped off the radio and jerked open the door.

A tall, blond man in a scarlet dressing-room stood in the doorway, smiling at me. His lean, white face was handsome if you like the profile type. A moustache, the size of a well-fed caterpillar, graced his upper lip. The pupils of his amber-coloured eyes were as big as dimes.

'Hello,' he said in a low, drawling voice, 'was that you ringing?'

'If it wasn't me, then the place is haunted,' I said, watching him. From the look of his eyes, he was full of reefer smoke, and I had an idea he needed watching.

'I can be funny too,' he said mildly. His hand flashed up, and the broken bottle he had been concealing behind his back whizzed towards my face

I managed to get my face out of the way more by luck than judgment. The impetus of his lunge brought him forward very conveniently for the right-hand punch I hung on his jaw. The smack of bone against bone, and the click of his teeth made a satisfying sound in my ears.

He spread out on the floor, the bottle still clutched in his fingers. I paused long enough to take the bottle from him, and then edged into the room. The air smelt of whisky fumes and marijuana smoke: the kind of smell you would expect to run into in any hole occupied by a man like Barratt. Several broken bottles of whisky lay in a heap in the fireplace. The all-steel-furniture was scattered around the room as if two husky steve-dores had been having a fight. The ten-foot polished-steel table lay on its side against a window that had a cracked pane.

Apart from the smell and the furniture, the room was empty. I moved silently over the blood-red carpet to a half-open door, and looked into a room that had the curtains drawn and the electric light on.

An ash-blonde girl lay on the bed. She had on a necklace of ivory beads, a thin gold chain around her left ankle, and nothing else. She was young and reasonably put together, but she didn't make a pretty picture as she lay on the crumpled sheet. Her mouth was puffed up as if someone had hit her recently, and there were several ugly-looking green-and-blue bruises on her arms and chest.

We looked at each other. She didn't move, nor did she seem surprised to see me. She gave me that silly, meaningless smile reefer-smokers hand out when they suspect they should be sociable, and the effort is too much for them.

She wasn't in any state to listen to a sales talk. I had to decide whether I should leave her there or take her home. Although her father wasn't anything a Boy Scout would want to hang on his totem pole, at least he wouldn't feed her hasheesh. I decided to take her home.

'Hello, Miss Wingrove. How about you and me going home?'

She didn't say anything. The smile remained fixed on the shiny red mouth. I doubted if she heard what I said, let alone understood what was happening.

I didn't like the idea of touching her, but it was pretty obvious she wasn't going to leave the apartment on her feet. She would have to be carried. I wondered what the bowler-hatted bouncer would say when he saw me manhandling her through the lobby.

There was another bed by the window. I stripped a blanket from it and dropped the blanket over the corrupt little body.

'Say so if you'd rather walk. If you don't feel up to it, I'll carry you.'

She stared blankly at me, her smile slipped, and she had to make a conscious effort to hitch it into place again. She hadn't any comments to make.

I bent over her and slid my hands under her knees and shoulders. As I lifted her she suddenly came alive. She grabbed me around the neck and flung herself back on to the bed, throwing me off balance so I fell on top of her. She was all arms and legs now, and I couldn't get away from her.

I didn't want to hurt her, but there was something pretty horrible in the way she was holding me, and I hated the feel of her hot, soft body. She was giggling in an inane way, and clung to me, her legs round my back and her finger-nails digging into my neck.

I seized her wrists and tried to break her hold, but she was surprisingly strong and I couldn't get enough leverage to free myself. We rolled off the bed on to the floor and she butted me with her head and tried to bite me in the face.

We wrestled around on the floor, knocking the furniture over, and after I had taken a couple of socks in the face that hurt I sank one into her midriff and winded her. She rolled away from me, gasping, and I got to my feet. I had lost my collar; one of my coat lapels had been ripped, and I was bleeding from a long scratch down the side of my face.

There was still plenty of fight left in her. She was squirming around on the floor, trying to get her breath back and trying to get at me when Barratt came into the room.

He came in quietly and cautiously, and there was a faded,

fixed smile on his white face. In his right hand he carried a long-bladed knife that could be and probably was a carving knife.

The enlarged pupils of his eyes gave him a blind look, but he could see me all right, and he was looking and moving towards me.

The sight of those sightless eyes, the fixed smile and the carving knife brought me out in a cold sweat.

'Drop that knife, Barratt!' I rapped out, and began to back away in search of a weapon.

He came on, slowly, rather like a sleep-walker, and I knew I should have to stop him before he cornered me. I made a sudden dive for the bed, grabbed up a pillow and flung it at him. It hit him in the face, sending him staggering, and I jumped for a chair, snatched it up as he came charging at me.

He ran slap on to the legs of the chair as I poked it at him. The collision sent both of us staggering, and as I recovered my balance and lifted the chair to hit him over the head, the girl jumped on my back, twining her arms round my throat, choking me.

I was getting rattled now and slammed against the wall with her as Barratt stabbed at me. I saw the flash of the knife and let out a yell, throwing myself sideways.

I and the girl sprawled on the floor. She was still clinging to me and her grip round my throat was making the blood hammer in my head.

I tore her hands away as Barratt bent over me. I thought I was a goner. I kicked out wildly, missed him, saw the blade flash up. I tried to roll clear, but knew it couldn't be done. The girl under me was holding me. I couldn't get my arms free; I couldn't turn. The blade was aimed for my belly when there was a rush of feet; Barratt half turned, the knife thudded down into the floor an inch from my body; a short, square-shouldered man who had appeared from nowhere hit Barratt savagely on the head with what looked like a sandbag.

Barratt arched his back, shot away from me and dropped down on hands and knees. He tried to rise, flattened out, dragged himself to a half-sitting position as the square-shouldered man sprang at him and hit him again.

All this took about five seconds. The girl was still trying to strangle me and now she started to scream. I rolled over on my face, bringing her uppermost. I felt her being wrenched away and I staggered to my feet, as, screaming wildly, she flew at the square-shouldered man, her fingers clawing at his face.

He stood his ground, swept her hands away and hit her very hard on the temple with the sandbag. She dropped at his feet as if she had been pole-axed.

He bent over her, lifted an eyelid, straightened and grinned at me.

'Hello. You seem to be having quite a time. I heard you yell. Was he going to knife you or were you two playing a game?'

I wiped my face and the back of my neck with my handkerchief before saying, 'He seemed a little worked up. I don't think he knew what he was doing. He's hopped to the eyes.' I looked a little anxiously at the naked heap of arms and legs on the floor. 'You hit her pretty hard. I hope you haven't damaged her. She belongs to a client of mine.'

He waved an airy hand.

'Don't worry about her. You have to treat these junkies rough. Besides, I've had a bellyful of them these past three days. They've been fighting and screaming at each other nonstop, and I like my sleep.'

I continued to wipe my face and neck. I was sweating quite a lot. The long carving knife on the carpet gave me the horrors.

'You live here?' I asked.

'For my sins. Just across the way. Nick Perelli's the name, in case it interests you.'

I told him who I was.

'I'm grateful to you. If you hadn't hit that goon he would have stuck that knife into me.'

Perelli smiled. His swarthy, thin face had a jeering, humorous expression. He wasn't a bad-looking guy: a little like George Raft, come to think of it. His clothes were good, and he wore them well.

'So you're the fella who runs Universal Services, are you? That's a nice racket. Wish it belonged to me.'

'It has its low moments. This is one of them. I'd like to put it on record if there's anything I can do for you now or in the future, let me know. It'll be on the house, and you'll get our Grade A service.'

'I'll remember,' he said, and grinned. 'Right now I'm pretty well fixed, but you never know.' He stuck his toe into the girl's side and gave her a little nudge. 'Is this one of the services?'

'One of the less pleasant ones. I came here to take her back to her father.'

'Think he'll be pleased to have her back? I wouldn't be if she belonged to me. I wouldn't want her back if she was given away with a yacht.'

I fetched the blanket and dropped it over her.

'Her old man's only one degree better than she is. What's the bouncer downstairs going to say when he sees me carrying her through the lobby?'

'Maxie?' Perelli laughed. 'He'll hang out the flags. He's been longing to get rid of her, only Barratt scares him. I'm on my way to meet my girl. We can go down together. I'll see he doesn't bother you.'

'Fine,' I said. 'I'd hate to be run in for kidnapping after what I've just been through.'

'The bathroom's through there if you want to tidy up,' he said, pointing. 'You look a bit of a wreck. I'll watch her until you get back.'

I went into the bathroom and repaired the damage as best I could. Even after a wash and I had pinned up the torn lapel I still looked as if I'd been wrestling with a wild cat.

I came out, gathered up the unconscious girl in the blanket and heaved her over my shoulder.

'Nice if she comes round in the car.'

'She won't,' Perelli said with confidence. 'When I sap them, they stay sapped.'

We got her into the elevator without anyone seeing us.

'Do you usually carry a sandbag when you go to meet your girl friend?' I asked as the elevator sank between floors.

He grinned.

'Never without one. I play cards for a living, and a cosh is the best way to settle *post mortems*. I get quite a few.'

'Well, you certainly know how to use one.'

'There's nothing to it. The secret is to hit them hard. A tap only makes them mad.'

The elevator came to a silent stop and we marched out into the lobby.

The girl behind the desk started out of her chair and gaped at us. Her hand fluttered along the desk and one finger poked into the bell-push. The bouncer in the bowler hat materialized from behind his pillar like a jack-in-the-box. He took one look at me and the girl draped over my shoulder, made a growling noise deep down in his throat and started purposely towards me.

'All right, Maxie; relax,' Perelli said. 'We're only clearing out a little garbage. There's no need to get excited.'

Maxie stopped in mid-stride. He stooped to peer at the girl, and as soon as he recognized her he lost his belligerent look.

'Oh, *her*! Where are you taking her?'

'What do you care so long as we take her?' Perelli inquired.

Maxie chewed this over in his mind.

'I guess that's right. Hasn't Barratt got anything to say about her going?'

'He's asleep at the moment,' I said. 'We thought it would be a shame to wake him up.'

Maxie eyed the scratches on my face and whistled softly.

'Yeah. I guess I haven't seen you two guys.' He looked across at the girl behind the desk. 'Did you hear, Gracie? We ain't seen nobody.'

The girl nodded and went back to her funnies. Maxie waved us to the door.

'Careful there're no cops around.'

We went down the steps into the sunshine. There were no cops around.

I laid the unconscious girl along the back seat of the Buick and closed the door.

'Well, thanks again. It wouldn't be an over-statement to say you saved my life.' I gave Perelli my card. 'Don't forget; anywhere, any time, I'll be glad to even the score.'

An easy thing to say, but the way it worked out I was scrabbling around like a monkey with a can tied to its tail, three weeks later, trying to make good my promise.

III

Jack Kerman, long, lean and dapper, lay full length on my divan; an immaculate figure in a bottle-green flannel suit, cream silk shirt and brown buckskin shoes. On his chest he balanced a highball, while he beat time a little drunkenly to the swing music coming from the radio.

Opposite him I relaxed in one of those down-to-the-ground easy chairs, and looked through the open windows at the moonlit Pacific, while I tried to make up my mind whether to go in for a swim or mix myself another drink.

Wingrove's daughter was an almost forgotten memory; Perelli

just another name. Ten days had gone past since I had returned the unconscious little junkie to the bosom of her family, and so far as I was concerned the case was closed.

'It's about time I had a vacation,' Kerman said suddenly. 'This continual grind is giving me ulcers. What we should do is to shut up the office for a couple of months and go to Bermuda or Honolulu. I'm bored with the local talent in this burg. I want a little more fire; grass skirts instead of lounging pyjamas: something with a little zing in it. How about it, Vic? Let's do it. We can afford it, can't we?'

'Maybe you can, but I'm damn sure I can't. Besides, what would we do with Paula?'

Kerman took a long drink from his glass, sighed, and reached for a cigarette.

'She's your funeral. That girl is a menace. All she thinks about is money and work. You might tell her not to keep picking on me. To hear her talk, you'd think I don't earn my keep.'

'Do you?' I said, shutting my eyes. 'Do any of us? Anyway, a vacation is out, Jack. We're getting on top and we've got to stay on top. If we shut the office, we'd be forgotten in a week. You can't stand still in a job like this.'

Kerman grunted.

'Maybe you're right. I've a redhead who's costing me a pile of dough. I don't know what's the matter with her. She thinks I'm made of money. Mind you, she's not a bad little thing. She's willing, and that's what I like about a girl. The trouble with her is . . .'

The telephone bell began to ring.

Kerman raised his head and scowled at the telephone.

'Don't answer it,' he advised. 'It might be a client.'

'Not at ten past ten,' I said, hoisting myself out of the chair. 'It's probably my past catching me up.'

'Then you'd better let me handle her. I have a very nifty line with women on the telephone.'

I shied a cushion at him as I picked up the receiver.

'Hello?'

A male voice asked, 'Is that Mr. Malloy?' A voice that would send an immediate prickle up most women's spines. A voice that conjured up a picture of a tall, powerfully built man, probably sun-tanned and handsome, who would rather drop in for an afternoon cup of tea when her husband's at the office than look in in the evening when he's at home.

Perhaps I was doing him an injustice, but that was the mental picture I got of him from the vibrating baritone voice.

'Speaking,' I said. 'Who is that?'

'My name is Lee Dedrick. I have been trying to get you at your office. There doesn't appear to be anyone there.'

'I'm sorry. The office closes at six.'

'And sweat-shop hours at that,' Kerman muttered, punching the pillow at the back of his head. 'Tell him we're in bed with the croup.'

The voice said sharply, 'But surely you have a night service?'

'You're talking to the night service now, Mr. Dedrick.'

'Oh. I see.' There was a pause, then he said, 'I would like you to come out to my place right away. It's rather urgent.'

In spite of the domineering tone, I had a sudden impression that he was frightened. There was a peculiar shake in his voice, and he seemed very breathless.

'Can you give me some idea what you want, Mr. Dedrick?' I asked, ignoring Kerman's frantic signals to hang up.

There was a moment's silence. I waited and listened to the uneven, hurried breathing.

'A few minutes ago some man rang me up and warned me an attempt would be made tonight to kidnap me. Probably a practical joker, but I thought it wise to take precautions. I happen to be alone here, except for my chauffeur; he is a Filipino, and would be quite useless in an emergency.'

This sounded screwy to me.

'Have you any idea why anyone should want to kidnap you?'

Again there was that pause. Again I listened to the hurried breathing. It was an eerie sound, and conveyed his fear to me as plainly as if I could see the fear on his face.

'I happen to be Serena Marshland's husband,' he said curtly. 'I'd be glad if you wouldn't waste time asking pointless questions. There'll be time enough to satisfy your curiosity when we meet.'

I didn't like his tone, but I knew he was scared. I didn't want to go out on this job. I had been working all day, and would much rather have spent the rest of the evening swopping drinks with Kerman, but that wasn't the way to build up a successful business. Besides, Serena Marshland was the fourth richest woman in the world.

'Where are you, Mr. Dedrick?'

'The house is called Ocean End. You probably know it. It's

rather isolated and lonely. I'd be glad if you would come quickly.'

'I know it. I'll be over in less than ten minutes.'

'There is a private road from Ocean View. You'll find the gates open. As a matter of fact, I have only just moved in here and ...' He suddenly stopped talking.

I waited, then as nothing happened, I said, 'Hello?'

I could still hear his quick, uneven breathing, but he didn't answer.

'Hello? Mr. Dedrick?'

His breathing went off the line. There was a long, silent pause, then a gentle click, and the line went dead.

IV

Ocean End is situated in the sand dunes, about three miles from my cabin. It was built in the late 'twenties for a millionaire who never lived there. Before he could take possession, he was caught in a financial smash and shot himself. For some years the place stood empty, then a syndicate bought it and made a pot of money out of it by renting it to visiting fleshpots and foreign nobility who considered themselves too grand to stay at the Orchid Hotel.

The Estate is quite a show place, and has been advertised as the millionaire's dream home. It has a hundred acres of terraced gardens and a swimming pool half outside the house and half under it. The house itself is Italian Baroque in style, and built of concrete and coraline stone. The interior is famous for some magnificent murals and works of art.

As I sent the Buick racing along the two miles of private road that leads to the Estate, a fine, wide road, lined on either side by Royal Palms, Kerman said, 'I've always wanted to see this joint.' He leaned forward to peer into the circles of light that fled before us. 'I've been kidding myself I'll rent it for a week myself one of these days. What do you think it'd cost me?'

'About ten years' pay.'

'Yeah, maybe you're right. Well, I guess I'd better just go on kidding myself. Pity, though. With a background like this, I'd have that redhead eating out of my hand.'

'Should have thought you'd have preferred her to eat off a plate. You know, I'm worried about this guy, Jack. What made him hang up like that in the middle of a sentence?'

'You know what these punks are like. They're so damn lazy it's an effort for them to breathe.'

'I have an idea someone came into the room, and he didn't want them to hear what he was saying.'

'But then you always try to make a mystery out of anything. My bet is he got bored talking to you and just hung up. All these rich jerks are alike. They don't have to watch their manners the way we do.'

Ahead of me were the main gates of the Estate. They were wide open. I didn't reduce speed. We flashed past them, and went storming up the road drive-way, banked on either side by enormous rhododendron shrubs.

'Must you drive as if we're going to a fire?' Kerman asked plaintively.

'He sounded scared, and I have a hunch he may be in trouble.'

I swung the Buick around a long, curving bend. The house seemed to leap at us in the light of the headlamps. Kerman gave a gasp of alarm as I slammed on the brakes. With a squeal of tortured tyres, I managed to bring the Buick to a skidding standstill a couple of inches from the balustrade that surrounded the courtyard.

'Why stop?' Kerman said, mopping his face. 'Why not drive slap into the house? You know I hate walking.'

'Your nerves are bad,' I said, a little pop-eyed myself. 'The trouble with you is you drink too much.'

I got out of the car and he followed me.

Parked to the left of the front entrance was a big, glittering battleship of a car with the parkers on.

Except for a light that spilled through an open casement doorway on to the far end of the terrace, the house was in darkness.

'Do we ring or go in that way?' Kerman asked, jerking his thumb towards the lighted window.

'We'll take a look in there first. If no one's around, we'll ring. Got your gun handy?'

'Here. You have it,' Kerman said generously, and thrust the .45 into my hand. 'It spoils the set of my suit.'

'What you really mean is if I have the gun I naturally go first.'

'What a sweet, charitable mind you've got. I honestly don't know why I work for you.'

'Probably for the money, and who but you calls it work?'

We were moving silently along the terrace while we whispered at each other, and as we neared the lighted window I motioned him to be quiet. He gave me a little shove forward, making signals for me to go ahead.

I went ahead while he watched me. When I reached the open casement door, I peered into a long rectangular room, furnished in Mexican style with rich rugs on the floor, saddles and bridles ornamenting the walls and big, lounging settees by the windows and before the vast empty fireplace.

On the table was the telephone and an untouched tumbler containing whisky and probably soda. A cigarette stub had fallen off the glass ash-tray and burned a scar on the highly polished table.

There was no one in the room.

I beckoned to Kerman.

'Pretty lush,' he said, peering over my shoulder. 'Imagine living in a joint like this. What do we do now?'

I walked into the room. The cigarette stub worried me; so did the untouched whisky.

Kerman sauntered in behind me and wandered around one of the settees before the fireplace to look at a Mexican saddle hanging on the wall. He took two steps towards it, then stopped with a start that flopped his hair into his eyes.

'Gawd!'

I came around the settee fast.

A man in the black uniform of a chauffeur lay on his back. I didn't have to touch him to know he was dead. There was a purple hole in the centre of his forehead, and a lot of blood had soaked into the Mexican rug on which he was lying. His yellow-brown hands were set rigid, his fingers were hooked like claws, and his small, brown face was twisted in a grimace of terror.

'Sweet grief!' Kerman said soberly. 'He gave me a hell of a fright.'

I bent to touch the claw-like hand. It was still warm. The arm dropped to the carpet when I lifted and released it. He couldn't have been dead for very long.

'Looks bad for Dedrick,' I said. 'They must have arrived while he was talking to me.'

'Think they've kidnapped him?'

'Looks like it. Go ahead and call the police, Jack. There's nothing we can do. You know how Brandon reacts to us. If he thinks we've been poking around, wasting time, he'll raise Cain.'

As Kerman reached for the telephone, he paused, cocked his head on one side, listening.

'Sounds like a car coming.'

I went out on to the terrace.

There was a car coming, and coming fast. I could hear the snarl of a powerful engine, and the whine of tyres as the car swept around the bends in the drive.

'Hold it a moment,' I said.

I could see the headlights of the car now through the trees. A moment later the car swept around the drive and pulled up a few yards from the Buick.

I walked along the terrace, and as I reached the head of the steps leading from the terrace to the garden a girl got out of the car.

In the dim, uncertain light of the moon and the combined parking lights of the three cars, I could just see she was tall, slender and hatless.

'Lee . . .'

She paused, looking up at me.

'Is that you, Lee?'

'Mr. Dedrick doesn't appear to be here,' I said, and came down the steps towards her.

I heard her catch her breath sharply, and she made a half turn as if she was going to run away, but she controlled the impulse and faced me.

'Who – who are you?'

'My name's Vic Malloy. Mr. Dedrick 'phoned me about a quarter of an hour ago. He asked me to come out here.'

'Oh.' She sounded both surprised and startled. 'And you say he isn't here?'

'He doesn't seem to be. There's only that light you can see showing. He isn't in there. The rest of the house is in darkness.'

By now I was close enough to get a vague idea what she looked like. I could see she was dark and youngish and in evening dress. I had an idea she was pretty.

'But he must be here,' she said sharply.

'May I ask who you are?'

For a fraction of a second she hesitated, then she said, 'I'm Mary Jerome; Mrs. Dedrick's secretary.'

'I'm afraid I have a shock for you. Mr. Dedrick's chauffeur

is in there.' I waved towards the lighted window. 'He's dead.'

'Dead?' I saw her stiffen.

'He's been shot through the head.'

She lurched forward, and I thought she was going to faint. I caught hold of her arm and steadied her.

'Would you like to sit in the car for a moment?'

She pulled away from me.

'No; it's all right. You mean he's been murdered?'

'It looks like it. It's certainly not suicide.'

'What has happened to Lee – Mr. Dedrick?'

'I don't know. He telephoned me, saying someone had warned him he was going to be kidnapped. I came out here and found the chauffeur dead.'

'Kidnapped? Oh!' She drew in a quick, shuddering breath. 'He said that? Are you sure?'

'Why, yes. We're just going to search the house. We've only been here two or three minutes. Will you wait in your car?'

'Oh, no! I'll look too. Why should they want to kidnap him?'

'I asked him that. He said he was Serena Marshland's husband.'

She pushed past me, ran up the steps and walked quickly along the terrace. I followed her.

Kerman came out and barred the way into the room.

'I don't think you should go in there,' he said mildly.

'Have you seen Mr. Dedrick?' she demanded, staring up at him. The light from the room fell on her face. She was lovely in a hard, cold way, with good eyes and a firm mouth and chin. At a guess she would be about thirty, and not the type I would have expected to be a rich woman's secretary. Her clothes were expensive-looking, and she wore a silk evening wrap over a wine-coloured, strapless evening dress with the confidence and grace of a model.

Kerman shook his head.

'Please look for him. Both of you. Search the house.'

I nodded to Kerman.

' 'Phone the police first, Jack.'

Whilst Kerman was using the telephone, the girl went to look at the chauffeur. I watched her, saw the colour leave her face, but as I went to her, she pulled herself together and turned away.

'Come out on to the terrace,' I said. 'Kerman will look for Mr. Dedrick.' I put my hand on her arm, but with a little shiver she shook it off and walked out on to the terrace again.

'This is dreadful,' she said. 'I wish you would try and find Mr. Dedrick instead of hanging around me. Why did he 'phone you? Does he know you?'

'I run Universal Services. He's probably seen one of our advertisements.'

She put her hand to her face, and leaned against the balustrade.

'I'm afraid that conveys nothing to me. What is Universal Services? I have only been in Orchid City for a few hours.'

'We handle any job from divorce to grooming a cat. Mr. Dedrick wanted a bodyguard, but I'm afraid we arrived a little late.'

I saw her flinch.

'I can't believe it. Please make sure he's not in the house. He must be here!'

'Kerman's looking now. I understood from Mr. Dedrick that he had only just moved in here, and was alone with his chauffeur. Is that right?'

'Mr. Dedrick has rented this house for the summer. Mrs. Dedrick and he have been staying for a few days in New York,' she explained, speaking rapidly. 'They have just come back from Paris. Mr. Dedrick flew from New York a few days ago. He went on ahead to make the arrangements about the house. Mrs. Dedrick arrives tomorrow. I came with him to make sure everything in the house was in order. We have rooms at the Orchid Hotel. Mr. Dedrick said he was going to look over the house this evening. I was to join him later.'

'I see.'

Kerman came out on to the terrace.

'No one in the house,' he said.

'Take a look around the garden.'

He gave Mary Jerome a quick, interested look and went off down the terrace steps.

'He's never mentioned being kidnapped to you, has he?'

'Oh, no.'

'What time did he leave his hotel?'

'At seven-thirty.'

'He called me at ten past ten. I wonder what he was doing for two hours and forty minutes here. Have you any idea?'

26

'I suppose he was looking over the house. I wish you would go after your friend and help him. Mr. Dedrick might be lying in the grounds – hurt.'

I began to get the idea that she wanted to get rid of me.

'I'll stick around until the police come. We don't want you kidnapped.'

'I – I don't think I can face any more of this. I'll go back to the hotel,' she said, her voice suddenly husky. 'Will you tell them, please? I'll see them at the hotel.'

'I think it would be better to wait until they come,' I said quietly.

'No; I think I'll go. He – he may be at the hotel. I think I ought to go.'

As she turned, I caught her wrist.

'I'm sorry, but until the police come, you must stay.'

She stared up at me, her eyes hard in the moonlight.

'If you think it is necessary.'

'That's the idea.'

She opened her bag.

'I think a cigarette . . .'

She did it very smoothly. I found myself looking down at a .25, aimed at my midriff.

'Go in there!'

'Now, look . . .'

'Go in there!' There was a dangerous note in her voice. 'I'll shoot if you don't go in!'

'You're playing it wrong, but have it your own way.'

I walked into the lounge.

The moment I heard her running down the terrace I jumped to the balustrade.

'Head her off, Jack!' I bawled into the darkness. 'But watch out; she has a gun!'

Then I legged it down the terrace after her.

There came a spiteful crack of the .25, and a slug buzzed past my head. I dodged behind a tub of palms. More gun-fire, and an excited yelp from Kerman. Then a car engine exploded into life; the gun fired again and the car went furiously down the drive.

I raced to the end of the terrace, intent on following her in the Buick, but she had taken care of that. Her last shot had gone through the off-side rear wheel.

Kerman came out of the darkness.

27

'What goes on?' he demanded indignantly. 'She tried to shoot me.'

V

We sat together before the empty fireplace in the library while a stony-eyed cop stood by the door and watched us without appearing to do so.

We had told our stories to Detective Sergeant MacGraw, and now we were waiting for Brandon. As soon as MacGraw learned who Dedrick was, he said the Captain of Police would want to see us. So we waited.

In the next room a squad of the Homicide boys were at work, dusting for fingerprints, photographing the body and the room, and prowling around for clues.

There was a considerable amount of telephoning and coming and going of cars. After a while I heard a barking voice and I nudged Kerman.

'Brandon.'

'What a thrill for him to find us here,' Kerman said, and grinned.

The cop scowled at him and moved restlessly. Unconsiously, he straightened his jacket and looked critically at his buttons. Captain of the Police Brandon was a martinet, and every cop on the Force was terrified of him.

Silence settled over us again like a film of dust. Another half-hour crawled past. The hands of my watch showed a quarter past midnight. Kerman was dozing. I longed for a drink.

Then the door jerked open and Brandon and Detective Lieutenant Mifflin of the Homicide Squad came in.

I gave Kerman a nudge and he opened his eyes as Brandon paused to survey us the way a grand duke would look at a set of muddy footprints on his bed.

Brandon was short and thickset, with a round, fat pink-and-white face, a mass of chalk-white hair and cold, inquisitive eyes. He was an ambitious cop without being a clever one. He got results because he used Mifflin's brains and took the credit. He had been Captain of Police for ten years. He owned a Cadillac, a seven-bedroom house; his wife had a mink coat, and his son and daughter went to the University. He didn't live in that style on his pay. There were the usual rumours that he could be bought, but no one had ever attempted to prove it as

28

far as I knew. He had been known to fake evidence and encouraged his cops to be brutal and ruthless. A man with a lot of power; a dangerous man.

'So you two have horned in on this, have you?' he said in his hard, rasping voice. 'I've never known such a pair of jackals.'

Neither of us said anything. Talk out of turn to Brandon and you're liable to find yourself behind bars.

He glanced at the cop who was as rigid as a wooden effigy.

'Out!'

The cop went out on tiptoe and closed the door as if it were made of egg-shells.

Mifflin gave me a slow, heavy wink from behind Brandon's head.

Brandon sat down, stretched out his short, fat legs, pushed his hard pork-pie hat to the back of his head and fumbled for the inevitable cigar.

'Let's have it all over again,' he said. 'There're one or two points I want to check. Go ahead, Malloy. Tell it the way you told it to MacGraw. I'll stop you when I've had enough.'

'Kerman and I were spending the evening in my cabin,' I said briskly. 'At ten minutes past ten the telephone bell rang, and a man who identified himself as Lee Dedrick asked me to come over here right away. He explained that some man had 'phoned him and warned him that an attempt was to be made tonight to kidnap him.'

'You're sure he said that?' Brandon asked, slitting the cellophane wrapping of his cigar with a well-manicured thumb-nail.

'Why, yes.'

'There's been no incoming calls to this house tonight. What do you make of that?'

'Maybe he had the call at his hotel.'

'He didn't. We've checked that too.'

'Any out-going calls from here, besides the one he made to me?'

Brandon rolled the cigar between his fat fingers.

'Yeah, one to a call-box number. What of it?'

Mifflin said in his slow, heavy voice, 'He could have been told during the day to call that number tonight, and got the warning that way.'

Brandon looked over his shoulder as if he wasn't aware

29

until now that Mifflin was in the room. Although he relied on Mifflin's brains, he always acted as if Mifflin had no business to be on the Force.

'Maybe,' he said, 'or Malloy could be lying.' He looked at me, showing his small even teeth. 'Are you?'

'No.'

'Tell me, why didn't Dedrick call the police instead of you?'

I had an answer to that one, but I didn't think he would like it. Instead, I said, 'He wasn't sure someone wasn't pulling his leg. Probably he was anxious not to make a fool of himself.'

'Well, go on. Tell me more,' Brandon said, setting fire to the cigar. He rolled it around between his thin lips and stared heavily at me.

'While he was talking, there was a sudden silence on the line. I called to him, but he didn't answer. I could hear him breathing over the line, then he hung up.'

'And that's when you should have called Headquarters,' Brandon snarled. 'You should have known something was wrong.'

'I thought maybe his chauffeur had come in, and Dedrick didn't want him to hear what he was saying. I'm not all that crazy to mix up a man like Dedrick with the police without his say-so.'

Brandon scowled at me and flicked ash off his cigar.

'You'd talk yourself out of a coffin,' he said sourly. 'Well, go on. You came out here and found Souki. That right?'

'Souki? Is that the chauffeur's name?'

'According to the letters he had in his pocket, it's his name. Did you see anyone on your way up; any car?'

'No. As soon as we found the body I told Kerman to 'phone your people. Before he could do so this girl arrived.'

Brandon pulled at his thick nose.

'Yeah, now about this girl: what did she call herself?'

'Mary Jerome.'

'Yeah; Mary Jerome.' He allowed a cloud of cigar smoke to obscure his face, went on, 'She said she was Mrs. Dedrick's secretary: right?'

'Yes.'

'She isn't staying at the Orchid Hotel.'

I didn't say anything.

'Did she strike you as the secretary type?'

'No.'

'Do you think she had anything to do with Dedrick's kidnapping?'

'I doubt it. She seemed genuinely startled when I told her. And, besides, why did she come back here after Dedrick had been taken away if she knew?'

'That's right, Malloy,' Brandon said, and gave me a foxy smile. 'You're on the right lines. She seemed upset, uh?'

'That's right.'

He sat farther down in the chair, stared up at the ceiling and rolled thoughts around in his mind. After a while, he said, 'Now, look, Malloy, I want you to get this straight. When the Press are told about this snatch there's going to be a lot of publicity and excitement. Dedrick's wife is an important woman. She's more than that: she's a household name. And another thing, she's got a lot of powerful friends. You and I could step off with the wrong foot if we're not very careful. I'm going to be careful, and you're going to do what you're told.'

I looked at him and he looked at me.

'It's my bet this Jerome girl is Dedrick's mistress,' Brandon went on. 'It sticks out a mile. He comes down here to rent this house. Mrs. Dedrick stays in New York. We don't know much about this guy, Dedrick. We haven't had much time since this broke, but we've already done a little digging. The wedding was secret. These two met eight weeks ago in Paris, and got married. Old man Marshland, Mrs. Dedrick's father, wasn't told until the two of them arrived at his house in New York as man and wife. I don't know why the marriage was secret unless Dedrick isn't anything to shout about, and she thought it would be better to present him to Marshland as her husband and not as her husband-to-be. I don't know, and it's not my business. But it looks as if Dedrick was playing along with another woman, and this woman is Mary Jerome. It is pretty obviously they intended to spend the night together here, only Dedrick got kidnapped before he could stop her turning up. The facts fit together. You can see why she didn't want to be questioned by the police, so she pulled a gun on you and cleared off before we turned up, and I don't mind telling you, I'm glad she did clear off.'

He waited to see if I had anything to say, but I hadn't. I thought it was likely he was right. The facts, as he had said, fitted together.

'That's why I wanted to have this little talk with you, Malloy,' he went on, his cold eyes on my face. 'Dedrick's been kidnapped. Okay, that's something we can do something about, but the other thing isn't our business. You're not to say a word about Mary Jerome, if you do, you'll be sorry. I'll take you both in as material witnesses and my boys will give you a working over every day you're with us. I promise you that if any information gets into the Press about this woman. I'm not going to have any muck-raking in this case. Mrs. Dedrick is going to receive every possible consideration from me. It's bad enough for her to lose her husband this way, but no one is to know her husband was cheating on her. Understand?'

I thought of Mrs. Dedrick's possible powerful friends. Probably the Governor, who could crack Brandon on her say-so. He wasn't looking after her interests or considering her feelings, he was safeguarding himself.

'Yeah,' I said.

'Okay,' Brandon said, getting to his feet. 'Keep your traps shut, or you'll regret it. You two get out of here, and stay out of here. If you try to horn in on this case, I'll make you wish you were never born.'

'That'll be no new experience,' Kerman said languidly as he drifted to the door. 'Most mornings when I wake up I wish just that very thing.'

'Get out!' Brandon barked.

We got out.

CHAPTER TWO

I

THE following evening, around ten o'clock, I was trying to decide whether to go to bed early or open a new bottle of Scotch and make a night of it, when the telephone bell rang.

The bell sounded shrill and urgent and startled me, probably because, up to now, the cabin had been as still and as silent as a poor relation at a wedding.

I lifted the receiver.

'Hello?'

Above the faint humming on the line I could hear a dance band playing a waltz. The high notes of the muted trumpet suggested Glyn Boos's Serenaders; that would make the call from the Country Club.

'Mr. Malloy?' A woman's voice: pitched low with a little drawl in it. A voice calculated to stimulate male interest. At any rate it stimulated mine.

'Speaking.'

'My name is Serena Dedrick. I'm at the Country Club just now. Can you come over? I can offer you a job if you want it.'

I wondered why she couldn't have waited until the morning, but then the Dedricks seemed to specialize in out-of-office hours. It didn't worry me. I wanted her custom.

'Certainly, Mrs. Dedrick. I'll be right over. Do I ask at the desk for you?'

'I'll be in my car in the parking lot. It's a black Cad. Will you be long?'

'A quarter of an hour.'

'I will wait that long, but no longer.' The drawl had sharpened.

'I'm on my way ...' I began, but she had hung up.

I went into the bathroom to inspect myself in the mirror, and decided I looked neat enough without being gaudy. As I straightened my tie, I wondered what she wanted: probably some first-hand information about the kidnapping. From the pictures I had seen of her and from the sound of her voice, she wouldn't be satisfied with anything second-hand.

I got the Buick out of the garage and drove fast up Rossmore Avenue that skirts the golf-course, where a couple of cranks were trying to play golf in the moonlight with the aid of luminous balls, turned left up Glendora Avenue and arrived at the imposing entrance of the Country Club with four minutes of the quarter of an hour in hand.

The wooded gardens were ablaze with lights, and as I drove up the drive I could see a bunch of half-naked men and women clustered around the swimming pool, while Glyn Boos's Serenaders played under the arclights in a flower-decked alcove nearby.

The car park was around the back of the clubhouse. I edged my way in, and parked in what seemed to be the only vacant space left. I got out, looked up and down the long rows of cars, and decided it would be easier to pick the needle out of the haystack than find one particular black Cad. from this collection of luxury cars. There must have been over three hundred of them, and probably a third of that number were Cadillacs.

Parking lights flickered on and off, away to my left. I set off hopefully towards them. They continued to go on and off until I drew close enough to see they were attached to the glittering black car I had seen outside Ocean End two nights ago.

I walked up to the car and looked in at the window.

She was sitting behind the wheel, smoking a cigarette. The cold, hard light of the moon fell directly on her, and the first thing I noticed was the string of diamonds that flashed and sparkled like fire-flies in her hair. The moonlight gave her a sculptured-in-alabaster effect. She was wearing a low-cut strapless creation in gold lamé, and she looked exactly what she was: the fourth richest woman in the world, from the diamonds in her hair to the cold, haughty expression on her rather long but distinctly lovely face.

While I was looking at her and thinking she had the largest eyes I have ever seen and that her long and silky eyelashes were probably her own, she was looking at me. In the few seconds of silence that followed we sized each other up with frank curiosity.

'I have about a couple of minutes in hand, Mrs. Dedrick,' I said. 'But even at that I seemed to have kept you waiting. I'm sorry. Do you want to talk here or somewhere else?'

'Where else is there?'

'Well there's a river view near the golf-course that isn't bad. At least it's quiet.'

'All right. We'll go there.' She moved along the bench seat. 'Perhaps you'll drive.'

I got in under the steering wheel, switched on and trod on the starter. As I manoeuvred the car out of the lot into the drive-way, I gave her a quick glance. She was looking away from me, remote and thoughtful, her face as expressionless and as smooth as an ivory mask.

I drove through the entrance gates, turned right, continued up the brilliantly lit avenue to the bridge, then swung the car on to the bridle path that led along the river. A few minutes' more driving brought me to the spot I had in mind. I slowed down, turned the nose of the car to face the glittering moon-lit river and parked. Except for the occasional croak of bull-frogs in the reeds farther up the river and the lap-lap-lap of water against the bank, there was no sound to disturb us.

'Do you want to get out?' I asked, breaking the silence that had brooded over us since we had driven from the club.

She roused herself, as if her thoughts had been miles away, tossed her cigarette end into the river and shook her head.

'No; we can talk here. It was you who found Souki, wasn't it?'

'Yes. Have you any news of your husband?'

'They 'phoned tonight. They want five hundred thousand. They told me he was well and was looking forward to seeing me again.' She spoke in a cold, flat voice that didn't quite conceal a frightened anxiety. 'The money is to be paid the night after next, and he will be released as soon as they have it.'

I didn't say anything. After a long pause, she turned to look intently at me.

'Someone has to deliver the money. I want you to do it. I'll pay you well.'

I was afraid she was going to say that. Dealing with kid-nappers could be a dangerous business. More often than not the stooge who hands over the ransom money gets himself knocked off.

'Have you made any arrangements with them yet?'

She shook her head.

'This is only the opening move. The money is to be in used

35

twenty-dollar bills. It is to be made up into three parcels, wrapped in oilskin. I shall get last-minute instructions where the money is to be delivered.' She turned to look at me. 'You're not frightened of the job, are you?'

'I'll tell you that when I've heard what the arrangements are.'

'Then you think it could be dangerous?'

'It could be.'

She opened her handbag and took out a cigarette case. As she offered it, she said, her voice a little unsteady, 'Do you think they'll send him back?'

I took the cigarette, tapped it absently on my thumb-nail before saying, 'The possibilities are that they will.'

I lit her cigarette, and for some moments we smoked in silence.

'I want you to tell me the truth,' she said suddenly. 'Will they send him back?'

'I don't know. It depends if he's seen them. If he hasn't, then there's no point in not sending him back.'

'But if he has seen them?'

'It depends on them. Kidnappers are about as ruthless as blackmailers, Mrs. Dedrick. Kdnapping carries the death penalty. They won't take chances.'

'There's nothing I wouldn't do or pay to get him back. It's all my fault this has happened. If it wasn't for my money, he wouldn't have been worth kidnapping. He's got to come back!'

There was nothing I could think of to say to that. My own feeling was she had seen the last of him: anyway, alive. With all that money at stake they were pretty certain to get rid of him. Most kidnappers prefer to kill rather than return. It is a lot safer for them. Too many kidnapped people in the past have given clues to the police that have led to the kidnappers being caught.

'Have you consulted the police about this development?' I asked.

'No; and I'm not going to! This man tonight said every move I make is being watched, and if I communicate with the police, Lee would be murdered. Besides, the police are useless. They haven't done a thing.'

'We have time to set a trap. The money could be marked in a way no one would spot it. At least, it would give the police a

36

chance to catch them after your husband's safe.'

'No!' she said emphatically. 'I gave them my word not to try any tricks. If I did that, and they found out, and Lee suffered, I'd never forgive myself. I don't care a damn about the money. It's Lee I want.'

'Who 'phoned you? Did you get an idea from his voice what kind of man he was? I mean was he educated? Did he have an accent? Was there anything about his voice that you would recognize if you ever met him?'

'I think he was talking through a handkerchief. His voice was very muffled. He didn't have an accent, but that's all I can tell you.'

'Did he talk tough?'

'Oh no. In fact, he was horribly polite.'

I stared thoughtfully at the river. Probably they had killed Dedrick as soon as they got him out of the house. They hadn't hesitated to kill his chauffeur, and they wouldn't hesitate to wipe me out after they had the money. It was a job I didn't want.

She was smart enough to guess what I was thinking.

'If you don't do this, I have no idea who else to ask. I'll come with you if you will do it.'

'Oh no. If I do it, I do it alone.'

'There will be no question of that. I've made up my mind to see the money delivered to them with my own eyes. If you won't go with me, I'll go alone.'

I turned to look at her, surprised by her vehemence. We stared at each other for about three seconds. I could see by the expression in her eyes no one would make her change her mind.

'Well, all right, if that's how you feel about it,' I said. 'I'll come with you.'

We sat for some moments in silence.

'There's one thing I wanted to ask you,' she said abruptly. 'What was this woman like who said she was my secretary?'

'You mean to look at?'

'Yes.'

'Well, she was about thirty or so, dark, good-looking and well dressed. I thought at the time she didn't look like anyone's secretary.'

'Was she very pretty?'

'I suppose she was, and she had character too. She hadn't

37

the usual vacant face of the usual pretty woman.'

'She called my husband by his Christian name. Is that right?'

'Yes.'

I saw her clench her fists.

'That fat fool of a policeman thinks Lee was having an affair with her,' she said, and she seemed to be speaking through locked teeth. 'Do you think that?'

'Does it matter what I think?'

'I'm asking you – do you think that?' Her voice was harsh and tight with emotion.

'I don't know. I know nothing about your husband. It looks like it, but she may have just been a friend of his.'

'He wasn't in love with her!' she said so quietly I could scarcely hear her. 'I know it! He wouldn't have done a thing like that. He wouldn't have taken another woman into my home. He wasn't that type.' She stopped, looked quickly away, her hand going to her face.

'Have the police found her yet?'

'No. They're not trying to. They're so sure she's Lee's mistress. They say it's better not to find her. I don't believe it! She must know something.'

I didn't say anything.

After a long, heavy silence, she said abruptly, 'Perhaps you'll drive me back to the club. I don't think there's anything else to discuss until the night after next. Will you come to the house at six? We may have to wait, but we must be ready to leave at a moment's notice.'

'I'll be there.'

We drove to the club in silence. As soon as I parked the car, she got out and gave me a meaningless, automatic smile as she said, 'The night after next then, at six.'

I watched her walk towards the clubhouse; a graceful, lovely figure in the gold dress; diamonds sparkling in her hair; fear and jealousy in her heart.

II

I toiled up the stone steps leading to Mifflin's small office on the fourth floor of Police Headquarters' building.

Mifflin was staring out of the window, his hat over his eyes, the stub of a cigarette stuck on his lower lip. He had a brooding, dismal look on his red face and his eyes showed the energy of his thoughts.

'You,' he said gloomily as I pushed open the door and edged my way into the small office. 'Funny thing, I was thinking about you. Come in, and park. I'm out of cigarettes, so don't ask me for one.'

I pulled up a hard, straight-backed chair, sat astride it, and folded my arms along the back of it.

'How's the kidnapping going?'

'Awful,' he said, and sighed. 'Nothing to work on, and Brandon's going around like a fiend. He reckons someone will make him Chief of Police if he catches the kidnappers.'

I searched in my coat pocket, fished out a package of cigarettes, offered him one.

We lit up and brooded at each other.

'Anything on the Jerome dame?'

Mifflin sighed.

'Have you come in here just to pick my brains?'

'No; nothing like that. I came here to swop some information.'

Mifflin's face lit up and he gave me a quick, searching look.

'You got anything?'

'Not much. It's confidential. Last night, Mrs. Dedrick called me up. You can guess what she wanted.'

'She's got the ransom demand, and you're to deliver the dough, is that it?'

I nodded.

'She doesn't want the police to know.'

'She wouldn't,' Mifflin said, bitterly; 'but she expects us to get her husband back. When?'

'Tomorrow night. They'll call her and give her final instructions.'

'Brandon will have to be told.'

I shrugged.

'That's up to you. There's nothing he can do about it, unless he moves in and grabs the guy who collects. If he does, he'll kill Dedrick as if he shot him himself.'

'It's my bet, Dedrick's dead already.'

'Maybe, but we don't know for sure.'

'Well. I'll have to tell him.'

'So long as he doesn't let Mrs. Dedrick know I've been here. What will you do – tap the telephone wire?'

'Could do,' Mifflin said, closed his eyes and frowned. 'If

that woman doesn't want us in this, the chances are Brandon won't do anything. He's scared to make a wrong move with her. Once the ransom's paid, our troubles will be over. The Federal Bureau will take charge.'

'Getting back to Mary Jerome; anything or nothing?'

'Brandon's leaving her alone, but I've traced her car. A patrolman spotted her coming from Ocean End and got the number. He's one of those freaks who remembers car numbers. He shoved in a report when he heard about the kidnapping. She rented the car from the Acme Garage. Maybe you know the joint. It's run by a guy named Lute Ferris. We've had our eye on him off and on for smuggling reefers, but have never pinned anything on him. He was in Los Angeles when I called, but I talked with his wife. She remembers this Jerome dame. She arrived the night before last – the night of the kidnapping – around eight o'clock and asked Lute for a car. She paid fifty dollars deposit and said she needed the car for a couple of days. She gave the Orchid Hotel as her address.'

'Trusting of Ferris to let her have a car without checking on her first, wasn't it?'

'Why should he care? The car's insured. Anyway, that's the story, and we're stuck with it.'

'You've checked the airport and the station to see if she came from out-of-town?'

'Yeah, we've done that, but can't get a line on her.'

'And that's as far as you've got?'

'That's as far as we'll ever get,' Mifflin said, stubbing out his cigarette. 'A kidnapping case is the worst kind of case you can get. If they knock off the guy who's kidnapped and the money ain't marked, you're up a tree. The only hope is for one of them to be dissatisfied with his cut and give the rest of them away. It makes it ten times as hard now Brandon's scared to move. This Jerome dame is our only lead, and I can't go after her.'

'Well, maybe you'll have another murder on your hands to cheer you up,' I said bitterly. 'It wouldn't surprise me if I don't get knocked off tomorrow night.'

Mifflin eyed me thoughtfully.

'That's the only bit of good news I've had this week,' he said. 'Yeah, come to think of it, it's an even bet that's what they'll do to you.'

I left him, rubbing his hands and whistling the Dead March in *Saul*.

III

'Have you made a will?' Jack Kerman asked as he watched me load a .38 from a box of shells on my desk. 'I hope you've left me all your money. I can do with it. That redhead of mine seems to think I'm made of the stuff.'

'Do be quiet, Jack,' Paula said sharply. She was trying not to show how worked up she was, but the worried expression in her eyes gave her away. 'Haven't you any sense of decency?'

'Oh, shut up, you two,' I said, scowling at them. 'You're giving me the shakes. Now, let's get this straight, Jack. The house will probably be watched, so you've got to keep out of sight. I'll let you know where we're going on my way out. Give us a good five minutes to get clear of the house, then follow on after us. Make certain no one sees you. We can't afford to slip up on this. Whatever you do, don't show yourself unless trouble starts, and then come out shooting.'

Kerman gulped.

'What was that last bit again?'

'I said come out shooting.'

'I thought that's what you said. Come to think of it, it mightn't be a bad idea if I made a will myself.'

'And for the love of Pete, try to shoot straight,' I went on, looked at my wrist watch, stood up and shoved the .38 into the shoulder holster under my coat. 'We'd better get off. If you don't hear from either of us, Paula, by midnight, get on to Mifflin and tell him the tale.'

'She'll hear from me,' Kerman said, looking worried. 'Well, damn it, I hope she will!'

'Be careful, Vic,' Paula said anxiously.

I patted her shoulder.

'I can't make you out. You worry over a little job like kidnapping, but think nothing of sending me into a room full of dope fiends. Be your age, Paula. Think of the money we're going to make.'

'Well, don't do anything silly,' she said, trying to smile, 'and for heaven's sake don't show off before that rich blonde.'

'You're making me nervous,' I said. 'Come on, Jack. Let's get out of here.'

41

'Together we went along the corridor to the elevator.

'Think we have time for a drink?' Kerman asked hopefully as we reached ground level.

'No; but there's a pint in the car. And, Jack, don't make any mistakes. This might turn out to be a nasty job.'

Kerman gave an exaggerated shudder.

'It's already nasty enough for me.'

He climbed into the back of the Buick and squatted down on the floor. I chucked a rug over him.

'I'm going to love every minute of this,' he said, poking his head out from the folds of the rug. 'How long do you reckon I'll be under this lot?'

'Oh, about three or four hours: not more.'

'With the temperature in the eighties, that should give me some idea what the Black Hole of Calcutta was like.'

'It'll get cooler in the evening,' I said heartlessly and started the car. 'You have a whole bottle of Scotch to help pass the time, only don't smoke.'

'Not smoke?' His voice shot up in a yelp of dismay.

'Listen; stop kidding yourself. If these guys find out you're in the back of the car, they'll steal up and slit your gizzard.'

That quietened him.

I drove up the two miles of private road a lot more sedately than the first time I came this way. I took the bend in the drive nice and slow, and pulled up within a yard of the balustrade surrounding the courtyard.

In the warm light of the evening sun, the house looked about as attractive as any house would look after a million dollars had been spent on it. The big black Cadillac stood before the front entrance. In the middle distance two Chinese gardeners were picking the dead roses off an umbrella standard. They worked as if the rose tree was their main source of income for the next nine months: probably it was. The big swimming pool glittered in the sun, but no one swam in it. Across the expanse of velvety lawn in the lower garden, below the terraces, six scarlet flamingoes stood looking towards me, stiff-legged and crotchety, as unreal as the blue sky of an Italian postcard.

There was everything to be had this day at Ocean End except happiness.

I looked towards the house. The grass-green shutters covered the windows; a cream-and-green striped awning flapped above the front door.

'Well, so long,' I said in a low voice to Kerman. 'I'm going in now.'

'Have a lovely time,' Kerman's voice was bitter from under the rug. 'Don't stint yourself. Have plenty of ice with your drinks.'

I walked along the terrace and screwed my thumb into the bell push. I could see through the glass panels of the door into a big hall and a dim, cool passage that led to the back of the house.

A tall, thin old man came down the passage and opened the front door. He looked me over in a kindly way. I had an idea he was pricing my suit and wishing he could buy me something a little better that wouldn't disgrace the house. But I was probably wrong. He may not even have been thinking about me.

'Mrs. Dedrick is expecting me.'

'The name, sir?'

'Malloy.'

He still stood squarely in the doorway.

'Have you a card, please?'

'Well, yes, and I have a birthmark too. Remind me to show it to you one of these days.'

He tittered politely like an aged uncle out to have fun with his sister's young hopeful.

'So many gentlemen of the Press have tried to see Mrs. Dedrick. We have to take precautions, sir.'

I had an idea I would be standing there till next summer if I didn't show him my card, so I got out my bill-fold and showed him my card : the non-business one.

He stood aside.

'Would you wait in the lounge, sir?'

I went into the room where Souki had been shot. The Mexican rug had been cleaned. There were no bodies lying about this evening to welcome me; no untouched whisky and soda, no cigarette stub to spoil the repaired surface of the table.

'If you could sneak me a double Scotch with a lot of ice in it, I'd appreciate it.'

'Certainly, sir.'

He drifted across the room to the sideboard on which stood a bottle of Haig and Haig, glasses, a bucket of ice and Whiterock.

I listened attentively as he moved, but I couldn't hear his bones creak. I was surprised. He looked old enough for them

43

to squeak. But, old as he was, he was no slouch when it came to mixing a drink. He handed me one strong enough to tip over a pony and trap.

'If you would care to look at some periodicals while you wait, sir, I will get some for you.'

I lowered myself into an easy chair that accepted me as if it was doing me a favour, stretched out my legs and balanced my drink carefully on the arm of the chair.

'You think there'll be a long wait?' I asked.

'I have no experience in these matters, sir, but it would seem likely they won't communicate with us until it is dark.' He stood before me, not unlike one of the flamingoes I had seen in the lower garden, and every inch of him dedicated to a life of service. Probably he would never see seventy again, but the blue eyes were still alert and clear, and what he lacked in speed he made up in experienced efficiency: a family retainer straight out of Hollywood, almost too genuine to be true.

'Yeah, I guess you're right. Looks like a good three-hour wait: probably more.' I dug out a package of cigarettes. He had a match flame ready before I got the cigarette into my mouth. 'I didn't get your name.'

The grizzled eyebrows lifted.

'Wadlock, sir.'

'Do you work for Mrs. Dedrick or Mr. Marshland?'

'Oh, Mr. Marshland, sir. I have been lent to Mrs. Dedrick for the time being, and I am very happy to be of service to her.'

'Have you been with the family long?'

He smiled benignly.

'Fifty years, sir. I was with Mr. Marshland senior for twenty years, and I have been with Mr. Marshland junior for thirty years.'

That seemed to put us on a friendly footing, so I asked, 'You met Mr. Dedrick when he was in New York?'

The benign expression went away like a fist when you open your fingers.

'Oh, yes, sir. He stayed a few days with Mr. Marshland.'

'I haven't seen him. I've spoken to him on the 'phone, and I've heard a lot about him, but there appears to be no photograph of him. What does he look like?'

I had an idea there was disapproval in the blue eyes now, but I wasn't sure.

'He is a well-built gentleman; dark, tall, athletic, with very

44

good features. I don't think I can describe him any better than that, sir.'

'Did you like him?'

The bent old back stiffened.

'Did you say you would like some periodicals, sir? You may find the wait a little tedious.'

I had my answer. Obviously for some reason or other this old man had as much use for Dedrick as I had for a punch on the jaw.

'That's all right. It makes a change to sit and do nothing.'

'Very good, sir.' He wasn't friendly any more. 'I will let you know when there is any news.'

He went away on his spindly old legs as dignified as an archbishop conferring a favour, and left me alone in a room full of bad memories. About a yard from my left foot Souki's head had bled on the rug. Over by the fireplace stood the telephone into which Dedrick had breathed hurriedly and unevenly while he talked to me. I turned to stare at the casement window through which the kidnappers had probably come, gun in hand.

A short, dapper figure in a white tropical suit and a panama hat stood in the doorway, watching me. I hadn't heard him arrive. I wasn't expecting him. With my mind full of murder and thugs, he gave me a start that nearly took me to the ceiling.

'I didn't mean to startle you,' he said in a mild, rather absent-minded way. 'I didn't know you were in here.'

While he was speaking he came into the room and put his panama hat on the table. I guessed he would be Franklin Marshland, and looked to see if Serena took after him. She didn't. He had a small, beaky nose, a heavy chin, dreamy, forgetful brown eyes and a full, rather feminine mouth. His wrinkled face was sun-tanned, and the thick fringe of glossy white hair, above which was a bald, sun-tanned patch, made him look like a clean-shaven and amiable Santa Claus.

I began to climb out of my chair, but he waved me to stay where I was.

'Don't move. I'll join you in a whisky.' He consulted a narrow, gold wrist-watch, worn on the inside of his wrist. 'Quarter past six. I don't believe in drinking spirits before six, do you?'

I said it was a good rule, but rules should be broken now and then if one was to preserve one's sense of freedom.

He paid no attention to what I was saying. There was a look of aloof disinterest on his face that hinted he seldom if ever listened to anything anyone said to him.

'You're the chap who's going to pay them the ransom money,' he went on, stating a fact and not asking a question.

I said I was as he carried a fair-size snifter to an arm-chair opposite mine. He sat down and stared at me over the rim of the glass the way you would stare at some curious animal at the Zoo.

'She tells me she's going with you.'

'So she says.'

'I wish she wouldn't, but nothing I say makes any difference.' He sipped the whisky, stared down at his white buckskin shoes. He had the smallest male feet I have ever seen. 'I never have been able to influence her one way or the other. A pity, really. Of course, old people are bores, but sometimes they are able to help the young if the young would only let them.'

I had the idea he was talking rather to himself than to me, so I didn't say anything.

He brooded off into a silence that lasted some time. I helped myself to another of my cigarettes, kept an intelligent expression on my face just in case he might think it worth while to speak to me and resisted the temptation to fidget.

In the middle distance I noticed the two Chinese gardeners had decided to call it a day. They had been staring at the umbrella standard for some time without touching it; now, having learned it by heart, they moved off to enjoy a well-earned rest.

'Do you carry a gun?' Marshland asked suddenly.

'Yes; but I don't expect to use it.'

'I hope not. You'll see she takes as little risk as possible, won't you?'

'Of course.'

He drank half the whisky. It didn't do much to cheer him up.

'These fellows have pretty big ideas. Five hundred thousand is an enormous sum of money.'

He seemed to expect me to say something so I said, 'That's why they snatched him. The risk is enormous too.'

'I suppose it is. Do you think they'll keep their side of the bargain?'

'I don't know. As I explained to Mrs. Dedrick, if he hasn't seen them . . .'

'Yes; she told me. You're probably right. I've been reading about some of the famous kidnapping cases of the past years. It would seem the higher the ransom the less likely is the chance of the victim surviving.'

I was suddenly aware that he wasn't mild or absentminded any more, and that he was staring at me with an intent, rather odd expression in his eyes.

'It depends on the kidnappers,' I said, meeting his eyes.

'I have a feeling we shan't see him again.' He got slowly to his feet, frowned round the room as if he had lost something. 'Of course, I haven't said anything to her about it, but I wouldn't be surprised if they haven't already killed him.' The white eyebrows lifted. 'What do you think?'

'It's possible.'

'More than possible, perhaps?'

'I'm afraid so.'

He nodded. The pleased, satisfied expression in his eyes jarred me to the heels.

He went out of the room, very spry and dapper, and humming a tune under his breath.

IV

It wasn't until the hands of my watch had crawled round to eleven that the telephone bell rang. The five-hour wait had been interminable, and I was so het-up I very nearly answered the telephone myself, but someone in some other part of the house beat me to it.

I had been pacing up and down, sitting on the settee, staring out of the window and chain-smoking during those five long hours. I had seen Wadlock for a few minutes when he had brought me dinner on a wheel wagon, but he hadn't had anything to say and left me to serve myself.

I had been out just after eight o'clock to have a word with Kerman and to drop him a cold breast of chicken through the car window. I didn't stay more than a minute or so. I was scared anyone who might be watching the house would hear his flow of bad language.

Now at last something was going to happen. Although Dedrick meant nothing to me, I was nervy after the long wait. I could imagine what Serena must be feeling like. She was probably fit to walk up a wall.

A few minutes later I heard movements outside and I went into the hall.

Serena, in black slacks and a short, dark fur coat, came hurrying down the stairs, followed by Wadlock, who was carrying three oilskin-wrapped packages.

She looked white and ill; there was a pinched, drawn look about her that told more clearly than words how she had suffered during those long hours of waiting.

'Monte Verde Mining Camp. Do you know it?' she said in a low, unsteady voice.

'Yes. It's on San Diego Highway. It'll take us about twenty minutes to get there if the traffic is light.'

Franklin Marshland appeared silently.

'Where is it?' he asked.

'Monte Verde Mining Camp. It's an old worked-out silver mine on San Diego Highway,' I told him. 'It's a good spot for them.' I looked at Serena's white face. Her lips were trembling. 'Any news of your husband, Mrs. Dedrick?'

'He – he is to be set free three hours after the money has been delivered. They will telephone us here where we will find him.'

Marshland and I exchanged glances.

Serena caught hold of my arm.

'Do you think they're lying? If we let them have the money, we'll have no hold on them at all.'

'You haven't a hold on them, anyway, Mrs. Dedrick. That's what makes kidnapping such a filthy business. You're entirely in their hands, and you just have to trust them.'

'Wouldn't it be better, my dear, if you let Mr. Malloy deliver the money, and you wait here for the second message?' Marshland asked.

'No!'

She didn't look at him.

'Serena, do be sensible. There's always a chance they might be tempted to kidnap you. I'm sure Mr. Malloy is quite capable. . . .'

She turned on him, distraught with misery and hysteria.

'I'm going with him, and nothing you say will stop me!' she cried wildly. 'Oh, you needn't pretend any more. I know you don't want Lee to come out of this alive! I know you hate him! I know you've been gloating with joy that this has happened to him! But I'm bringing him back! Do you hear? I'm bringing him back!'

'You're being absurd . . .' Marshland said, a faint flush coming to his face. His eyes looked hard and bitter.

She turned away from him to me.

'Are you coming with me?'

'Whenever you're ready, Mrs. Dedrick.'

'Then bring the money and come!'

She ran to the front door, jerked it open and went out on to the terrace.

Wadlock gave me the three packages.

'You'll take care of her, sir,' he said.

I gave him a crooked grin.

'You bet.'

Marshland walked away without looking at me.

'She's very upset, sir,' Wadlock murmured. He looked upset himself.

I ran along the terrace, down the steps to the Cadillac.

'I'll drive,' I said and tossed the packages into the back of the car. 'I won't be a moment. I want my gun.'

I left her getting into the Cad. and ran over to the Buick.

'Monte Verde Mine,' I said. 'Give us five minutes, then come on – and watch out, Jack.'

A soft moan came from under the rug, but I didn't wait. I went back to the Cadillac and climbed under the steering wheel. Serena sat huddled up in a corner. She was crying.

I sent the car shooting down the drive.

'Don't let it get you down.'

She went on crying quietly. I decided perhaps it was the best thing for her, and drove as fast as I could without taking risks, and ignored her.

As we drove along Orchid Boulevard I said, 'Better get hold of yourself now. You haven't told me yet what was said. If we make one false move, we may spoil his chance of getting back to you. These guys will be a lot more scared than we are. Now, come on, pull yourself together, and tell me. What did they say?'

It took her some minutes to control herself, and it wasn't until we were shooting up Monte Verde Avenue that she told me.

'The money is to be left on the roof of a shed standing before the old shaft. I don't know if you know it?'

'I know it. What else?'

'Each parcel is to be placed at least a foot apart and in a row. After we have placed the parcels we must leave immediately.'

'That the lot?'

She gave a little shiver.

'Except for the usual threats about setting a trap.'

'They didn't bring your husband to the 'phone?'

'No. Why should they?'

'Sometimes they do.'

The fact they hadn't made it look bad for Dedrick, but I didn't tell her so.

'Was it the same man who spoke to you before?'

'I think so.'

'The same muffled voice?'

'Yes.'

'All right. Now this is what we do. I'll stop the car at the entrance to the mine. You stay in the car. I'll take the money and put it on the roof. You'll be able to see every move I make. I'll come straight back and get into the car. You will drive. At the beginning of Venture Avenue you'll slow down and I'll drop off. You carry on and get back to the house.'

'Why are you dropping off?'

'I may catch sight of them.'

'No!' She caught hold of my arm. 'Do you want them to kill him? We're leaving the money and doing what they tell us. You've got to promise.'

'Well, all right; it's your money. If they double-cross you, you'll stand no chance of catching up with them. I'll guarantee they won't see me.'

'No!' she repeated. 'I'm not going to give them any opportunity to go back on the bargain.'

I swung the long black nose of the Cad. into San Diego Highway.

'All right, but it's the wrong way to play it.'

She didn't answer.

There was a lot of traffic belting along the Highway, and it took me some minutes before I could swing the car across to the dirt track leading to the mine. We went bumping over the uneven surface of the track. It was dark and forlorn up there, and the headlamps bounced off great clumps of scrub and dumps of rubbish. Although only a few hundred yards or so off the main Highway, once on this track it was as lonely and as dark as the inside of a tomb.

Ahead of me was the entrance to the mine. One of the high wooden gates had been blown off its hinges. The other still stood upright, but only just. I pulled up before the gateway. The headlights sent a long, searching beam along the cracked concrete driveway that led directly to the head of the shaft.

We could see the shed. It was not more than seven feet high; a rotten, derelict building where probably at one time the time-keeper had sheltered while he checked in the miners.

'Well, that's it. Now you wait here. If anything happens get out of the car and run for it.'

She was staring at the shed as if she expected to see Dedrick come out of it. Her face looked as if it was carved out of ice.

I got out, opened the rear door and collected the three parcels. Holding them under one arm, I loosened the .38 in its holster and set off down the driveway towards the shed.

Only the distant rumble of traffic on the Highway disturbed the silence. Nothing moved. No one jumped out on me with a gun. It seemed a long way to the shed, and the brilliant head-lamps made me a nice target for anyone with a trigger itch. I was glad when I got there. My right hand slid inside my coat and rested on the gun butt as I peered through the half-open door.

Only a broken chair, a lot of dirt and scraps of paper on the floor greeted me. The headlights of the car went through the doorway and made two pools of light on the spider-in-fested wall.

I was reluctant to leave all that money on the roof of the shed. I had a feeling Serena would never see it again; nor would she buy Dedrick back with it. But I had been hired to put the money there, so I put it there. I placed the packages along the rusty, corrugated roof in a row, spacing them carefully a foot apart as she had been instructed. There was nothing more to do. I would have liked very much to have hidden near-by and watched, but if I was spotted and Dedrick died, I would have his death on my conscience. She was right. Her one hope was to trust them to carry out their end of the bargain.

I walked towards the car, my flesh creeping a little, still a nice target for anyone who wanted to shed a little blood. I wondered if they were watching. There were any number of places to hide in this ruined mine.

I reached the Cadillac, jerked open the door and slid under the wheel.

She was crying again.

'If you're sure you don't want me to watch, I'll take you back,' I said, not looking at her.

'Take me back,' she said in a muffled voice and turned away from me.

As I drove through the gates I caught sight of a shadowy figure that ducked behind a pile of old railway sleepers. I thought it was Kerman, but couldn't be sure. If it was Kerman, he would probably hang around and see something. I looked quickly at Serena, but she was busy with her handkerchief and hadn't noticed anything.

In a more optimistic mood I headed for Ocean End.

v

The hands of the clock on the mantelpiece showed a quarter past two. I sat alone in the lounge, nibbling at a whisky and soda, staring at a silver-and-gold inlaid Mexican saddle that was hanging on the wall without particularly noticing it.

Serena was upstairs somewhere.

We had been waiting for two and a half hours.

A sudden soft whistle from behind me jerked me round and spilt my whisky.

'Lousy nerves you've got,' Kerman said, coming in. 'Is that whisky you've spilt?'

'There's plenty more. Help yourself. You look as if you could use it.'

'I can.' He crossed to the wagon and mixed himself a long, stiff drink. 'Phew! Think we'll get any sleep tonight?'

'Never mind sleep. Did you see anything?'

He flopped into an armchair opposite me.

'No. At least I didn't see them, but I did see the money go.'

'But didn't you see who took it?'

He shook his head.

'The guy's smart. He kept hidden. I think he was probably standing on one of the girders that support the shaft head. It was pitch dark up there. Anyway, he must have been above the roof of the shed. He had a fishing rod. One of those deep-sea rods, I should imagine. It would have to be something pretty hefty to take the weight of those parcels. He just dropped a hook on the parcel and fished it off the roof into the darkness. I never heard a sound or caught a glimpse of him. It was damned spooky seeing those parcels take off in the moonlight until I tumbled to what he was doing.'

'Yes, that's smart. Did he see you, Jack?'

'Not a chance.'

'Don't be too sure. I saw you.'

'I'll bet my life you didn't. Besides, I didn't arrive until you were driving away. I saw your tail lights. And when I reached the mine I was crawling around like a Red Indian.'

'Well, I saw someone as I was leaving.'

'It couldn't have been me.'

I tried to remember what the shadowy figure had looked like. It had certainly reminded me of Kerman, so that would make it tall, broad-shouldered and lean. Not much to go on, but something.

'Must have been one of the gang. I wish I had seen more of him.' I looked at my wrist-watch. 'In another quarter of an hour we should hear: if we're going to hear.'

Kerman rubbed weary knuckles into his eyes.

'I feel whacked. That five-hour wait in the car nearly killed me. Think they'll turn him loose?'

'I don't know. I can't see them doing it. It'll be a lucky break for him if they do.'

'Brandon's going to love this if he doesn't come back,' Kerman said, stifling a yawn.

'It's her responsibility.'

'But we are accessories. He'll be scared to curse her, but he'll have something to say to us.'

'Well, let him say it,' I said, got up and tramped across to the wagon to make another drink. My hand hovered over the bottle as Franklin Marshland came silently into the room.

'So you've got back safely,' he said. 'I must say I was very worried.' He looked inquiringly at Jack Kerman.

I introduced them.

'A very long, unpleasant wait,' Marshland went on. 'Surely it's time they communicated with us?'

'It needs five minutes to the three hours,' I said, giving Kerman another drink and going back to the settee. 'If they've released him, they'll make sure he doesn't get back here until they are well out of town.'

He half turned to stare at me.

'I think it's extremely unlikely they will release him,' he said. 'If we don't hear in another half-hour I propose calling the police.'

'That's up to you,' I said, 'but as we've waited so long, I

53

think we should wait until daylight. Even now any false move might be dangerous for him.'

'I think he's dead.'

I felt tired, and beyond making aimless small-talk.

'Just what is it you dislike so much about Lee Dedrick, Mr. Marshland?'

He ignored this question, and stepped out on to the terrace. He remained out there for three or four minutes, then came in again and headed for the door.

'I'd better see how my daughter is,' he said, more to himself than to us. 'This wait is very hard on her.' At the door he paused, looked back at me. 'A man who marries a woman for her money is always worthy of contempt, Mr. Malloy.'

He went out of the room, and we listened to his footsteps on the stairs.

Kerman made a grimace.

'Did he marry her for her money?' he asked in a whisper.

'I don't know.' I jerked my thumb at the clock. 'Five minutes overdue.'

'Doesn't look very healthy, does it?'

'There's nothing we can do except wait. I swung my legs up on the settee. 'I like that girl. Maybe she is a little over-rich and probably spoilt, but she's got a tender heart.'

Kerman grunted.

'I like 'em hard and shiny,' he said, and closed his eyes.

Minutes ticked by. We began to doze. We finally slept.

The first rays of the morning sun brought me upright with a start. I looked at the clock. It showed a quarter to seven. Kerman slept soundly. I heard no sound except the gentle beating of the surf on the low ridge of coral stone that made a natural harbour at the end of the garden.

I swung my legs off the settee and walked on to the terrace.

The two Chinese gardeners were at work, staring at the umbrella standard. The flamingoes were grouped around the lily pond, hunting up some breakfast. On a balcony at the far end of the terrace, Serena Dedrick, still in her black slacks and her short fur coat, sat staring out to sea. There was a lost look on her white face: a look that told me no one had telephoned while we slept, and no one had sent him back.

I walked quietly into the lounge and left her alone with her misery.

CHAPTER THREE

I

THE next four days were a sustained and shattering bedlam that shook the usually placid, unruffled calm and quiet of Orchid City to its foundations.

When the news broke that five hundred thousand dollars had been paid to a gang of kidnappers and the kidnapped man had not been returned, the country as far north as San Francisco and as far south as Los Angeles sprang into action.

For the first few hours, Brandon had it all his own way, and revelled in the commotion. He began to organize what was to be the greatest man-hunt of the century, but he had scarcely begun to issue orders when a dozen sharp-eyed Federal agents descended on him from San Francisco and snatched away his command.

State troopers, regular Army units, aircraft, television and the radio were all pressed into service.

Kerman and I spent hours at Police Headquarters being questioned and crossed-questioned by a furious, purple-faced fist-pounding Brandon, and later by two quiet Federal agents who took us apart, laid us on the desk, poked us about with long inquisitive fingers, and weren't over-fussy how they put us together again.

We were bullied and threatened and cursed. We had fists shaken in our faces. Necks swelled, eyes turned bloodshot and spittle flew in all directions with the intensity of trying to get a clue out of us. But we hadn't a clue to give out.

I couldn't move ten yards on the streets without some visiting Pressman letting off a camera in my face. Kerman, described as 'the man who saw the ransom taken,' was badgered from dusk to dawn for his autograph, his nail-parings, locks of his hair and clippings from his suit by wild-eyed, sensation-hungry souvenir-seekers until he was scared to leave the safety of the office.

The massive gates of Ocean End were closed. The telephone was disconnected. A quiet, deathly hush hung over the place.

Rumour had it that Serena Dedrick had collapsed and was seriously ill.

All day long aircraft circled overhead, searching the sand dunes, the foothills and the approaches of the city. Every road was patrolled. A house-to-house inquiry was set on foot; suspicious characters were rounded up and questioned; a squad of police went into Coral Gables, the east-end district of the city, and checked over the more disreputable inhabitants.

The activity was enormous, but for all the efforts made by the Federal agents, the police, state troopers, the Army and hundreds of amateur investigators, neither Lee Dedrick nor the kidnappers were found.

Then, on the fifth morning, Serena snapped out of her grief and took a hand in the hunt herself. It was announced through the Press and over the radio that she would pay a twenty-five-thousand-dollar reward to anyone giving information that would lead to the arrest of the kidnappers, and a thousand-dollar reward for any information remotely connected with the kidnapping.

The result of this announcement turned practically every citizen, except the wealthy, into amateur detectives and made Orchid City a temporary hell on earth.

It was on the sixth night after the ransom had been paid that I let myself into my quiet little cabin, thankful to get away from the strident hubbub of the hunt, with the intention of locking the door and getting myself a little peace and an early night in bed.

My cabin is situated in the sand dunes, facing the sea, and is a quarter of a mile from the nearest house. It has a small weed-infested garden which I pay Toni, my good-for-nothing house-boy, to keep neat; a veranda with faded sun blinds, one big living-room, two bedrooms, a bathroom and a kitchen big enough to swing a cat in, providing it is a Manx cat.

The charm of the place to me is that it is lonely and quiet, and you can't hear anyone's radio and you can sing in your bath without getting a brick through your window. But because it is so isolated it is also an ideal spot for anyone who wants to slit my throat. My yells for help would be as futile as a short-tempered man trying to slam a revolving door.

I was sinking the key in the lock when I heard a soft foot-fall behind me. Normally my nerves will pass in a crowd with a light behind them, but the excitement and strain of the past five days had made them a little edgy. I swung around with a quick intake of breath to find a shadowy figure right on top of me.

The right-hand punch that automatically started got no more than half-way when I saw that my visitor was a woman. I lowered my fist, gulped in a little of the hot night air and said as even as I could, 'Must you sneak up like that and scare me out of my wits?'

'Your name Malloy?'

I peered at the slim figure before me. It was too dark under the veranda roof to see much of her, but what I could see appeared to be worth looking at.

'Yeah. Who are you?'

'I want to talk to you. Let's go in where we can park.'

As I led the way into the main room, I thought it was a pity she had a voice hard enough to crack a rock on. We stood in the darkness, close together while I groped for the light switch. I found it, thumbed it down and looked into a pair of wide brown eyes that knew all the answers and most of the questions too.

She was around twenty-four or five, and dark. Her thick glossy hair was parted in the middle and framed a face of standard prettiness that was a shade paler than it should have been and too hard and bitter for the number of years she had been using it. Her over-bright red lips, put on square, and the faint smudges under her eyes gave her a sexy look that would make men stare at her and wonder, but probably they'd get no farther than wondering. Her figure under the fawn-and-green silk windbreaker and the highwaisted slacks was good enough to advertise the best foundation garment in the business.

'Hello,' I said, staring at her. 'Sure it's me you want?'

'If your name's Malloy, I'm sure,' she said, and moved past me to the fireplace. She faced me, her hands thrust deep into her trouser pockets, her eyes searching my face. 'Nick Perelli told me to come to you.'

'Why, sure,' I said, and looked sharply at her, wondering who she was. 'Has he been sandbagging anyone recently?'

'No, but he's in trouble,' the girl said. She took out a crumpled package of Lucky Strike, flicked one into her mouth, scratched a match alight with her thumbnail and set fire to the cigarette. 'He's been pinched for the Dedrick snatch.'

In the pause that followed, the clock on the mantelpiece ticked busily and the refrigerator in the kitchen gave an irritable grunt.

The girl continued to watch me, not moving, her head tilted a little on one side so the smoke of her cigarette wouldn't get into her eyes.

'Perelli?' I said, as blank as I sounded.

She nodded.

'He said you were a bright boy. Well, go ahead and be bright. Someone's got to be if he's going to beat this rap.'

'When did they take him?'

'An hour ago.' She glanced over her shoulder to look at the clock. 'An hour and five minutes to be exact.'

'The Feds?'

She shook her head.

'A smooth, well-dressed fatty and a couple of hard-faced dicks. There were two bulls outside with the car.'

'Was it Brandon? Short, fat, white-haired?'

'That makes him Brandon. Who's he?'

'Captain of Police.'

She drew on her cigarette, examined her nails and frowned.

'I didn't know police captains made arrests.'

'They do when there's a lot of money hanging to the pinch, and a lot of juicy publicity as well. Besides, Brandon would want to get in front of the Feds.'

'Well, he's got in front of them.' She moved away from the fireplace and sat down on the divan. 'Nick said you'd get him out of it. Can you?'

'I don't know. I owe him something, and if there's anything I can do, I'll do it. What does he expect me to do?'

'He didn't say. He was a little rattled. I've never seen Nick rattled before. When they found the gun, he told me to come to you.'

I went to a cupboard, took out a bottle of Scotch and two glasses and set them on the table. I fetched a jug of ice water from the refrigerator.

'Let's start from the beginning. It'll be quicker that way. Do you like your whisky straight or with water?'

'For a bright boy, you haven't much imagination. Right now they're beating his brains out. Do you think I want to drink whisky when I know that's going on?'

I made myself a stiff drink and sat down.

'You don't know for certain, and worrying about it won't help him.'

She jumped to her feet and took three or four quick paces across the room, turned and went back to the divan. She sat down again and began to pound her first into the palm of her hand.

'Who are you, anyway?' I asked.

'Myra Toresca. Nick's girl.'

'All right. Now let's take a look at it. Give me the details, but make it fast.'

'I arrived with them,' she said, and went on practically in one breath: 'Nick and I were going to the movies. He was late. I 'phoned and he said to come over while he changed. I went over. I rode up in the elevator with the three of them. I knew they were cops. We got off at the fourth floor, and I let them go ahead. When they turned the corner, I went after them. They were standing outside Nick's door. Two of them had guns in their hands. I watched. They didn't notice me. The fat one rapped on the door. I guess Nick thought it was me. They jumped him, and had the cuffs on before he knew what had hit him. Then they started to ransack the place. The front door was pushed to, but not closed. I looked in. Nick was standing by the wall watching them take the place to pieces. He looked my way and made motions for me to keep out of the way. I stuck around, watching. Then they found the gun down the side of the settee. Brandon got awfully excited. He said it was the gun that had killed Dedrick's chauffeur. Nick got rattled then. He and I play cards for a living. We can lip-read. It helps when the cards don't fall right. He told me to come to you. I left them shouting at him.'

'How did Brandon know the gun killed Dedrick's chauffeur?' I asked.

She shook her head.

'I don't know.'

'What happened then?'

'I waited across the other side of the street. After about half an hour, they brought him out. He could scarcely walk, and there was blood on his face and his clothes.' She got up to grind the cigarette out in the ash tray. 'They took him away in a police car. Then I came on here.'

I sat staring at her for a second or so.

'Do you know anything about the kidnapping?'

The brown eyes met mine.

'Only what I've read in the papers.'

'Nothing else?'

'No.'

'Does he?'

'No. He wouldn't touch a thing like that. All right, maybe we are a little tricky with a deck of cards, but that's as far as we go.'

'Has he ever been caught?'

Her eyes hardened.

'Now and then.'

'Has he a police record?'

'I guess so. He drew two years in San Francisco. He hasn't been out more than four months.'

'Anything before that?'

'You want to know a lot, don't you?'

'I want to know his record. It's important.'

'Six months, a year and two years. Spread over eight years.'

'Card-sharping?'

She nodded.

'Did he ever hurt anyone with that cosh of his?'

'No one's ever complained.'

'You're quite sure about the kidnapping? You don't think he pulled it without telling you?'

'He didn't do it! It's not his line. Can't you understand that?'

I decided to believe her.

'All right. I'll see what I can do.' I reached for the telephone and dialled a number. After a while a polite voice said, 'This is Mr. Francon's residence.'

'Mr. Francon in? This is Vic Malloy.'

'Yes, sir. I'll put you through.'

After more delay, Francon came on the line. 'Hello, Vic, what's on your mind?'

'An hour ago, Brandon, with a couple of dicks, picked up a guy named Nick Perelli at his apartment on Jefferson Avenue. They searched the rooms and found a gun. Brandon said it was the gun that had killed Lee Dedrick's chauffeur. They've arrested Perelli for the Dedrick kidnapping. I want you to represent him, Justin. Expense no object, and I want you to get over to Headquarters and look after him. They're pushing him around and I want it stopped. Will you do it?'

'Has he anything to do with the kidnapping?'

'I don't know. His girl, who ought to know, says he hasn't. It looks like a frame to me. Brandon couldn't know the gun was the death gun by just looking at it. He either brought it with him and planted it or he's guessing.'

'You can't say a thing like that!' Francon's voice was shocked.

'Off the record I can. It would be a terrific boost for Brandon if he could crack this case and steal a march on the Feds. I wouldn't put anything past him.'

'Who is Perelli, anyway?'

'He's a card-sharper with a record.

'That doesn't help. What's he to you?'

'He did me a good turn once. As a personal favour, Justin, I want you to get down there right away and stop them working on him.'

There was a long pause on the line while he chewed it over. I didn't hurry him.

Finally, he said, 'I'm not sure I want this job. Brandon must have something more solid to work on than the gun.'

'Maybe he has, but that isn't the point. You're not going to let him hang something on this guy just because he's got a record, are you?'

'Well, no. All right, Vic. I'll go over there and see him. But I warn you, if I think he's guilty, I'm pulling out. There's too much publicity tied to this business to be in on the losing end.'

'I still think it could be a frame. Take a look at him, anyway. And don't worry too much about what they've got on him. I'm going to take a hand in this, Justin.'

'Well, all right. I'll see what I can do. Better see me to-morrow morning at my office.'

'I'll ring you tonight.'

I hung up before he could protest.

Myra was watching me, an intent expression in her eyes.

'Who's that?'

'Justin Francon. The smartest criminal lawyer on the Pacific Coast. If he believes Perelli is being framed, he'll never stop fighting until he's freed him.'

'Is he going down there?'

'You bet he is, and he'll block Brandon off.'

She lit another cigarette. Her hand was noticeably unsteady.

'I guess Nick knew what he was doing when he told me to come to you.'

From her that would be praise.

I finished my drink and stood up.

'Where can I reach you?'

'245 Monte Verde Avenue. It's a little green-painted shack on the left-hand side as you go up. I live alone.'

While I was writing the address down, she went on, 'This will take some money, won't it?'

'I told Perelli I'd be glad to help him any time, and it'd be on the house. That still goes.'

'Thanks.'

'Forget it. I owe him a stab in the belly. Now look. I'm going down to Police Headquarters right away. There's not much I can do until I find out just how much they have on him. I might even have a word with him if I'm lucky.'

'You mean they'll let you talk to him?'

'I don't know. The Homicide Lieutenant is a friend of mine. He might swing it.'

Just for a second the hardness went out of her eyes, and the red-painted mouth trembled.

'Give him my love,' she said.

II

The news of Perelli's arrest had broken by the time I reached Princes Street and Centre Avenue.

I couldn't get within five hundred yards of Police Headquarters. As I tried to take the turn a raving, purple-faced cop waved me back into Centre Avenue. Three other cops were barring the way to other cars.

I managed to catch a glimpse of a seething crowd that overflowed the sidewalks of Princes Street into the road before I drove on down to Orchid Boulevard.

I parked the car and walked back.

There was a big crowd of people standing before Police Headquarters, and it was growing every second. No amount of swearing and pushing from the sweat-soaked patrolmen made any impression on them. They had come to gape, and no cursing cop was going to stop them.

A bunch of Brandon's special tough squad stood in the doorway of the building with their nightsticks drawn. I knew I had about as much chance of getting past them as a nudist has of gate-crashing the White House: probably less.

I fought my way into a near-by drug-store. It was empty except for a white-coated night clerk who stood in the doorway wistfully watching the crowd.

'I just wanted to 'phone,' I said as he reluctantly tore himself away and moved back into the store.

'Some excitement,' he said, licking his lips. 'They say Brandon's grabbed the kidnapper. Think he'll get the twenty-five grand? Jeepers! I wish it was me. I could use that amount of dough.'

I made grunting noises and shut myself in a call-box. I asked the operator to connect me with Police Headquarters.

'I can't,' she said. 'Every line's jammed. I've been trying to get them for the past twenty minutes. What goes on down there?'

'Some cop's cleaned his buttons, and the whole force's gone on strike,' I said sourly and hung up.

I came out into the quiet and cool of the store again. The clerk was standing on a stool so that he could see over the heads of the crowd. By now they were jammed up against his windows. It looked as if I'd have trouble in getting out.

'The Feds have arrived,' he told me, sucking in his breath excitedly. 'But this has wiped their eyes. That guy Brandon's a smart cop. Best Captain of Police we've ever had.'

'How do I get out of here?' I said impatiently after trying to shove through a bunch of backs facing me in the doorway.

'You don't want to get out, do you? Grab a stool. You won't get a better view than here.'

'View of what?'

He frowned down at me.

'Maybe they'll bring him out. Maybe that Dedrick dame will come down to look him over. Anything can happen. I wish my girl was here. She'd love this.'

'Is there a back way out of here?'

'Through that door. Takes you into Orchid Boulevard.'

'Thanks.'

As I jerked open the door, the crowd lurched back. There came a tremendous crash of breaking glass as one of the plate-glass windows of the store gave up the unequal struggle.

I didn't wait to see what the damage was. A passage at the back of the store brought me to a dark alley that led eventually to Orchid Boulevard.

Mifflin had a small house on Westwood Avenue. He lived with his wife, two children, a Boxer dog, two white cats and a bullfinch. Apart from his police duties, he was a highly domesticated man, and rumour had it he was even more scared of his wife than he was of Brandon.

I decided to go out there and wait for him. I was determined to see him tonight, come rain, come sunshine, so I drove out there and parked before his front door.

The time was twenty minutes past ten. I had no idea when he went off duty, but with the rumpus going on at Headquarters he was pretty certain to be late.

I settled down with a cigarette and prepared for a long wait. There was a light showing in one of the lower rooms of the house, and from time to time I saw a woman's shadow on the blind. Around quarter to eleven the light went out, and then a light flashed up in one of the upper rooms. After a while that went out in its turn, and the house was dark.

I closed my eyes and tried not to think about Perelli. I didn't want to get any false ideas until I knew more facts. Francon was probably right when he said Brandon would have more than the gun on Perelli. It was my bet someone had tipped the police: someone with an eye on the twenty-five grand; a temptation to anyone to manufacture a few lies if he could.

A car came grinding up the hill. A few seconds later headlights came through the windshield to dazzle me, and a car came to a standstill.

I poked my head hopefully out of the window. It was Mifflin all right. He was looking out of his window, a scowl on his face.

'Take that lump of rusty iron out of my way and drop it in the sea,' he said testily. 'You're blocking my gates.'

'Hello, Tim,' I said, and got out of the Buick.

He gaped at me.

'What the hell are you doing here?'

I opened his car door, slid in and sat beside him.

'Felt lonely, so I thought I'd cheer myself up with your company.'

'Beat it! I've had enough for one night. I'm going to bed.'

'Let's have it, Tim. Why did Brandon pick up Perelli?'

'So you know that, do you?' Mifflin snorted. 'Read about it in the morning newspapers and don't bother me. I've had all I want of it for one night. They've gone crazy down there: like a lynch mob.'

'I know. I've seen them. Now look, Tim, Perelli happens to be a friend of mine. He didn't kidnap Dedrick. It's not his line.'

Mifflin groaned.

'Gimme a butt. I've smoked all mine.'

I gave him a cigarette and lit it for him.

'Do you think he's the kidnapper?'

'I don't know. Maybe, but probably not. Was it you who sent Francon down?'

'Yeah. Did he get in?'

'Can you imagine anyone keeping him out? He got in, all right. I reckon he saved Perelli's life. They were certainly working over him.'

'Was it a tip?'

Mifflin nodded.

'Yah. And that's what makes me think it's a phoney. Whoever it was, asked for Brandon; nobody else would do. Brandon talked to him. This guy wouldn't say who he was, and that means he's gypped himself out of the reward. To me that stinks. No one in their right senses would pass up a reward that big unless he was scared of getting involved. He told Brandon to go right away to Perelli's apartment, where he'd find the death gun down the side of a settee and other evidence that would pin the kidnapping on to Perelli. Brandon tried to find out who he was, but he got jittery and hung up. We've traced the call to a call-box in Coral Gables, but that's as far as we've got.'

'Someone who must hate Perelli's guts.'

'Could be, or maybe one of the kidnappers with cold feet. I don't know. Anyway, Brandon made the pinch himself. Know what he found?'

'He found the gun.'

'He found that. He also found three oilskin wrappers, a hundred thousand grand in used twenty-dollar bills and a fishing-rod which was probably used to take the money off the shed roof.'

I whistled softly.

'Where did he find them?'

'The money was in a suitcase in a cupboard. The oilskin wrappers were at the back of a drawer and the rod was under the bed.'

'As if anyone in their right minds would keep evidence as

hot as that in their apartment. Can't he see it's a plant?'

'Look, Brandon wants the Feds out of the city pronto. Perelli's got a police record. This is a gift to him. If he stares at it all day and all night, it wouldn't be a plant to him.'

'Has Perelli an alibi for the kidnapping?'

'One full of holes. He says he was playing cards with Joe Betillo in a private room in Delmonico's Bar. We've talked to Joe. He says Perelli played cards with him until nine-thirty. Joe remembers the time because Perelli was winning and suddenly said he had a date. Joe was sore because he wanted to get back some of his losses. Perelli swears he played on until ten-thirty. The kidnapping, if you remember, took place at ten past ten.'

'Anyone see Perelli leave?'

Mifflin shook his head.

'He went out the back way.'

'Well, who'd believe a rat like Betillo, anyway?'

'Brandon does. He'd believe anyone as long as he gets the Feds out of town. The money worries me, Vic. Everything looks like a plant until you come to the money. A hundred grand is an awful lot of money to throw away to frame a man. A couple of grand would have been enough.'

'That's just the reason why it was planted. The kidnapper has still four hundred grand to keep him warm. Leaving an amount that big in Perelli's place would make people think just what you're thinking.'

'It's throwing money away. I can't see anyone doing it.'

'That's because you're badly paid. A lot of people in this city wouldn't think anything of passing up a hundred grand.'

'Juries are badly paid too. They wouldn't believe it.'

I flicked my cigarette out of the window and shrugged. He was right, of course.

'How is he, Tim?'

'Perelli? Not so bad, considering. They didn't shake his story, and they certainly tried. I think he'd have croaked if Francon hadn't breezed in. Those two punks, MacGraw and Hartsell, get under my skin. They like nothing better than to be turned loose on a guy in handcuffs.'

'Yeah. They tried to bash me once. Any chance of my seeing him?'

'Not a hope. He's Brandon's special prisoner. Even the Feds

had to get tough before he'd let them look at him.'

I lit another cigarette and passed him the pack.

'I don't think he did it, Tim.'

'Well, you'll be about the only one by the time they get him before a jury. Wait 'til you see the morning newspapers. As far as they're concerned, he's been tried and found guilty already. The only way to get him off is to produce the real kidnapper.'

'I've got to do something for him. What'll Brandon do now?'

'Nothing. As far as he's concerned, the case is closed. He's got Perelli, and he's got all the evidence he needs. It's in the bag.'

I opened the car door and slid out.

'Well, at least it gives me a clear field. I'm going to start in and dig.'

'I wish you luck,' Mifflin said. 'But you've got a sweet job on your hands. Where will you dig? What have you got to work on?'

'Not much. I'm going after Mary Jerome. I have a feeling she knows more about this than you think.'

'Maybe, but I doubt it. If she had anything to do with the kidnapping, she wouldn't have come back like that.'

'She may have left something in the room and had to come back. She wasn't to know I'd be there. The chances are she doesn't know anything, but I'm going to find her and make sure.'

'Okay, anything I can do, let me know. I think Perelli's been framed myself, but that's strictly off the record.'

'Thanks, Tim. I'll probably have something for you. So long for now.'

I climbed into the Buick, waved my hand to him and drove fast to Centre Avenue. Half-way down the broad thoroughfare I spotted a call-box and swung to the kerb. I dialled Justin Francon's number.

He answered the telephone himself.

'What do you make of him, Justin?'

'I don't think he did it,' Francon said briskly. 'But that doesn't mean I can get him off. I'll try, but it looks pretty hopeless. The frame's too good. Whoever planted the evidence knew his business. The money is damning. Shall we get together tomorrow morning at my office? We'll have a look at it from every angle and see what we can do. Make it ten. All right?'

'I'll be there,' I said.

'Don't expect too much, Vic. I don't like to say it, but I think he's a dead duck.'

'He isn't dead yet,' I said shortly and hung up.

III

Justin Francon sat in his desk chair with his legs hanging over one of the arms, his thumbs hooked into the armholes of his vest, a dead cigar jutting out of his face.

He was a thin, small, leathery man with a straggly black moustache, high cheekbones, a big, bony nose and small, bright black eyes. He reminded me of a ferret. You wouldn't think to look at him he was the smartest lawyer on the Pacific Coast, but he was. He was in a class of his own, and had more millionaire clients in his fee-book than any other lawyer in the country.

Paula, Kerman and I sat in a half-circle before the massive desk. Francon allowed us the doubtful privilege of studying his profile while he stared out of his office window at the golden beach stretched out twenty storeys below him. The silence mounted in the big air office while he turned the facts over in his mind.

Finally, he shrugged, swung his legs off the arm of the chair and faced us.

'Nothing you've told me would convince a jury that Perelli didn't murder Souki or kidnap Dedrick,' he said. 'You'll have to get me some ammunition. Right now we haven't a damn thing. There's enough evidence on Perelli to convict him without the jury leaving the box. You've got to face it. Feeling is running high. He won't get a fair trial. His record's against him. Unless you hand me something pretty substantial to hit the D.A. with, there's nothing I can do for him except talk a lot of hot air that won't get him anywhere. They intend to indict him on Souki's murder, but if, in the meantime, they find Dedrick's body, they'll hook the two killings together, and it'll be all over bar the gas chamber.'

He stared at his dead cigar, frowning, then dropped it into the trash basket.

'Now let's see what they've got on him. They've found the

68

gun in his apartment. If I worked hard enough, I could convince a jury the gun was a plant. The fishing-rod could be disposed of too. Anyone can have a fishing-rod. But the money is something no one will believe was planted. That's where the fellow who planted it showed he has brains. A hundred thousand is a whale of a lot of money. We're agreed on that, aren't we?'

I nodded.

'All right. Well, so far the one thing we can't get around is the money. The oilskin wrappers could have been planted, but once the jury makes up its mind the money wasn't planted, then there's no reason why the gun, the oilskin wrappers or the rod should have been also planted, and that makes the D.A.'s case watertight. You see that, don't you?'

'Yeah, but all the same, we know the money was planted. Couldn't you persuade the jury that the kidnapper, to save his own dirty hide, would be willing to part with a fifth of his spoils?'

Francon shook his head.

'I don't think so. It'd be too much of a risk. If Perelli had a good alibi, we might get away with it, but he hasn't. And another thing, his fingerprints are on the gun.'

'I heard that, but I don't believe it.'

Francon nodded his head.

'It's a fact. I've seen them.'

'But Perelli didn't handle the gun.'

'He says Brandon gave him the gun and asked him if he could identify it. He handled it all right, but he handled it after it was found.'

'For Pete's sake! You're not going to let Brandon get away with that, are you?'

'It's Perelli's word against the Captain of Police. Who do you think would be believed?'

There was a long pause, then he went on, 'So you see how it stacks up. I've got to have something hot and meaty to go into court with, and if I don't get it, I'm passing up the case. That's the position. I've got to have something to work with. It's up to you to give it to me.'

'I'll dig up something if it kills me,' I said. 'The only way for us to crack this case is to start right from the beginning and dig until something turns up. I have an idea at the back of my mind that this isn't just a gang of kidnappers at work. I may

69

be right off the beam, but it's a hunch that's growing stronger every day.'

'I don't follow you,' Francon said, frowning at me.

'I don't exactly follow myself,' I said and grinned. 'I do know that Franklin Marshland's damn' pleased that Dedrick is among the missing. I'm going to find out why. He looks a harmless little guy, but every now and then you catch a look in his eyes and you suddenly realize he could be dangerous. The wedding was secret. Why? Suppose Marshland's at the back of the kidnapping? Suppose he realized that Serena had married a crook who was only after her money? Suppose he decided to get rid of Dedrick and staged a faked kidnapping? I'm not saying this happened, but it's an idea. Suppose this Mary Jerome is hooked up in some way to Dedrick's past. You see what I mean? If this is an ordinary kidnapping job, and the kidnappers are just a gang from anywhere, then we're sunk. But if this is an inside job, if Marshland's at the back of it, then maybe we can crack it.'

Francon was looking interested now.

'You might have something there, Vic. It's worth trying.'

'It's the only thing we've got. I'm going after Mary Jerome. She was first seen at the Acme Garage, and that's where I'm going to start to look for her. If I can trace her from the garage to Ocean End on the night Dedrick was kidnapped then I may come across something on the way. I'm going to dig into Souki's past. No one's bothered with him yet. Then there's Dedrick himself. I'm sending Jack to Paris right away to get hold of every scrap of information about Dedrick he can find. All this may be a waste of time, but it's our only chance. We're digging a big plot of ground in which something valuable may or may not be buried. If we don't dig, we won't find it, and if it's not there to find then, it's just too bad.'

'I think Mary Jerome's a good line of investigation,' Francon said, pulling at his long, bony nose, 'but I can't see any point in bothering about Souki.'

'That's just why I'm going to do it. No one's bothered to look at Souki. He's just the corpse. I'm leaving nothing to chance. I can't afford to.'

'Well, all right, but don't waste too much time on it. You wouldn't know if Perelli had an enemy, would you? Someone must have hated him pretty badly to have hung that frame on him.'

'Yeah. I've been thinking about that. There's one man who's tailor-made for the job. A nasty little rat named Jeff Barratt. He's a reefer-addict and a thorough bad egg. He has an apartment opposite Perelli's. I went on to tell Francon how I had called on Barratt and how Perelli had saved my life.

'Does Brandon know this?' Francon said, interested.

'No; but if he did, it wouldn't make him change his mind. I'm going to dig into Barratt's background. That fishing-rod is something you couldn't easily conceal. Someone had to carry it into Perelli's apartment. I'm hoping whoever it was was seen.' I stood up. 'Well, we'd better get moving. As soon as I have something for you, you'll have it.'

'The sooner the better,' Francon said.

Outside in the corridor Kerman said, 'What was that again about me going to Paris?'

'Yeah. I want you to get off right away. Paula will fix the details. You can have what spending money you want within reason. You won't object to a trip to Paris, will you?'

Kerman rolled his eyes and tried to conceal his excitement.

'I'll put up with it,' he said. 'It's in a good cause. Besides, from what I hear these French wrens are pretty accommodating.'

'They'll need to be if you're going to hum around them,' Paula said tartly.

IV

Mrs. Martha Bendix, Executive Director of the Bendix Domestic Agency and an office neighbour of mine, was a big, hearty woman with a male haircut and a laugh like the bang of a twelve-bore shotgun.

She was coming out of her office as I was coming out of mine, and, as soon as I saw her, I knew I wanted to talk to her.

'Hello there, Vic,' she boomed. 'Where have you been hiding yourself? Haven't seen you in days.'

'I want to see you, Martha. Can you spare a moment?'

She looked at her wrist-watch, about the size of a cartwheel, decided after all she wasn't in any hurry and opened the office door.

'Come on in. Suppose you want to pick my brains again, huh? I gotta date, but it's nothing important.'

She led the way through the outer office where a pale blonde with a face like a happy rabbit pecked at a typewriter and gave her a coy little smile as she passed.

'If Mr. Manners calls, Mary, tell him I'm on my way down,' Martha said, and breezed into her cream-and-green office.

I followed her in and closed the door.

'Turn the key,' Martha said, lowering her voice. It probably could still be heard at the far end of the corridor, but she imagined she was speaking in a conspirator's whisper. 'I've a bottle of Vat 69 that wants breaking open, but I wouldn't like Mary to think I drink in office hours.' She hoisted a bottle into sight as I sank into an armchair. 'I wouldn't like her to think I drink at all, for that matter.'

'What makes you so positive she doesn't know?'

'What makes you so damn positive she does?' Martha said and grinned. She slapped a three-inch snifter down on the desk in front of me. 'Rinse your phlegm out with that.'

'There are times, Martha, when I don't believe you're even civilized, to hear you talk,' I said, collecting the glass. 'Well, bung-ho.'

'Fungus on your adenoids,' she boomed, and downed her drink at a gulp. 'Not bad, huh? Want another?'

I shook my head, and accepted the three coffee-beans she dropped on the blotter before me.

'Well now, what's your trouble?' she asked, sitting down and getting to work on the beans herself. 'What do you want to know this time?'

'I'm trying to find out something about a Filipino named Toa Souki; Serena Dedrick's chauffeur. She engaged him in New York, and I'm wondering if your New York office handled the job.'

Martha looked insulted.

'My good man! I'll have you know we don't handle coloured people. You're not sticking your nose into that case, are you?'

I said I was sticking my nose into that case.

'How can I get a line on Souki?'

Martha scratched her head with the paper-knife while she thought.

'I suppose I could find out for you,' she said, a little grudgingly. 'Syd Silver runs the biggest colour agency in New York. He's a friend of mine, the dirty little rat! I'll ask him. If his boils aren't bothering him, he might find out for you. Anything in it for him?'

'A hundred bucks.'

Martha's eyes popped.

'Why, for a hundred bucks that guy would drown his mother in a quart of beer.'

I said I didn't want him to drown his mother in a quart of beer. All I wanted was the low-down on Souki.

'Consider it done. I'll have some dope for you in a couple of days. Will that do?'

'I'll make it a hundred and fifty if I can get it by tomorrow morning and if the dope's worth having.'

'You'll get it,' Martha said, climbing to her feet. 'That guy's a genius at stirring up dirt. That all?'

'Yeah. Well, thanks, Martha, you're always helpful. I don't know what I'd do without you.'

Martha grinned.

'Tell me something, Vic. When are you marrying that dark-eyed lovely you keep in frustration in your office?'

'If you mean Paula, I'm not marrying her. I wish you wouldn't keep harping on that subject whenever we meet. Haven't I told you she isn't the marrying type?'

She gave me a nudge that nearly dislocated my spine, and let off a laugh that rattled the windows.

'You ask her and see,' she said. 'There's no such animal as a non-marrying woman. Those who aren't married haven't been asked.'

v

I parked the Buick in the forecourt of the apartment house on Jefferson Avenue and walked into the quiet of the lobby.

A girl, not the foxy-faced Gracie, was sitting behind the counter, the telephone harness hitched to her chest. She was chewing gum and reading the funnies, and from the bored expression on her face I concluded they were no funnier than those Gracie had been reading the first time I had come in here.

Maxie, the bowler-hatted bouncer, popped out from behind his pillar and scowled at me.

'Hello,' I said, and gave him the teeth. 'Where do we talk?'

His small eyes, set deep in the fat-veined face, showed suspicion and surprise.

'What do we want to talk for?' he growled, his moustache bristling. 'I ain't anything to say to you. Besides, I'm busy.'

That seemed to be the cue for the mercenary theme, so I took out my bill-fold and hoisted a ten-dollar bill into sight.

'Let's go somewhere quiet and talk,' I said.

He studied the ten-dollar note thoughtfully, groped with a thick, dirty finger amongst his back molars, fished out a slab of something and deposited it on the seat of his trousers. Then he looked at the girl behind the counter.

'Hey! I'll be downstairs if you want me. Don't let anyone up.'

She didn't bother to drag her eyes away from the funnies, but she did manage to incline her head a couple of inches to show she heard and understood.

Maxie plodded off towards the elevator.

We stood side by side, breathing over each other as the elevator took us down to the basement.

He led the way along a white-tiled passage, lit by lamps in wire baskets to a small office that consisted of a desk, two chairs and a signed photograph of Jack Dempsey over a soot-filled fireplace.

He sat down behind the desk, pushed his bowler hat to the back of his head and relaxed, breathing gently through his thick, fat nose. His eyes never left the ten-dollar bill for a second.

I gave it to him. I knew he wouldn't concentrate on anything else until he had it. Fat, nicotined fingers closed on it and stowed it away in a pocket somewhere in his rear.

'Perelli,' I said.

He wiped the end of his nose on his coat-sleeve, puffed out a small quantity of garlic and beer fumes and sighed.

'Aw, hell! Not him again?'

'Certainly. Why not?'

'Every cop in the City has been talking to me about Perelli. I've got nothing to tell you I haven't told them.'

'That doesn't mean a thing, since I don't know what you told them. Suppose you answer a few questions: questions I bet the police didn't ask you.'

'Well all right,' he said with no enthusiasm. 'So long as you pay for my time I don't care.'

I rolled a cigarette across the desk to show him this wasn't going to be a hurried session, and he wasn't to get any false ideas about the value of his time, and lit one for myself.

'Do you think Perelli kidnapped Dedrick?'

The small eyes blinked. He hadn't been expecting that one. 'What's it matter what I think?'

'Plenty. And, look, don't let's waste time. If you don't want to answer questions, just hand back my dough and I'll find someone who will.'

We stared at each other across the desk, and he decided I meant business.

'Beer?' he asked. 'Might as well make ourselves comfortable.'

He produced two cans of beer, levered off the caps with a jack-knife and handed me one.

'Happy days.'

'Happier nights.'

We drank, sighed as men will, and set the cans on the desk. 'I don't reckon he did it. It wasn't in his line.'

'That's what he told me.' I leaned forward and began to make patterns on the desk with the wet bottom of the can. 'I want to help him if I can. Anything you might tell me could turn the trick.'

Maxie started to explore his back molars again, changed his mind and poked about inside his ear instead.

'Not a bad guy. A free-spender. No trouble. Nice girl friend. You seen her?'

I said I had seen her.

He closed one small eye, then opened it again.

'The best figure I've ever seen on a woman. Think it's real?'

'Could be. Did you see him bring that fishing-rod in here?'

He shook his head.

'No; and I know he never had a fishing-rod. I asked the girl who cleans his room. She's never seen one.'

'Did she look under the bed?'

'She cleans under it.'

'The cops found it last night. Did she clean under the bed yesterday morning?'

He nodded.

'What time?'

'She was late. Perelli didn't leave the apartment until twelve-thirty. She didn't start cleaning until one.'

'What time did the police find it?'

'Seven-thirty.'

'So between one-thirty in the afternoon and seven-thirty in the evening someone planted it. That's right, isn't it?'

'If anyone planted it.'

'Well, we won't argue about that. Sometime between one-thirty and seven-thirty either Perelli or someone brought a fishing-rod into this building. That's right, isn't it?'

He couldn't find any fault with that reasoning.

'Yep.'

'Are there any other entrances except the main one?'

'There's a rear entrance to the basement.'

'Can anyone get up to the apartments that way?'

'No.'

'Sure?'

'Certainly, I'm sure. The way this place is built, you either come in the main entrance or up the stairs from the rear entrance. Either way you have to cross the lobby and you'd be seen.'

'Where were you between one-thirty and seven-thirty last night?'

'At the movies.'

'You mean you weren't here yesterday afternoon and evening?'

'I was at the movies.'

'Your day off?'

'My day off.'

'Who was in charge of the lobby?'

'Gracie Lehmann.' Maxie took another pull at his can of beer, added, 'It's her day off today.'

'Have the police questioned her?'

'Why should they?'

'Didn't they want to know about the rod? I mean how it got into Perelli's room?'

'Why should they?'

I drank a little beer myself. He was right, of course. They had found the rod in Perelli's room, and that was good enough for them. They wouldn't bother to find out how it got there. It was there, and as far as they were concerned that was all that mattered.

'She could have seen someone bring the rod in, then?'

'If anyone brought it, she saw it.'

'She might have gone out to wash her hands or something?'

Maxie shook his head.

'The lobby ain't to be left a second. That's the rule of the house. She has a retiring room behind the switchboard. If she goes in there she turns down a switch connected with buzzers under the front and rear mats. Anyone coming in from the main entrance or up the stairs from the basement would sound the buzzer. It's foolproof. We had a lotta burglaries here one time. Now we really have to watch out. If anyone brought in the rod, she would have seen it.'

'We've just proved either Perelli or someone did bring it in. So she must have seen it.'

'That's right.'

I drained the can of beer and lit another cigarette. I was faintly excited.

'Want another?' Maxie asked, helping himself.

I nodded, and watched him hoist two more cans into sight.

'Well, I guess I'd better talk to Gracie,' I said as he knocked off the cap of the can. 'She could be my star witness.'

'She'll be in tomorrow. Watch her. She'll come a mite expensive.'

'Where does she live?'

He brooded over this, then shook his head.

'Can't give you her address. It's against the rules.'

I nursed the can of beer and stared past him at the photograph of Jack Dempsey.

'It's my bet Jeff Barratt brought in that rod.'

He was drinking from his can, and the beer went down the wrong way. I had to get up and thump him on the back or he would have choked. I thumped him a little harder than necessary. I thought I might as well get something for my money.

'Barratt?' he wheezed when he could speak. 'What are you talking about?'

'Barratt hates Perelli's guts. The guy who planted the rod hates Perelli's guts. Barratt lives opposite Perelli. Barratt's a first-prize rat. Not evidence in court, but evidence to me.'

He chewed this over and finally nodded his head.

'Could be.'

We drank some more beer.

'Don't waste your time on Gracie if you expect her to squeal on Barratt,' he said, lowering his voice. 'She's very, very strong for him.'

Now, perhaps, I was going to get value for my money.

'What gives?' I asked. 'Why should Barratt want to bother himself with a girl like that?'

'The guy who owns this building tries to keep it respectable. Don't ask me why. He's funny that way. We've got instructions that all women visitors are to check out before one o'clock or it has to be reported. Gracie works a night shift every other week. Barratt's women visitors don't check out at one o'clock and don't get reported.'

'So what does he do? Feed her five bucks a week? I'll pay for information.'

Maxi finished his beer, dusted the ash off his trousers and stood up.

'Well, I guess I gotta get back to work.'

'Sit down and give. I haven't had anything like ten dollars' worth of information.'

'At my rates you have. Make it another ten, and I'll tell you something that'll sit you on the edge of your can.'

'Five.'

'Ten.'

'Seven and a half.'

We closed at eight.

I gave him the money and he sat down again.

'She's a reefer-smoker, see? Barratt keeps her in weeds. You ain't got a chance.'

I thought this over, and decided perhaps I hadn't, but there was no harm trying.

'Give me her address.'

The extra money persuaded him to break the rules.

'274 Felman Street: it's one of those rooming-houses.'

I stood up.

'Keep this under your bowler, Maxie. If anyone asks you, you've never seen me.'

Maxie grunted, thumped himself on the chest and eyed me sourly.

'You don't have to worry. I'm fussy who I claim as a friend.'

I left him sitting there, breathing gently and staring absently at the empty beer cans.

VI

The entrance to 274 Felman Street was sandwiched between a tobacconist's shop and a third-rate café. There was a dirty brass plate on the door that read: *Rooms for Business Women. No Service. No Animals. No Men.* A card with several dirty thumb-prints on it was pinned above the brass plate and read: *No Vacancies.*

The next-door café had four tables on the sidewalk. They were presided over by an elderly waiter whose long, lean face carried an expression of infinite sadness, and whose tail coat, in the hard sunlight, looked green with age. He watched me park the Buick before the entrance to the rooming-house and hopefully flicked at one of the tables with a soiled cloth, but the gesture didn't sell me anything.

I climbed the three stone steps to the glass-panelled doors of 274, pushed one open and entered a dark, smelly lobby full of silence and neglect. Along the left-hand wall was a row of mail boxes. I went over and read the names mounted in grimy brass frames above each box. There was a surprising number of Eves, Lulus, Dawns and Belles among the three dozen names, and I wondered if the brass plate on the door was entirely truthful. The fourth frame from the right read: *Miss Grace Lehmann. Rm. 23. Flr. 2.*

Stairs, carpeted with coconut matting, faced me. I puffed gently up thirty of them before I reached the first-floor landing and a long corridor that went away into a quiet dimness surveyed on either side by numerous doors before which stood bottles of milk and newspapers. As the time was ten minutes past noon, it seemed to me the business women were neglecting their business, if they had a business, which on the evidence didn't seem very probable.

As I began to mount the second flight, a lean, hard-faced man appeared at the head of the stairs. He wore a fawn flannel suit, a white felt hat and sun-glasses. He gave a nervous start when he saw me, hesitated as if in two minds whether to retreat or not, then came down the stairs with a studied air of nonchalance.

I waited for him.

He scratched his unshaven jaw with a thumb-nail as he passed me. I had an idea the eyes behind the sun-glasses were uneasy.

'No animals and positively no men,' I said softly as he walked across the landing to the lower flight of stairs.

He looked hastily over his shoulder, paused, said aggressively. 'Ug-huh?'

I shook my head.

'If you heard anything, it was probably the voice of your conscience.'

I went on up the stairs, leaving him to stare after me, pivoting slowly on his heels until we lost sight of each other.

The second floor was a replica of the lower floor, even to the bottles of milk and the newspapers. I walked along the corridor, treading softly, studying the numbers on the doors. Room 23 was half-way down and on the right-hand side. I paused before it, wondering what I was going to say to her. If what Maxie had told me was true, and it probably was, then this girl could clear Perelli if she wanted to. It now depended whether or not I could persuade her to throw Barratt to the wolves.

As I raised my knuckles to knock on the door I heard a quiet cough behind me. I looked furtively over my shoulder. There was something in the atmosphere of the place that would have made an archbishop feel furtive.

Behind and opposite me a door had opened. A tall, languorous redhead lolled against the doorway and surveyed me with a smile that was both inviting and suggestive. She wore a green silk wrap that outlined a nice, undulating hip, her legs were bare and her feet were in swan's-down mules. She touched her red-gold hair with slender fingers that had never done a day's work in their lives, and her neat, fair eyebrows lifted in a signal that is as old as it is obvious.

'Hello, Big Man,' she said. 'Looking for someone?'

'Huh-uh,' I said. 'And I've found her. Don't let me keep you from your breakfast.'

The smile widened.

'Don't bother with her. She's not even up, but I am, and the safety catch's off too. I'm all ready to fire.'

I raised my hat and gave her a courteous bow.

'Madam, nothing would please me more than to pull the trigger, but I am committed elsewhere. Perhaps some other time? Regard me as food for your dreams, as I most certainly will regard you. Bear your disappointment as I am bearing mine, remembering that tomorrow is another day, and we too can have fun even if it is fun postponed.'

The smile went away and the green eyes hardened.

'Awe hell, just another nut,' she said, disgusted, and shut the door sharply in my face.

I blew out a little air, rapped on Gracie's door and waited. A half a minute later I rapped again; this time much louder. Still nothing happened. No one opened the door.

I looked to right and left, put my hand on the doorknob and turned it gently. The door moved away from me as I pushed.

I looked into a room that was big enough to hold a bed, two armchairs, a wardrobe and a dressing-table fitted with a swinging mirror. There was no one in the room. The bed hadn't been made, and the sheets hadn't been changed, by the look of them, for probably six months. They were grey and crumpled and as uninviting as only dirty sheets can be. There was a film of dust on the mirror and cigarette ash on the carpet. From where I stood I could see bits of fluff under the bed. Not a clean room: a room that gave me an itchy feeling down my spine as I looked at it.

At the head of the bed was another door that probably led to the bathroom. I stared at it, wondering if she was in there and knocked sharply on the panel of the open bedroom door to see if anything happened. Nothing did, so I stepped inside, and in case the redhead opposite became curious, I closed the door.

On one of the armchairs was a pile of clothes: a frock, stockings, a grey-pink girdle and a greyer pink brassière.

There was a distinct smell of marijuana smoke in the room. Not new, but of many months' standing. It had seeped into the walls and the curtains and the bed and hung over the room like a muted memory of sin.

I moved silently past the bed to the closed door, rapped sharply and listened. I heard nothing. No one called out, and I was suddenly aware of a drop or two of sweat running down my face from inside my hat.

I turned the handle and pushed. The door opened heavily and sluggishly, but it opened. Something behind the door bumped against the panels and sent my heart jumping like a frog on a hot stove. I looked into the empty bathroom, saw the soiled pink bath, the mussed-up towels, the loofah, the cake of toilet soap and the half-squeezed tube of toothpaste.

I knew she was behind the door. She had to be.

I stepped into the bathroom, my nerves creeping up my spine. She was there all right: hanging from a hook in the door, in a blue, crumpled nightdress, her knees drawn up, her head on one side, the knot of her dressing-gown cord carefully under her right ear, the cord imbedded in the flesh of her neck.

I touched her hand.

It was cold and hard and lifeless.

CHAPTER FOUR

I

I LOOKED up and down the corridor. There was no one in sight. A faint and far-off sound of movement told me that at least some of the occupants behind the many doors were beginning to greet the day; even if they went no farther than rolling over in bed.

I moved cautiously out of Room 23 and closed the door. Then I took off my hat and wiped my face with my handkerchief. I lit a cigarette and drew in a lungful of smoke. That helped a little, but not much. What I needed was a large whisky, neat, and in a hurry.

I stepped across the corridor to the redhead's door. On the left-hand panel with a card that read: *Miss Joy Dreadon. At home weekdays after five.*

I tapped with my finger-nails on the door, making no more noise than a mouse makes when it is nibbling at the wainscotting, but it was loud enough.

The door opened about eight inches and Miss Dreadon peered at me through the opening. She seemed to have lost her *bonhomie* and her trustful air of welcome.

'Well?'

Her big green eyes were suspicious and watchful.

I decided to waste no time and to talk to her in a language she would understand and appreciate.

'I want to buy a little information,' I said, and pushed my card at her. 'Twenty dollars buys ten minutes at my rates: nice clean bills and secrecy guaranteed.'

She read the card with that pained expression people usually wear who don't read a great deal and are still bothered by long words. She had to make an obvious effort not to move her lips while she spelt out the letters to herself.

Then she opened the door a couple more notches and pushed the card back at me.

'Let's see the money.'

A simple, direct soul, I thought, who gets straight to the

point of interest and doesn't bother to ask unnecessary questions.

I took out my bill-fold and showed her two crisp clean ten-dollar bills. I didn't give them to her. I just showed them to her.

She eyed them the way a small child eyes Santa Claus's sack, and opened the door.

'Come on in. I don't care who you are, but those berries certainly make my palms itch. Sure it's information you want?'

I stepped past her into a room a little larger than 23, and much more pleasant and comfortable. There was a divan, a settee, two armchairs, a couple of expensive Chinese rugs on the grey fitted carpet and a bowl of red-and-yellow begonias on a table in the window recess.

I put my hat down on a chair and said I was sure it was information I wanted.

She held out a white hand with dark red, polished nails.

'Let's have half. It's not that I don't trust you, but it's a good principle. You can have a drink if you like, or coffee.'

I gave her one of the ten-dollar bills, thinking this case was costing me plenty. I seemed to be spending the entire morning giving my money away.

She folded the bill and hid it in her brassière as I said a Scotch would adequately meet the case.

She wasn't niggardly about it. She gave me the bottle and glass and told me to help myself.

'Give me a second to get my coffee.'

By the time she was back I was two drinks ahead of her.

She set a tray on the table near her and flopped on the settee, showing me a pair of long, slender legs that might have given me ideas if my head wasn't already full of ideas of a different kind. Seeing the direction of my studied stare, she flicked the wrap into place and raised her eyebrows.

'What are you: a private dick or something?'

'Something like that. Not quite, but it'll do.'

'I knew it. As soon as I saw you, I knew you weren't the usual prowler. You've got nice eyes. Sure you wouldn't like a little fun?'

I started to make a courteous speech, but she stopped me with a wave of her hand and a wide, friendly grin.

'Forget it, honey, I was only kidding. It's not often I get a good-looking man in here who doesn't start climbing up the wall immediately the door shuts. It's a novelty, and I like it. What do you want to know?'

I made a third drink.

'The subject of the inquiry is Gracie Lehmann. Do you know her?'

Miss Dreadon's face hardened.

'For crying out loud! You're not wasting good money to find out about *her*, are you?'

The Scotch had set me up. In fact it was so good it nearly set me up on my ear.

'I'm working for a client who's in trouble with the police. Gracie could have cleared him. No other reason.'

'Well, go and ask her. Why come to me?'

'I doubt if she's going to be much help now. She's dead.'

She started and spilt some coffee on her bare knee, she swore softly under her breath, put down the coffee cup and wiped her knee with her handkerchief.

'Must you say things like that?' Then, as I didn't say anything, but looked at her, she went on, 'You don't mean she's really dead?'

'She's dead all right. I've just been in there. She's hanging at the back of the bathroom door.'

She gave a little shudder, grimaced, gave another little shudder and reached for the whisky bottle.

'She was a stupid little fool, but I didn't think she'd be that stupid. The trouble with her was she couldn't leave reefers alone.'

'I guessed that. I could smell the stuff in the room.' I took out my cigarette case and offered it.

She took one and we lit up, then she poured a shot of whisky into her coffee and drank it.

'Now I've got the jitters,' she confessed. 'I hate hearing things like that.'

'Did you see her last night?'

'Yes; I'm always running into her.'

'When?'

'Oh, when I went out to dinner she was coming in, and we met again on the stairs when I returned. She must have gone out again while I was having dinner. We both came in together.'

'What time was this?'

Miss Dreadon suppressed a yawn, not very successfully.

'It was late. About three-thirty I guess. I didn't particularly notice, but it was plenty late enough.'

'Was she alone?'

She shook her head.

'Oh no. She had a man with her as usual. What they can see in that dirty little ...' She broke off, frowning. 'Oh well, I'd better not talk like that now she's dead.'

'What was he like?'

'Much too good for her. The kind of man I'd go for in a big way: like Clark Gable. Not like him in looks, but his style.'

'How was he dressed?'

'He had on a snappy number in fawn flannel suiting, a white felt hat and a hand-painted tie. He wore big doughnut sized sun-glasses. I guess he put those on in case any of his friends spotted him going in with her. The tricks men get up to.'

I was sitting on the edge of my chair now, trying very hard to keep calm.

'Did he have a thin, black moustache and hard, lean face?'

'Certainly he had. Do you know him?'

'I ran into him coming down the stairs this morning.'

'This morning?' Her eyes opened very wide. 'But if she's dead ...?'

'Yeah. She's been dead some time. I'd make a guess and put it at about eight hours.'

'You mean she went into the bathroom and hanged herself while he was in the other room?'

'I saw him coming downstairs about twenty minutes ago. She died eight hours ago; say about four o'clock in the morning. Obviously she died while he was in her room, unless he left before four and came back this morning for some reason or other.'

She sank back on the cushions of the settee and fanned herself with her hand.

'He could have done that, couldn't he? Gee! I was getting all worked up.'

I remembered the lean man's unshaven chin. If he had left last night, why hadn't he shaved this morning before coming out on to the streets? There might be a perfectly good answer to that one, but until I heard it it seemed to me he had spent the night in Gracie's room.

This was too important to let slide. I had to find out for certain.

I got to my feet.

'Here's the other ten I owe you. Thanks for the help. Take my tip and keep out of this. Let someone else find her.'

'Uuugh! I won't sleep a wink thinking of her in there.'

'You'll sleep even less if some tough cop takes you down to Headquarters and gets to work on you. Keep out of it.'

'Aren't you going to tell them?'

I shook my head.

'I haven't the time to waste on a suicide case. You'll be surprised how quickly someone will miss her. They always do.' I took out my bill-fold and another ten-dollar bill. 'If they ask questions, keep me out of it. Tell them about this guy in the fawn suit, but not until they ask you.'

She took the bill and stowed it away in her brassière.

'I'll keep you out of it.'

I left her sitting on the settee, biting her under-lip and frowning. She looked a lot less happy and a lot more worried than when I had first seen her.

Out in the corridor again, I peeped to right and left, satisfied myself no one was watching me, then stepped across the corridor into Room 23. I closed the door and began a quick but systematic search of the room.

I was looking for some proof that would tell me the lean man had spent the night here. I didn't know what I was looking for, but I looked just the same.

First I examined the bed and found a couple of black hairs on the pillow. Gracie was blonde. If he had rested his head on the pillow, it didn't mean he had stayed in the room all night. But it certainly hinted he had.

It wasn't until I had covered practically every inch of the apartment and was giving up that I found what I wanted. There were two cupboards in the kitchenette: one contained cups and saucers and plates; the other, jugs and dishes and cooking utensils. There was a cup and saucer amongst the jugs. They shouldn't have been in that cupboard. They should have been in the adjacent cupboard. That gave me an idea. I turned my attention to the trash basket. Dumped on top of the usual refuse was a small pile of coffee grounds; and they were luke-warm. There was no mistake about that. They had been emptied out of a percolator some time this morning.

Gracie hadn't made coffee this morning. That was certain. If the lean man had returned because he had forgotten something he wouldn't have made himself coffee. That I wouldn't believe. But if he had slept there the night, he might have made himself coffee before leaving. It would be a cold-blooded thing to have done, as he must have known Gracie was hanging dead in the bathroom. Come to think of it, he probably knew she was dead before he went to bed; and that was even more cold-blooded.

Then suddenly it was as obvious as a neon light on a dark night. This wasn't suicide: it was murder.

II

There was a call-box in the darker part of the lobby. I opened the door and stepped inside. It smelt as if someone had kept a goat in there at one time, and not a particularly nice goat at that.

Holding my breath, I hung my handkerchief over the ancient mouthpiece, lifted off the receiver and dialled.

After a while a voice bellowed: 'Police Headquarters. Sergeant Harker talking.'

'Connect me with Lieutenant Mifflin,' I said, speaking away from the mouthpiece. I probably sounded at the other end like Hamlet's father's ghost.

'Who's that?'

'Harry Truman,' I said. 'Make it snappy. You may not think it, but time's money to me.'

'Hold on,' the sergeant said. I heard him call across the room. 'Is the Lieutenant in? There's a guy wanting him. Says his name is Harry Truman. That's familiar, ain't it? I've heard it before somewhere.'

Someone called the sergeant a very rude name.

Then Mifflin came on the line.

'Lieutenant of the Police talking,' he said sternly. 'Who's that?'

'I'm reporting a hanging in Room 23, second floor, 274 Felman Street. If you get over there fast you'll find a clue in the refuse bin. Don't be too sure it's suicide, and take a little trouble in checking on the woman. It'll pay dividends.'

'Who's that talking?' Mifflin demanded.

I could hear the scratch of his pen as he wrote down the address.

'I haven't the faintest idea,' I said, and hung up.

I pushed my handkerchief into my pocket and took quick,

silent steps to the front door. I had about three minutes, not more, to get clear. The city police might not be over-bright, but in emergencies they were fast.

As I slammed the Buick door, a boy in a ragged windbreaker and a pair of dirty flannel trousers jumped on the running board. He pushed his grimy little face through the open window.

'Hey, mister, you're to go to 2 Coral Row; right away: it's urgent.'

I started the engine, my eye on the driving mirror, expecting to see a police car come pounding up behind me.

'Who says so?'

'Some guy gave me a dollar to tell you. Says it's urgent, and you'd know.'

He dropped off the running board and bolted off down the street. I hadn't time to go after him. I wanted to, but the need to get away from 274 was more pressing. Already I could hear the distant sound of a police siren. I sent the car shooting towards Beach Road.

I had never heard of Coral Row, but it would be somewhere in Coral Gables. I headed that way because I was curious. Right at this moment I had a lot on my mind. I was wondering if the old waiter would remember me, and if he had noticed the number of my car. I was particularly anxious not to get tied up with Mifflin at this time. He could work out the problem of Gracie's murder without my help. I had other more pressing things to do. But if he began asking questions and got around to the waiter, he might get a description of me. I knew he wouldn't be pleased I had left before he arrived.

At the bottom of Beach Road I turned left on to the waterfront, and parked in a vacant space hedged in on either side by coils of rope and oil drums.

Coral Gables is no place to wander around in unless you have an escort or carry a gun. Even the cops go around in pairs, and scarcely a month passes without someone is found up an alley with a knife in his back.

As I got out of the Buick and looked up and down the long harbour, crammed with small boats and fishing trawlers, I was aware that I was being stared at by groups of men who lounged in the sun, picturesque enough in their soiled canvas trousers and various coloured sweat-shirts, their shifty, dark eyes weighing me up.

I picked on one who was on his own, aimlessly whittling a piece of wood into the shape of a boat.

'Can you put me on to Coral Row?'

He eyed me over, leaned away from me to spit into the oily water of the harbour and jerked his thumb over his shoulder in the direction of the coffee-shops, the sea-food stalls and the like that faced the waterfront.

'Behind Yate's Bar,' he said curtly.

Yate's Bar is a two-storey wooden building where, if you aren't fussy who you eat with, you can get a good clam-chowder and a ten-year-old ale that sneaks up on you if you don't watch out. I had been in there once or twice with Kerman. It's the kind of place where anything can happen, and very often does.

'Thanks,' I said, and crossed the broad water-front road to the bar.

Alongside the wooden building was an alley. High up on the wall was a notice that read: *Leading to Coral Row.*

I paused to light a cigarette while I regarded the alley with a certain amount of caution and no enthusiasm. The high walls blocked out the sunlight. The far end of the alley was a black patch of smelly air and suspicious silence.

I slid my hand inside my coat to reassure myself I could get the .38 out fast in case of an emergency, then I walked quietly towards the darkness.

At the end of the alley, and at a sharp right-angle to it, was Coral Row: a dismal, dark courtyard flanked on three sides by derelict-looking buildings that had at one time or another served as marine storehouses. By the look of them now they were nothing better than rat-infested ruins.

High above me I could see the stark, black roofs of the buildings sharply outlined against a patch of blue sky.

I stood in the opening of the alley, looking at the buildings, wondering if I was about to walk into a trap.

Opposite, a worm-eaten door sagged on one hinge. A dirty brass number, a 2, was screwed to the central panel.

There it was: 2 Coral Row. It now depended on myself whether I'd go in there or not. I took a drag at my cigarette while I looked the place over. It would probably be as dark as a Homburg hat inside, and I hadn't a flashlight. The boards would be rotten, and it would be impossible to move silently. But I decided to go ahead and see what happened.

Throwing my cigarette away, I walked across the courtyard to the sagging door. I wasn't any calmer than a hen chased by a motor car, and my heart was banging against my ribs, but I went ahead because I'm a sucker for discipline, and I feel, every now and then, it is good for one's morale to do things like this.

I gum-shoed up the stone steps and peered into a long, dark passage. Facing me was a flight of stairs, several of them crushed flat as if some heavy foot had been too much for the worm-rotten timber. There were no banisters, and the stairs looked unpleasantly suicidal. I decided to leave them alone, and investigate the passage.

The floor creaked and groaned under my feet as I walked slowly and cautiously into the stale-smelling darkness. Ahead of me I heard a sudden rustle and a scamper of rats. The sound brought me to a standstill, and the hair at the back of my neck stiffened. To be on the safe side, and probably to bolster up my courage, I eased out my gun.

There was an open door at the end of the passage. I paused before it and peered in. There wasn't much to see except darkness. I was in no hurry to go in, and after a few seconds I made out tiny chinks of light coming in through the boarded walls. Even at that, it was much, much too dark in there.

I took a couple of very cautious steps forward, and paused just inside the doorway. There seemed no point in going farther, and no point in staying longer. If someone was hiding in there, I couldn't see him, and I doubted if he could see me, but in this I was wrong.

A board creaked suddenly close to me. The swish of a descending sap churned the air. I threw myself forward and sideways.

Something very hard and that hurt hit my shoulder, driving the gun out of my hand: a blow aimed at my head, and which would have sent me to sleep for a long, long time if it had landed.

I fell on my hands and knees. Legs brushed against my side, fingers groped up my arm, touched my face and shifted to my throat: lean, strong fingers, damp against my skin, and cold.

I shoved my chin into my collar so he couldn't get a proper grip, straightened, groped in my turn for a hold. My hands touched a coat, went up a powerful bicep. That gave me an idea where his face was. I slammed in a short, hard punch that connected with what felt like an ear.

There was a grunt, then a weight that could have been around fourteen stone dropped on top of me, driving me flat on to the floor. The fingers dug into my neck; hot, hurried breathing fanned my face.

But this time he wasn't dealing with a girl. Probably he hadn't had a great deal of trouble in handling Gracie, but he was going to have some trouble handling me.

I caught hold of his thumbs and bent them back. I heard him catch his breath in a gasp of pain. He jerked his thumbs out of my grip only because I let him, and as he straightened up I clouted him on the side of the head with a round-house swing that sent him away from me with a grunt of anguish.

I was half up, with my fingers touching the floor, as he launched himself at me again. I could just make out his dim form in the darkness as he came, and I lurched towards him. We met with a crash like a couple of charging bulls. He reeled back, and I socked him in the belly: a going-away punch that hadn't the beef to put him down, but that brought the wind out of him like the hiss of a punctured tyre.

At the back of my mind I could see that screwed-up figure in the soiled blue nightdress hanging on the back of the bathroom door, and it made me mad. I kept moving in, belting him with right and left punches, not always landing, but taking good care when they did land they'd hurt. I took one bang on the side of the jaw that sent my head back, but it wasn't hard enough to stop me.

He was gasping for breath now, and backing away as fast as he could. I had to stop throwing punches, because I lost sight of him. I could only hear his heavy breathing, and guess he was somewhere just ahead of me. For a moment or so we stood in the darkness, trying to see each other, listening and watching for any sudden move.

I thought I could just make out a shadow in the darkness about a yard to my left, but I wasn't sure. I stamped my foot, and the shadow swerved away like a scared cat. Before he could recover his balance, I jumped in, and my fist caught him on the side of his neck. The impact sounded like a cleaver driving into a hunk of beef.

He gave a wheezing gasp, fell over on his back, scrambled up and backed away. He now seemed very anxious to break up the meeting and go home. I dived forward to finish him, but instead, my foot landed on a rotten plank that gave under me, and I came down with a crash that shook the breath out of me.

He had me cold then, but he wasn't interested. All he could think of was getting home.

He bolted for the door.

I struggled to get up, but my foot was firmly held in the rotten flooring. I caught a glimpse of a tall, broad-shouldered figure outlined in the dimness of the doorway; then it vanished.

By the time I got my foot free I knew it would be useless to go after him. There were too many bolt-holes in Coral Gables to find him after such a start.

I limped to the door, swearing to myself. Something white lying in the passage caught my eye. I bent to pick it up.

It was a white felt hat.

III

The barman in Yate's Bar looked like a retired all-in-wrestler. He was getting old now, but he still looked tough enough to quell a riot.

He served me with a slice of baked ham between rye bread and a pint of beer, and while I ate he rested hairy arms on the counter and stared at me.

At this hour of the day the bar was slack. There were not more than half a dozen men at the various tables dotted around the room: fishermen and turtle men waiting for the tide to turn. They took no notice of me, but I seemed to fascinate the barman. His battle-scarred face was heavy with thought, and every now and then he passed a hand as big as a ham over his shaven head as if to coax his brain to work.

'Seen yuh kisser some place,' he said, pulling at a nose that had been stamped on in the past. 'Been in here before, ain't yu?'

He had a high, falsetto voice that would have embarrassed a choirboy.

I said I had been in before.

He nodded his shaven head, scratched where his ear had been, and showed a set of very white even teeth.

'Never forget a kisser. Yuh come in here fifty yars from now, and I'd remember ya. Fact.'

I thought it wasn't likely either of us would live that long, but I didn't say so.

'Wonderful how some people remember faces,' I said. 'Wish I could. Meet a man one day, walk through him the next. Bad for business.'

'Yah,' the barman said. 'Guy came in yesterday; ain't been in here for three yars. Give him a pint of old ale before he could ask for it. Always drank old ale. That's memory.'

If he had served me old ale without asking me I wouldn't have argued with him. He didn't look as if he had a lot of patience with people who argued.

'Test your memory on this one,' I said. 'Tall, thin, broad-shouldered. Wears a fawn suit and a white felt hat. Seen him around here?'

The squat, heavy body stiffened. The battered, hairy face hardened.

'It ain't smart to ask questions in dis joint, brother,' he said, lowering his voice. 'If yuh don't want to lose yu front teeth, better keep yu yap shut.'

I drank some beer while I eyed him over the rim of the glass.

'That scarcely answers my question,' I said, put down the glass and produced a five-dollar bill. I kept it between my fingers so only he and I could see it.

He looked to right and left, frowned, hesitated, then looked to right and left again: as obvious as a ham actor playing Hard-iron, the spy, for the first time.

'Give me it wid a butt,' he said, without moving his lips.

I gave him a cigarette and the bill. Only five of the six men in the bar saw him take it. The other had his back turned.

'One of Barratt's boys,' he said. 'Keep clear of him: he's dangerous.'

'Yeah; and so's a mosquito if you let it bite you,' I said, and paid for the beer and the sandwich.

As he scooped up the money, I asked, 'What's he call him-self?'

He looked at me, frowning, then moved off down to the far end of the bar. I waited a moment until I was sure he wasn't coming back, then I slid off the stool and went out into the hot afternoon sunshine.

Jeff Barratt: could be, I thought. I didn't know he had any boys. He had a good reason to shut Gracie's mouth. I began to wonder if he was the master-mind behind the kidnapping. It would fit together very well if he was; possibly too well.

I also wondered, as I walked across to where I had parked the Buick, if Mary Jerome was hooked up in some way with Barratt. It was time I did something about her. I decided to run up to the Acme Garage and ask some questions.

I drove fast up Beach Road into Hawthorne Avenue and turned left into Foothill Boulevard.

The sun was strong, and I lowered the blue sunshield over the windshield. The sunlight, coming through the blue glass, filled the car with a soft, easy light and made me feel as if I was in an aquarium.

The Acme Garage stood at the corner of Foothill Boulevard and Hollywood Avenue, facing the desert. It wasn't anything to get excited about, and I wondered why Lute Ferris had selected such an isolated, out-of-the-way spot for a filling station.

There were six pumps, two air- and water-towers in a row before a large steel and corrugated shed that acted as a repair shop. To the right was a dilapidated rest-room and snack bar, and behind the shed, almost out of sight, was a squat, ugly-looking bungalow with a flat roof.

At one time the station might have looked smart. You could still see signs of a blue-and-white check pattern on the buildings, but the salt air, the sand from the desert, the winds and the rain had caught up with the smartness, and no one had bothered to take on an unequal battle.

Before one of the gas pumps was a low-slung Bentley coupé; black and glittering in the sunshine. At the far end of the ramp leading to the repair shop was a four-ton truck.

There seemed no one about, and I drove slowly up to one of the pumps and stopped; my bumpers about a couple of yards from the Bentley's rear.

I tapped on the horn and waited; using my eyes, seeing nothing to excite my interest.

After a while a boy in a blue, greasy overall came out of the repair shop as if he had the whole day still on his hands, and wasn't sure what he was going to do with it now he had it. He lounged past the Bentley, and raised eyebrows at me without any show of interest.

At a guess he was about sixteen, but old in sin and cunning. His oil-smudged face was thin and hard, and his small green eyes were shifty.

'Ten,' I said, took out a cigarette and lit it. 'Don't exhaust yourself. I don't have to be in bed until midnight.'

He gave me a cold, blank stare, and went around to the back of the car. I kept my eye on the spinning dial just to be sure he didn't short-change me.

After a while he reappeared and shoved out a grubby paw. I paid.

'Where's Ferris?'

The green eyes shifted to my face and away.

'Out of town.'

'When will he be back?'

'Dunno.'

'Mrs. Ferris about?'

'She's busy.'

I jerked my thumb towards the bungalow.

'In there?'

'Wherever she is, she's still busy,' the boy said and moved off.

I was about to yell after him when from behind the repair shop came a tall, immaculate figure in a light check lounge suit, a snap-brimmed brown hat well over one eye and a blood-red carnation in his buttonhole: Jeff Barratt.

I sat still and watched him, knowing he couldn't see me through the dark blue sunshield.

He gave the Buick a casual stare before climbing into the Bentley. He drove off towards Beechwood Avenue.

The boy had gone into the repair shop. I had an idea he was watching me, although I couldn't see him. I waited a moment or so, thinking. Was it a coincidence that Barratt had appeared here? I didn't think so. Then I remembered Mifflin had told me Lute Ferris was a suspected marijuana smuggler. I knew Barratt smoked the stuff. Was that the hook-up between them? Was it also a coincidence that Mary Jerome should have picked on this out-of-the-way garage from which to hire a car? Again I didn't think so. I suddenly realized I was making discoveries and progress for the first time since I started on this case. I decided to take a look at Mrs. Ferris.

I got out of the Buick, and set off along the concrete path that led past the repair shop to the bungalow.

The boy was standing in the shadows, just inside the door of the repair shop. He stared at me woodenly as I passed. I stared right back at him.

He didn't move or say anything, so I went on, turned the corner of the shed and marched up the path to the bungalow.

There was a line of washed clothes across the unkept garden: a man's singlet, a woman's vest, socks, stockings and a pair of ancient dungarees. I ducked under the stockings, and rapped on the shabby, blistered front door.

There was a lengthy pause, and as I was going to rap again the door opened.

The girl who stood in the doorway was small and compact and blowsy. Even at a guess I couldn't have put her age within five years either side of twenty-five. She looked as if life hadn't been fun for a long time; so long she had ceased to care about fun, anyway. Her badly bleached hair was stringy and limp. Her face was puffy and her eyes red with recent weeping. Only the cold, hard set to her mouth showed she had a little spirit left, not much, but enough.

'Yes?' She looked at me suspiciously. 'What do you want?'

I tipped my hat at her.

'Mr. Ferris in?'

'No. Who wants him?'

'I understand he rented a car to Miss Jerome. I wanted to talk to him about her.'

She took a slow step back and her hand moved up to rest on the doorknob. In a second or so she was going to slam the door in my face.

'He's not here, and I've nothing to tell you.'

'I've been authorized to pay for any information I get,' I said hurriedly as the door began to move.

'How much?'

She was looking now like a hungry dog looking at a bone.

'Depends on what I get. I might spring a hundred bucks.'

The tip of a whitish tongue ran the length of her lips.

'What sort of information?'

'Could I step inside? I won't keep you long.'

She hesitated. I could see suspicion, fear and money-hunger wrestling in her mind. Money won, as it usually does. She stood aside.

'Well, come in. It's not over-tidy, but I've been busy.'

She led me into a back room. It was shabby and dirty and sordid. The furniture looked as if it had come from the junk-man's barrow; the threadbare carpet sent out little puffs of dust when I trod on it. There were greasy black finger-prints on the overmantel and the walls. The least one could say of it was, it was not over-tidy.

She sat down in an easy chair that sagged under her weight and stared at me, uneasy and suspicious.

'The boy said your husband is out of town. I didn't believe him,' I said.

'I don't know where he is.' Her eyes suddenly filled with tears and she turned her head. 'I think he's skipped.'

I felt a prickle run up my spine.

'What makes you think that?'

She rubbed her eyes with the back of her hand.

'What about this money? I haven't a damn cent. He went off, owing money everywhere. I haven't enough even to buy food.'

'You'll get it if you have anything worth while to tell me.'

Her face hardened.

'I could tell you plenty. They think I don't know anything, but I do. I keep my ears and eyes open. I know all about them. I've had enough of this hole. I'll sell them out if you give me enough to get away from here.'

'Sell who out?'

'Lute and Barratt.'

I took out my bill-fold. It felt very lean. I had only thirty dollars left. I took out a twenty-dollar bill and dangled it before her.

'There's more where this comes from. How much do you want?'

She leaned forward and snatched the bill out of my hand.

'Five hundred and I'll give you the works.'

'What do you think I am – made of money? A hundred.'

She gave me a cold, fixed stare.

'That's my price; take it or leave it. I'm going to get out of here. I'll give you a signed statement. It'll blow the lid off their racket. Take it or leave it.'

'I've got to know what I'm buying. You'll get your five hundred if what you've got is what I want. Tell me.'

She hesitated, staring at me.

'Who are you working for?'

'Perelli. Let's have it.'

'I'll give you a little of it,' she said at last. 'I'll give you the whole of it when I have the money. Lute, Barratt and Dedrick are running the biggest smuggling racket on the coast. They're

97

supplying millions of reefers all over the country and to Paris, London, and Berlin. Lute looks after Los Angeles and San Francisco. Barratt takes care of London and New York. Dedrick supplies Paris and Berlin. How's that for a sample?'

'You're sure about Dedrick?'

She gave me a sneering little smile.

'I'm sure. I've heard them talk. They think I'm dumb, but I'm not. If they had treated me right I would have kept my mouth shut. I know where they keep the reefers. There's not much I don't know. You'll get it all for five hundred bucks, and it'll be cheap at the price.'

'What do you know about Mary Jerome?'

She chewed her underlip, her eyes hard.

'I know all about her. I know where she is too.'

'Where is she?'

'She was at the Beach Hotel, but she isn't there now. I'm not giving you any more until I get the money. I know why Dedrick was kidnapped. I tell you, I can lift the lid right off this racket, but I'm going to be paid first.'

'Okay. I have a car outside. Come down to my office. You'll have your money and can talk in comfort.'

'I'm not moving from here. You might take me anywhere.'

'I'll take you to my office. Come on.'

'No! I'm not all that crazy.'

'What did Barratt want just now?'

'I don't know. He comes to see the boy. That'll show you how they treat me. He doesn't bother to see me. He just talks to the boy and goes away again. Lute hasn't been near me since he went off with that woman.'

'You mean Mary Jerome?'

'I don't know who it was. It might have been her. I didn't see her. She telephoned. I heard Lute talking to her. He said, "All right, baby, don't get so excited. I'm coming right over." He didn't even bother to say good-bye. He took the car and went, and I haven't seen him since.'

'When was this?'

'The night Dedrick was kidnapped.'

'What time?'

'Just before eight o'clock.'

'Had Barratt anything to do with Dedrick's kidnapping?'

She looked at me and smiled slyly.

'That's the lot, mister; get me the money and you'll hear the rest. I know it all, but I'm not saying another word until I get the rest of it.'

'Suppose I call the cops? You'd have to talk to them for nothing.'

She laughed.

'I'd like to see anyone try to make me talk for nothing. I wouldn't be talking to you if it wasn't for the money.'

'You'd better come with me. If I leave you here, one of them might fix you. They fixed Gracie Lehmann because she knew too much.'

'I'm not scared. I can look after myself. Go and get the money.'

I decided I was wasting time trying to make her tell me more.

'I'll be back in half an hour.'

'I'll wait.'

I went out of the sordid room, down the path to the Buick.

IV

Paula looked up sharply from her paper-strewn desk as I burst into her office.

'I want five hundred dollars right away,' I said breathlessly. 'Things are really popping. Grab a notebook and pencil, and let's go. I'll tell you about it on the way.'

There was no flustration. Paula always kept calm. She got to her feet, went over to the office safe, counted out twenty-five twenty-dollar bills, opened a drawer, took out her notebook, picked up her handbag and the little skullcap affair she calls her hat and was ready to go: all inside twelve seconds.

On our way out, she told Trixy to wait until she got back. Trixy looked doleful, but neither of us paid any attention.

I hurried Paula along the corridor.

'Hey!'

Martha Bendix's sergeant-major voice hit me at the back of the neck.

I looked over my shoulder.

'Can't wait: I'm in a hurry.'

'That party of yours: Souki. Just heard. No skeleton. First-rate man. Been with Marshland ten years,' Martha bellowed. 'When do I get my money?'

'You'll get it,' I shouted back and crowded Paula into the elevator.

'That woman would win a hog-calling contest,' Paula said tartly as the elevator hurtled down to the ground floor.

'That's a hundred and fifty dollars down the drain,' I said gloomily. 'I hoped to dig up some dirt on that chauffeur. Well, well, can't be helped. With any luck, I've cracked this case.'

I talked solidly as I rushed the Buick along Orchid Boulevard, up Beach Road and Hawthorne Avenue. It was surprising how much there was to tell her since I had last seen her.

Finally, as I swung into Foothill Boulevard I got around to Mrs. Ferris.

'This is really something,' I said. 'Dedrick a reefer smuggler! What do you know? For five hundred she'll give me a signed statement.'

'But how do you know she's telling the truth?'

'I'll get the statement and then shanghai her to the police. She'll get her money all right, but every word she's signing is going to be checked.'

I slowed down and pulled up outside the filling station. The boy didn't show up. I got out of the car, followed by Paula.

'The bungalow's around the back.'

We walked down the path, past the repair shed. I paused to look in. The boy wasn't there. I felt a sudden tightness around my chest, and I broke into a run. I was rapping on the door of the bungalow by the time Paula caught me up.

No one answered. Nothing happened.

'Well, I warned her,' I said savagely, drew back and slammed my shoulder against the door.

It wasn't built for such treatment and flew open.

We stood, side by side, in the dark little hall.

'Mrs. Ferris!' I shouted. 'Mrs. Ferris!'

Silence.

'Well, that's that. These rats work fast. You'd better stay here, Paula, while I look the place over.'

'You don't think she changed her mind and bolted?'

I shook my head.

'Not a chance. She wanted the money too badly. The boy must have tipped them off.'

Leaving her in the hall, I went from room to room. I didn't find her.

I came back to the hall.

'Not here. If they haven't taken her away, they've frightened her away.'

I was thinking of the screwed-up figure in the blue night-dress, hanging on the back of the bathroom door. If Mrs. Ferris knew as much as she hinted she did, her life now wasn't worth a dime.

'Take a look in her bedroom and see if she's taken any clothes,' I said. 'She can't have many.'

While Paula went into the bedroom, I went into the back room where we had talked. I hunted around, but didn't find anything that told me why she had disappeared.

Paula came in after a while.

'As far as I can see, she hasn't taken anything. There're no gaps in the cupboards and the drawers aren't disturbed.'

'I wish I knew where that boy is. If I could get him to talk—'

'Vic!'

Paula was looking out of the window. I joined her.

'What's that, by the shed? Isn't it—?'

At the end of the strip of garden was a tool shed. The door was ajar. I could see something white lying on the floor.

'Wait here. I'll look.'

I went to the back door, opened it, and walked quickly down the garden. As I approached the shed, I pulled out my gun. I pushed open the door, looked into the dim darkness.

She was there, lying on her face, her hands covering her head as if to protect it.

I imagined her seeing them coming up the front way, losing her head and running wildly down the path to the shed. They had probably shot her from the back door, not even bothering to come down and see if she was dead.

I turned and walked quickly back to the bungalow.

v

There were several well-bred, well-dressed and overfed men lounging in the lobby of the Beach Hotel. All of them stared fixedly at Paula's ankles as we walked over to the reception desk.

The reception clerk was a tall, willowy young man with blond, wavy hair, a pink-and-white complexion and a disillusioned expression in his pale blue eyes.

'Good evening,' he said, giving Paula a little bow. 'Have you made reservations?'

'No; it's not that kind of a party,' I said, and laid my business card on the counter. 'I'm hoping you can give me some information.'

Blond eyebrows lifted. He peered at the card, read it, picked it up, and read it again.

'Ah, yes, Mr. Malloy. What can I do for you?' He glanced at Paula again, and unconsciously fingered his tie.

'We're trying to find a young woman who we think stayed here on the 12th or maybe the 11th.'

'We don't encourage inquiries about our visitors, Mr. Malloy.'

He was as stiff as a Dowager watching a bubble dance.

'That I can understand. But she happens to be this young lady's sister.' I waved to Paula, who gave him a look from under her eyelashes that made his knees buckle. 'She ran away from home and we're anxious to trace her.'

'Oh, I see.' He hesitated. 'Well, perhaps, in that case I might . . . What is her name?'

'We think she was staying here under an assumed name. You don't get many unattached young women staying here, do you?'

He shook his head regretfully.

'Actually, not. I think I know the one you mean. Miss Mary Henderson, if I remember rightly.' He flicked the pages of the register, ran a well-manicured finger down a page, paused. 'Yes; Miss Henderson. Tall, dark, distinctly pretty. Would that be the one?'

'Sounds like her. She wore a wine-coloured evening gown and a black silk wrap on the evening of the 12th.'

He nodded, patted his lips with a snow-white handkerchief and gave Paula a dazzling smile.

'That's Miss Henderson.'

'Fine. When did she book in?'

He consulted the register.

'Six o'clock on the 12th.'

'Any forwarding address?'

'I'm afraid not.'

'When did she leave?'

'On the 13th. I remember now. I was rather surprised. She had booked the room for a week.'

'Did she have a car?'

The clerk frowned, studied Paula's lovely, intent face,

seemed to draw inspiration from it for he said, 'Actually, not. At least, not when she arrived. But before she went up to her room, she arranged to hire a car. She said she wanted it that evening as she was going out.'

'Did you hire the car for her?'

'Oh, yes. We deal with the Acme Garage. You may know it?'

I said I knew it.

'Ferris brought the car around at six-thirty or seven, and left it for Miss Henderson.'

'Did he see her?'

The clerk lifted his eyebrows.

'Why, no. That wasn't necessary.'

'You're quite sure he didn't see her?'

'Yes.'

'What happened to the car?'

'As a matter of fact, it's still in our garage. I'm glad you reminded me. Ferris usually comes and takes it away. I must remind him.'

'Mind if I look at it?'

'Why, certainly.'

'What is it?'

'A black Lincoln. The attendant will show it to you.' He was looking puzzled.

'Well, thanks. One more thing; did Miss Henderson have any visitors while she was here?'

He thought for a moment.

'One gentleman. Yes, that's right. He came to see her in the afternoon on the 13th. She cancelled her room after he had gone.'

I lit a cigarette before I asked, 'Did you see him?'

'Certainly. He came to the desk and asked for her.' Again he patted his lips with his handkerchief and gave Paula a quick, admiring glance out of the corners of his eyes.

'Can you describe him?'

'He was an elderly gentleman. Well dressed; obviously well-to-do. He said his name was Franklin Marshland.'

I drew in a slow deep breath, asked, 'Short, suntanned, beaky nose and very small feet?'

'I didn't notice his feet, Mr. Malloy, but the rest is right.'

'And Miss Henderson left almost immediately after? Did she seem upset?'

'I wouldn't say upset, but perhaps a little flustered. She

seemed very anxious to go. I was rather surprised. I think I told you. She had reserved the room for a week.'

'Did she take a taxi?'

'I believe she did. The porter will remember her.'

'If we could find the taxi-driver, he might know where she went.'

The clerk was taking a lot of interest by now.

'I'll ask the porter. Just wait a moment.'

When he crossed the lobby to the porter's desk, Paula and I exchanged glances.

'Well, we are certainly making progress,' I said. 'I wonder what Marshland wanted with her. You know, I'm beginning to think my idea that Marshland has something to do with the kidnapping isn't such a scatty one at that.'

'Do we know where he was at the time of the kidnapping?'

'I don't think that matters. He wouldn't have had anything to do with it himself. He would have hired someone to do it.'

The clerk came back.

'No luck, I'm afraid. The porter remembers Miss Henderson, but has no idea who the driver was. The cab was cruising when he stopped it.'

'Well, thanks for giving me so much of your time. I'll take a look at the car now. The garage's around the back?'

He said the garage was around the back.

'I hope you find her,' he said to Paula.

Paula thanked him with a smile that had him running his hand over his curly blond hair.

As we walked across the lobby the well-fed loungers again paused in their conversations to stare at Paula's ankles.

The attendant in the garage took us over to a black Lincoln.

'That's the job. Can't understand why Ferris hasn't collected it yet,' he said. He too seemed smitten with Paula.

'Do you remember what time she brought it in on the night of the 12th?' I asked.

'I can tell you. We log all cars as they come in.'

While he went over to the office, I examined the car, pushing my hands down the sides of the seats, turning up the floor mats, and going through the pockets, hoping to find something she might have dropped or forgotten. I didn't find a thing.

The attendant came back.

'She booked in at twenty minutes to eleven.'

'Did you see her?'

'I must have, but I don't remember.'

It would have been too good to be true if he had.

'Okay,' I said, and gave him a buck. 'Well, thanks.'

We went back to the Buick. The time was now half-past six.

'I'll drop you off at the office. Get Trixy off home,' I said.

'And you?' Paula asked.

'I'm going to talk to Marshland.'

CHAPTER FIVE

I

As I drove towards Ocean End, I laid out my discoveries in my mind and brooded over them.

In actual fact, I was no nearer to getting Perelli out of jail, but I had a feeling that if I kept on digging, sooner or later I'd get the necessary proof. At least, I had something to work on: which was more than Mifflin had.

Gracie had been murdered because she knew who had framed Perelli. That meant Perelli was innocent, and up to now I hadn't been 100 per cent convinced. It made a difference.

If I was to believe Mrs. Ferris, Dedrick had been smuggling reefers into Paris before he met Serena. Was this the clue to his kidnapping? Had he decided to give up working for Barratt now he had married Serena, and had Barratt killed him: staging a fake kidnapping to get money out of Serena? That was possible.

My mind shifted to Marshland. Had he anything to do with the kidnapping? Suppose Souki had found out that Dedrick was hooked up with Barratt and had told Marshland? That would have been a nice item of news: the fourth richest woman in the world married to a reefer-smuggler. Marshland might have gone to any lengths to save his daughter from such publicity. He might have hired someone to get rid of Dedrick. It might have been his idea, and not Barratt's, to fake the kidnapping. For all I knew, Dedrick might have been buried somewhere in the grounds of Ocean End. No one had thought of looking for him under four feet of earth.

Where did Mary Jerome come in on all this? Who was she? Brandon had made a feeble attempt to find her, but apparently Marshland had had no difficulty in tracking her down. How had he found out where she was? Why had he gone to her? Why had she bolted after they had talked?

I ran my hand over my hot, tired face, and said, 'Aw, nuts!' I knew I was within touching distance of the key to this business, but my arm wasn't quite long enough. I had to get more information.

How was I going to tackle Marshland? He wasn't going to be easy. After thinking about it, I decided the only way was to be tough. He could either talk to me or to Brandon. The reception clerk would identify him. He couldn't deny he had gone to the Beach Hotel. Either me or Brandon.

I drove down the private road to Ocean End with the evening sun reflecting on the windshield.

The big black Cadillac was parked on the tarmac as it had been parked on my first visit to the house. The two Chinese gardeners were weeding a rose bed as enthusiastically as a man sitting down in a dentist's chair. They poked about in the rich, dark soil with their handforks, lifting the odd weed and sneering at it, dropping it into a basket and poking again.

The flamingoes were moving about, stiff-jointed, on the lawn below the terraces. Like the Chinese gardeners, they paid no attention to me.

I walked along the terrace, thumbed the bell-push and waited, feeling the sun hot on my back.

Wadlock opened the door. His bushy eyebrows contracted and the eyes under them registered disapproval when he saw me.

'Hello,' I said. 'I'd like to talk to Mr. Marshland. Would you tell him?'

'Will you come in, Mr. Malloy?' He stood aside. 'I am not sure if Mr. Marshland is in.'

I walked into the hall. It was cool and dim after the hot terrace. I took off my hat, looked inside it for no reason at all, said, without looking at the old man, 'The password is Beach Hotel. Will you tell him?'

'Beach Hotel?'

'That's right. You'll be surprised how he'll react. Do I go in the lounge?'

'If you will, sir.'

'How is Mrs. Dedrick?' I asked. 'I heard she hasn't been well.'

'Considering the circumstances, sir, she is as well as can be expected.'

I looked at him thoughtfully, but the old face gave nothing away, so I went into the lounge. It seemed a long, long time ago since I had last been here. I moved on to the terrace again, and looked expectantly up at the veranda where Serena had sat mourning for her loved one. No one was up there. I returned to the lounge, picked a comfortable chair and sat down. The day had been an exciting one. I felt very tired: probably nervous excitement, I told myself. I lit a cigarette and blew smoke at the Mexican saddle hanging on the wall. An enormous bowl of sweet peas filled the room with an overpowering scent. It made me feel a little drowsy.

After a while, probably ten minutes, I heard footsteps coming down the stairs.

Serena Dedrick came into the lounge. She was wearing a simple white-linen dress and a rose in her hair. There were dark smudges under her eyes and a drawn, hard look about her mouth. She looked steadily at me as I got to my feet, smiled without warmth, waved me back to the chair.

'Don't get up. Would you like a whisky and soda?'

'Well, not just now, thank you. I wanted to see your father. Didn't Wadlock tell you?'

She went over to a big cocktail cabinet and poured two whiskies. She gave me one, motioned to a box of cigarettes on the occasional table by my side and sat down opposite me.

'My father went back to New York yesterday,' she said, looking anywhere but at me. 'What did you want to see him about?'

I sipped the whisky. It was Four Roses, and very good. I wondered why Wadlock hadn't broken the news and saved her the trouble of seeing me. It occurred to me that perhaps she wanted to see me.

'I wanted to ask him something, Mrs. Dedrick,' I said, 'but as he isn't here it doesn't matter. Could I have his New York address?'

'Is it so important?'

'It's something I want to ask him. I could telephone him.'

'He is going away. This – this business has upset him. I don't think you could reach him,' she said after a long silence.

I drank half the whisky, set down the glass and stood up.

'It doesn't matter. It isn't all that important.'

She looked at me now, surprise in her eyes.

'But can't you tell me what it is?'

'The day after your husband was kidnapped, Mr. Marshland called on the woman who said she was your secretary,

Mary Jerome. The meeting took place at the Beach Hotel, where the woman was staying. I wanted to ask him what was said, and how he knew she was there.'

'My father?'

She stood so still she could have been a statue.

'Yes. He gave his name to the hotel clerk, who would be able to identify him.'

'But I don't understand. How could it be my father? He doesn't know the woman.'

'He's seen her and talked to her. I want to know what was said. If he won't tell me, I'll have to put the information in Brandon's hands.'

Her eyes lit up.

'Are you being threatening?'

'Call it that if you like.'

'My father flies for Europe this evening. He's probably gone by now. I have no idea where he is spending his vacation. He often goes off like that when he wants a rest.'

'He's gone at a convenient time – for himself.'

She moved to the terrace window and stared out into the garden.

'You have no idea why he went to see her, have you?'

'No.'

'You can't even guess?'

'No.'

I joined her at the window.

'Mrs. Dedrick, there's a question I would like to ask you.'

She continued to stare out of the window. The flamingoes were looking towards the house, stiff, upright and crochety.

'Well?'

'Do you think Nick Perelli kidnapped your husband?'

'Of course.'

'Why of course? Why so sure?'

She made an impatient movement.

'I don't wish to talk about it. If there is nothing else you want, perhaps you will excuse me.'

'I don't think Perelli kidnapped him,' I said. 'Has it occurred to you that your father has a very sound motive for getting rid of your husband?'

She turned swiftly. Her face had drained of colour. Fear looked at me out of her big eyes.

'How dare you! I won't listen to you. You have no right

to come here making insinuations and asking questions. I shall complain to the police.'

She went out of the room. She was crying as she mounted the stairs.

I stood there, brooding out into the twilight. Why had she been frightened? Did she know for certain that Marshland had engineered the kidnapping?

A faint cough behind me made me turn.

Wadlock was waiting at the door.

I crossed the room, paused before him.

'Apparently Mr. Marshland has gone off to Europe,' I said.

The old eyes were expressionless as he said, 'Apparently, sir.'

'Was it Souki who told you about Dedrick or did you find out for yourself – that he was a reefer-smuggler?'

I got past his guard, as I meant to. It was a shame to do it to him; he was a little too old to control his reflexes, but I wanted to know.

His mouth fell open and his eyes popped.

'Why, Souki told me . . .'

He stopped; a little late. A faint flush rose to his face: but he was too old to be really angry.

'Your hat, sir.'

I took it and slapped it on the back of my head.

'Sorry about that,' I said, and meant it. 'Think no more about it.'

He closed the door behind me. Looking back, I could see him watching me through the glass panels. I felt he was still watching me by the time I reached the end of the terrace.

If Souki had told him, Souki had also told Marshland. I wasn't getting ahead very fast, but I was making progress. I got into the Buick, started the engine and stared across the terrace garden at the Pacific. I couldn't go on like this. I would have to do something that would bring the secrets out into the open. But what?

I lit a cigarette and flicked the match out of the car window. Then I drove slowly down the private road, thinking.

Perelli had told Francon he was playing cards with Joe Betillo at Delmonico's bar on the night of the kidnapping. He had said he left Betillo at ten-thirty. Betillo had said it was nine-thirty. Why? Was Betillo in this or was he bribed? If he was bribed, who had bribed him? The evening was before me.

Maybe it might be a good idea to check Perelli's alibi. I was in the mood for trouble. Two girls had been murdered this day. A tall, unknown gentleman in sunglasses had tried to lay me among the sweet peas. The fourth richest woman in the world had told me a number of lies. It might be an idea to top off the day with a visit to Delmonico's Bar, the toughest dive on the Coast.

I felt in the mood to be tough. I decided to go there.

II

Paula's cool voice floated over the line: 'Good evening. Universal Services.'

'Are you all alone there?' I asked, pushing my hat to the back of my head and wiping my forehead. The call-box was as hot as a circus tent, and the last occupant had fallen in a vat of Night and Day, the aristocrat of perfumes, to judge by the smell she had left behind.

'Oh, Vic; yes, I'm alone. How did you get on?'

'Nothing to get excited about. Promise me something, will you?'

'What?'

'Never wear Night and Day perfume. It's horrible stuff.'

'Why bring that up? I wouldn't wear it if they gave it to me.'

'That's fine. This call-box stinks of it. I'm feeling stifled.'

'What happened, Vic?'

'Marshland has suddenly rushed off on a vacation in Europe. That's what Serena tells me. It's my bet he was lurking upstairs somewhere, probably biting his nails. I told her he was possibly at the bottom of the kidnapping. She chucked an ingbing and ran off, piping her eye.'

'Seriously?'

'Well, she looked scared. I think she's thought that all along. These rich, well-connected families have a horror of being dragged out of their shells. The butler was revealing too. Nice old boy: one of the old school. I jumped him about Souki, and before he could stop himself he admitted Souki had told him Dedrick was a smuggler. How do you like that?'

'It doesn't help Perelli very much, does it?'

'You're quite right. It doesn't help him a bit. I'm going to do something about him right now. There's a small point you might take care of. Will you send a cable to Jack and tell him what I've found out about Dedrick? Tell him to get hustling.'

Paula said she would get the cable off right away.

'When you've done that, shut up and go home,' I told her.

'What are you doing?'

'I'm digging a little more. The night's young yet.'

'Don't be reckless, will you, Vic?'

I said I'd handle myself as carefully as I'd handle a Ming vase, and hung up before she could ask any more questions.

I got into the Buick again and drove to Monte Verde Avenue. No. 245 was, as Myra Toresca had said, a small, painted bungalow with crazy paving where the garden should have been and a high, overgrown hedge to foil inquisitive neighbours.

I parked the Buick outside, pushed open the low wooden gate and walked up the path. A light showed in one of the windows; a shadow crossed the blind as I rapped on the front door.

The door opened a few inches. Myra asked, 'Who is it?'

'Malloy.'

She slid off the chain, opened the door. The passage behind her was dark.

'Come in. I was wondering when you were coming.'

I followed her into the lighted sitting-room. I was surprised to see her taste ran to frilly cushions, china masks and ornamental dolls.

She was wearing her windbreaker and slacks. Her eyes were heavy-looking and her face pallid. She didn't look as if she had had much sleep since last I saw her.

'What's cooking?' she asked as she fetched out a bottle of Scotch, glasses and ice. 'I've been walking the floor since last night.'

Last night! It didn't seem possible that so much had happened in twenty-four hours.

I dropped into an easy chair.

'Plenty, but I'm not sure that it does us any good. I've a little job on you might like to help me with, but before I go into that, I'll get you up to date on what's happened so far.'

She stood before the empty fireplace, her hands in her trouser pockets, a cigarette between her lips, her face set and cold while I talked.

I didn't leave out any of the details, and the story took the best part of a half an hour.

'I have a lot of facts,' I concluded, 'but no proof; and it's proof we must have. I must build up a case that'll stand up in court. What I've told you makes a good yarn, but Francon couldn't use it as it stands. The next move is to get the proof, and the only way we can get it is to fight Barratt with his own weapons. The first and easiest move is to try to establish Nick's alibi. He told Francon he was playing cards with Joe Betillo from eight-thirty to ten-thirty. Betillo said he left Delmonico's at nine-thirty. Betillo is a notorious character in Coral Gables. He'd sell his own mother for a dollar. I'm going out there to-night and see if I can find anyone who saw Perelli leave. Maybe someone did, but is scared to get in bad with Betillo. If I can't find anyone, then I'm going to get hold of Betillo, bring him here and persuade him to change his mind about the time Nick left. That all right with you?'

She gave a hard little smile.

'That's fine,' she said. 'If you can't make him talk, perhaps I can.'

'We'll both try. Has Nick any friends? Anyone big and tough who'd help me handle Betillo? He'll need a lot of handling.'

Myra shook her head.

'Nick doesn't make friends easily. We haven't long been here. I'll help you.'

'No. This isn't the kind of outing you take a girl on. Never mind. I'll get hold of Mike Finnegan. He's always ready for trouble.'

'I'm doing it,' Myra said. 'I'm a little tired of sitting here, doing nothing. I can handle a gun. I have more incentive than your friend; a lot more incentive. Tell me what to do, and I'll do it.'

I studied her, decided to take a chance.

'Look, don't let's have any misunderstanding. We don't want to kill this guy: we just want to make him talk.'

She gave me a look that sent a prickle up my spine.

'Get him here, and I'll make him talk.'

I stood up.

'Well, come on. Let's go.'

She pulled open a drawer and took out a .25, checked the clip and pushed the gun into her hip pocket. She finished her whisky, glanced at herself in the mirror.

'Jeepers! I look a fright. I'm glad Nick isn't here to see me.'

'He'd be glad to see you however you look,' I reminded her, and went to the door.

She turned out the light, and together we walked down the garden path to the Buick.

'Suppose we collect Barratt and make him talk,' she said as she settled herself in the car beside me. 'Wouldn't that save a little time?'

'I'm not too sold on the idea of forcing a guy to talk,' I said, driving towards the water-front. 'It might work with Betillo, but not with Barratt. He's too important. He could give us the works, then swear we forced him to confess under torture when he got in the box. That kind of evidence doesn't stand up.'

'If you don't save Nick, I'm going to get Barratt,' she said, in a hard, tight voice. 'That's something I've promised myself.'

I parked the car in the shadows, a few yards from Delmonico's Bar.

'Let's concentrate on saving Nick,' I said. 'There'll be plenty of time to take care of Barratt if we can't do it the legal way. Have you ever been in this joint?'

'Of course I have. Nick used to come here practically every night.'

'I want to look at the room in which Nick and Betillo played cards. Can you swing that?'

'I can if no one's using it.'

'Let's go in and find out.'

We walked up the five wooden steps that led into the bar. Inside was brightly lit and full of people. A juke-box was churning out the *Harry Lime Theme*. Big, tough-looking men propped up the bar. At the tables scattered around the room girls in halters and shorts were trying to convince their male companions that there was more fun upstairs than sitting in this smoke-laden room, drinking rot-gut whisky. They didn't seem to be getting anywhere.

It was the kind of scene you can see in any Warner Bros. movie. All you needed was a tracking shot up to Humphrey Bogart and you'd feel at home.

Myra seemed to know her way around. She walked across the sawdust-covered floor up to the bar and crooked a finger at one of the barmen.

I stood behind her, waiting for trouble.

Four or five men, as wide as they were tall, who were up at the bar, stopped talking and looked at her.

They looked over their shoulders at me, sneered, turned their attention to Myra again.

'Hello, girlie,' one of them said softly.

This, of course, I thought, is where trouble starts. I was a fool to have brought her here. Instead of getting evidence, I was going to get into a fight with a bunch of toughs as big as Carnera.

Myra turned slowly, looked the four men over, said four words with unbelievable viciousness that froze them in their tracks, turned back to the bar again.

Silently, as if they had peeped into a room in which something was going on that shocked even their unshockable minds, they drifted away from the bar and sat at one of the tables.

Myra whispered to the barman, who looked at her narrowly, nodded his head and jerked his thumb to the stairs.

'Come on,' she said to me. 'We can go up.'

We pushed our way through the crowd to the stairs.

'You have quite a way with you when you're aroused,' I said as we mounted the stairs.

'I can take care of myself. The bigger they are the softer the centre. I haven't kicked around with men all my life for nothing.' There was a cold, brooding look on her face. 'The barman says Betillo's got a poker game up here in half an hour.'

'Will he tip him?'

She shook her head.

'He's a friend of mine. What do we do? Wait until he shows and grab him?'

'Let's look the territory over first.'

We reached the head of the stairs. Before us stretched a long passage, lined on either side by doors.

'Room 15,' Myra said, walked along the passage, paused outside a door, turned the handle and pushed the door open. She groped for the light switch, turned it on and we went in together.

The room was big. Under green-shaded lights was a round table, equipped with decks of playing cards and two wooden racks containing poker chips. There were about ten chairs grouped round the table; a couple of brass spittoons completed the furnishing.

'Okay,' I said. 'Now where's the back exit which Nick used?'

She turned out the light and we went to the far end of the

passage. A door opened on to a veranda, overlooking an alley. A steep flight of wooden steps linked the veranda with the alley.

'Right. We'll wait for him inside. If he shows fight, I'll rap him on the dome, but if we can, we'll try to persuade him to walk. He's no light weight.'

We moved back into the passage again.

'Any of these other rooms empty, do you know?'

'Look and see,' she said, opened the first door she came to and groped for the light switch. There was an angry yell, and a flood of violent language, and she turned off the light hurriedly.

'That one isn't,' she said, moved to the next door.

'Wait a minute,' I said, grabbing her arm. 'We'll have a riot up here if you keep doing that. Let's try the door opposite 15.'

We went farther down the passage and paused outside the door opposite 15. I rapped gently. There was a sound of movement and the door opened.

A tall, tired-looking blonde in a none-too-lean wrap peered at me. Her painted face brightened a little, the smudged lips forced a smile.

'Hello, honey, looking for me?'

Then she saw Myra and her face turned to stone.

'What do you want?'

Her face was familiar. My mind groped back into the past, remembered a night when I'd been in trouble, had come through the skylight into this passage and the blonde had saved me.

'Remember me? We had a little fun about two years back,' I said, moving so the light from her room fell on my face. 'I went out of the window with half the cops in Coral Gables after me.'

She stared, frowned, then her face brightened again.

'Jeepers! I'd forgotten you. I remember. You spoilt one of my best sheets, sliding out of that window. What are you doing here? More trouble?'

'Could we come in and talk?'

She looked at Myra.

'She too?'

'Yeah; this is business.'

She must have remembered I hadn't been tight-fisted last time we met, and she stood aside.

'Well, come on in. It's not much of a place for visitors,' and she meant Myra.

We went into the room which was small and stuffy and skimpily furnished. A bed, a chest of drawers, a toilet basin and a threadbare rug were the only luxuries it could boast of.

'I never got your name last time,' I said, propping myself up against the wall.

'Lola,' the blonde said and sat on the bed. She wasn't at ease with Myra in the room.

Myra rested her hips against the toilet-basin. She looked around the room with unconcealed curiosity. Lola watched her, waiting for some remark that didn't come.

'I'm after Betillo again,' I said quietly. 'Remember? The last time we met I'd been to see him with a club in my hand.'

'What's he done to you this time?' Lola asked, looking interested. 'I still hate that heel.'

'Nothing to me personally, but to her boy friend,' I said, waving a hand towards Myra. 'Nick Perelli.'

Lola's eyes opened.

'The guy who snatched Dedrick?' she asked. 'Gee! I've been reading about that business.' She looked enviously at Myra. 'Did your honey get away with five hundred grand?'

'Wait a minute,' I said hastily as Myra's pale little face hardened. 'You're on the wrong number. Perelli didn't pull the Dedrick snatch. He was framed for it. He was playing cards with Betillo at the time of the kidnapping, but Betillo has sold him to the cops. That's why I want Betillo.'

'That rat would sell his first-born to the cops,' Lola said in disgust.

I had a sudden idea.

'You didn't see Perelli leave, did you?'

'Leave where? What do you mean?'

'He was playing cards with Betillo in Room 15. He said he left Betillo at ten-thirty. Betillo said it was nine-thirty. The kidnapping took place just before ten.'

Lola closed her eyes in the effort to think.

'I don't remember seeing him,' she said at last. 'But then I see so many men during the evening, honey.'

'He wore a white linen suit,' Myra said. 'A navy blue shirt and a white, hand-painted tie.'

Lola gaped.

'Was that the guy? Why, sure I know him. He told me his name was—' She broke off suddenly and, probably for the first time in twenty years, she blushed.

There was a heavy, electric silence.

Myra said, 'Go ahead: don't mind me. Was he with you on that night?'

Lola jumped to her feet; her face still red, but her eyes angry and hard.

'Get out, you two! I'm talking too much. Go on, beat it! I've said all I'm going to say.'

'Don't get excited,' I said soothingly. 'This is important, Lola. Perelli's in a jam. If you can help him, you've got to do it. If you know he left here at ten-thirty, you can save his life. Was he with you on that night?'

Lola gave Myra a quick, calculating look.

'I'm not talking,' she said curtly. 'Get out; both of you!'

'All right, Myra,' I said, and went to the door, opened it and jerked my thumb. 'Wait for me in the car. I have a little business deal to settle with Lola. I'll join you in a couple of minutes.'

'How about Betillo?' Myra said. 'He'll be up here any minute now.'

'Never mind Betillo. Wait for me in the car.'

She went out, her back very straight, her face white. I closed the door.

'That was a bit of bad luck,' I said, took out a pack of cigarettes and offered it to her.

She looked at me, grimaced, and took the cigarette.

'Think twice the next time you make up your so-called mind to bring a woman into a hole like this,' she said savagely. 'What kind of spot do you think you've put me in?'

'Yeah; I'm sorry, but I wasn't to know. As it turns out, it may be a lucky break. Don't be coy with me, Lola; was Perelli with you?'

'Of course he was. He played cards with Betillo and then came over to me. I was always seeing him. He's one of my regulars.'

'Remember what time he left you?'

'It would be about half past ten. I don't remember to the minute.'

'That's swell,' I said sarcastically. 'So Betillo was telling the truth and Perelli was lying.'

She didn't say anything.

'I guess he didn't want Myra to know what he was up to,' I said, and shook my head. 'He must have gambled on Betillo backing up his story. You may have to be a witness, Lola. He's got to have an alibi.'

'I don't care,' she said, shrugging, 'but she will. I know her type. She thinks once a man falls in love with her he's hers for keeps. It doesn't work out that way.'

I took out a hundred-dollar bill.

'I owe you this for spoiling that sheet of yours. Keep your mouth shut about Perelli, Lola. I'll tell you if we want you at the trial.'

She took the bill, folded it and pushed it down the top of her stocking.

'What pigs men are,' she said, and threw the half-smoked cigarette contemptuously into the fireplace.

III

I opened the Buick door, slid under the wheel and trod on the starter.

Myra was smoking, a brooding look on her face.

'So we don't touch Betillo?' she said in a low, flat voice.

'As it happened,' I said, not looking at her, 'he was telling the truth. Nick parted company with him at nine-thirty.'

'And spent an hour with that awful, washed-out blonde,' Myra said. 'Lovely for him. I hope he enjoyed himself.'

I drove with exaggerated care up Monte Verde Avenue.

'He's risking his neck to keep it quiet,' I said. 'There's that in his favour.'

'Oh, shut up!' Myra said, her voice unsteady. 'You don't have to make a case out for him. There wasn't a damn thing I wouldn't have done for him: not a thing. When he was in jail, I waited for him. When he came out, I was right on the doorstep. When he was short of money, and he was always short of money, I kept him going. I've been walking the floor all last night, worrying about him. And he has to cheat with a hustler like that in a sordid little room, and pay for it.'

'You're breaking my heart,' I said. 'Okay, so he cheated on you. So what? You don't have to stand by him now. You're free. There're hundreds of men who'll give you a good time. What are you worrying about?'

She swung round in her seat, catching her breath, her face tight with rage.

I grinned at her.

'Get off your high horse, honey. It doesn't suit your complexion.'

She started at me, bit her lip and managed a wry smile.

'I guess you're right. They're all alike. I wish I didn't love the heel. If he ever gets out of this mess, I'll have something to say to him. He'll be allergic to blondes for the rest of his life by the time I've finished with him!'

I pulled up outside her bungalow.

'Go to bed and get some sleep. I have to do a little more thinking.'

'What's the matter with going to the police and getting them to talk to that blonde? Won't her evidence get Nick out?'

I shook my head.

'Not a hope. They wouldn't believe her, for one thing. A woman like that hasn't any standing in a court of law. There're no other witnesses. Nick realized that.'

'So tonight's been so much waste of time?'

'That's right. I've got to cook up another angle. I'll keep in touch.'

I leaned across her and opened the door.

'Don't worry. You may not think it, but we're making progress. We'll have made some more by tomorrow. So long for now.'

She put her hand on my arm.

'Thanks for what you've done so far. Keep trying. I want that heel back.'

I watched her walk up the path to the dark little bungalow, then engaged gear and drove away.

IV

As I drove along the wide track that led through the sand dunes to my cabin, the headlights of the Buick picked out a big battleship of a car parked outside my front gate.

I slowed down, threw out the clutch, shifted into neutral and cruised to a standstill.

I got out of the Buick and walked over to the car. The light from the dashboard reflected on Serena Dedrick's pale, set face. She turned her head and we looked at each other through the open window.

'I hope you haven't been waiting long,' I said, startled to find her here outside my cabin.

'It doesn't matter. I want to talk to you.'

'Come in.'

I opened the car door.

She got out, holding a crimson silk wrap closely to her. She made a lovely, impressive figure of beauty in the moonlight.

Silently, we walked together up the path that led to the veranda.

I opened the front door, switched on the light and stood aside, wondering what she wanted.

She went into the lounge. I followed, closed the door, and turned on the standard lamp by the settee.

'Would you like a drink or coffee?'

'Nothing,' she said curtly, and sat down on the settee. The wrap fell open. She had certainly dressed for the occasion. The white satin dress, the skirt heavy with gold brocade, was fit for a State ball. Diamonds glittered at her throat. A diamond bracelet, four inches wide, imprisoned her left wrist. She seemed determined I shouldn't forget she was the fourth richest woman in the world.

I poured out a stiff whisky, carried the glass to my favourite armchair and sank into it. I felt tired and a little depressed. All the way from Myra's bungalow I had been racking my brains to find a way of cracking this case, but it was like hammering my head against a brick wall.

Then, being suspicious by nature, an idea floated into my mind. I considered it, decided it was a sound one, got to my feet again, crossed the room and thumbed down an electric switch on the wall. Then I came back to the chair again and sat down.

Serena watched me, under down-drawn eyebrows.

'I have a telephone connection in my bedroom. It wasn't switched through,' I explained; went on, 'Well, now, Mrs. Dedrick, what can I do for you?'

'I want you to stop interfering with this kidnapping case,' she said.

I sipped a little whisky, stared at her, not very surprised, but making believe I was.

'Are you serious?'

Her mouth tightened.

'Of course I am. You're being a nuisance. You're prying into things that don't concern you. The police have made an arrest. I am satisfied that this man kidnapped my husband. There is no point in you stirring up more trouble.'

I lit a cigarette, tossed the match into the fireplace, and blew a little cloud of smoke to the ceiling.

'The man the police have arrested didn't do the job, Mrs. Dedrick. He happens to be a friend of mine. I shall continue to investigate this business until I have cleared him.'

She went very pale and her eyes lit up. Her hands became fists in her lap.

'I am willing to pay you to stop being a nuisance,' she said in a hard, tight voice.

'The number of times beautiful women with more money than ethics have tried to bribe me to give up a case really astonishes me,' I said. 'Sorry. I'm not interested.'

'You can name your price,' she said, her voice edged with anger.

'Yeah, I'm sure, but I'm still not interested. If that's all you have to say, I'll turn in. I'm tired.'

'Fifty thousand dollars,' she said, watching me.

I grinned at her.

'We're bargaining for a man's life, Mrs. Dedrick. If I don't go on working on this case, Perelli will go to the gas chamber. Do you seriously mean that's what you want?'

'I know nothing about Perelli. I'm not interested in him. If he is tried and found guilty, then he is guilty. I will give you fifty thousand dollars to go away for a month. Will you take it?'

'I can't go away for a month, Mrs. Dedrick. I'm busy trying to find out who kidnapped your husband.'

'Seventy-five thousand!'

'What are you scared of? What don't you want me to find out?'

'Seventy-five thousand!' she said.

'What's happened to Dedrick? Did someone hit him too hard? Have you discovered your father's at the back of this, and you want to buy his life? Or is it purely selfish motives and you don't want the great American public to know you were taken for a ride by a reefer-smuggler?'

'A hundred thousand!' she said, through white lips.

'Not a million!' I said, getting to my feet. 'So save your breath. I'm going ahead with this job, and I'm going to finish it. Good night!'

She stood up. There was a dangerous stillness about her that made me look quickly to see if she had a sandbag with her, but she hadn't. In the mood she was in now I wouldn't put it past her to shoot me.

'Are you sure?' she said.

'I said, good night. You can't expect always to get your own way. Run along, Mrs. Dedrick. You bore me.'

'There's another way of taking care of you,' she said with a cold, set smile. 'I'll give you one more chance. Two hundred thousand.'

'Get out!' I said, and crossed the room to throw open the door.

She went quickly to the telephone, dialled, waited a second then screamed in a voice that made me nearly jump out of my skin :'Police! Help! Come at once!'

She dropped the telephone and turned to me, the set smile still on her lips.

'Very smart,' I said, and sat down. 'What am I supposed to be doing? Criminal assault?'

She put her hand on the front of her dress and ripped it down. Then she dug her nails into her shoulder and clawed into her white flesh, leaving four angry red marks on her skin. She ran her fingers through her hair. She kicked over a table, pushed the settee into the fireplace, scuffed up the rug. As she walked across the room to disarrange more furniture, I reached for the telephone, dialled, and waited.

'Hello?' Paula said.

'I'm in trouble. Come over here fast. You know what to do, collect Francon and get down to Police Headquarters as fast as you can. In five minutes I'll be on a charge of criminal assault. Mrs. Dedrick is setting the stage now.'

'I'll be with you,' Paula said and hung up.

I dropped the receiver back on its cradle and lit a cigarette.

'While you're about it, I'd let my stockings down if I were you. It always gives a more authentic picture,' I said gently.

'You'll be sorry you didn't take the money, you stupid fool,' Serena said. 'They'll give you two years for this.'

'Pity you scratched yourself,' I said, shaking my head at her. 'Rather a wasted effort. They won't find your skin under my nails, and they always look.'

A car drew up outside with a squeal of brakes. Serena gave a wild, piercing scream and went staggering out on to the veranda.

I didn't move.

Feet pounded up the garden path.

'All right, lady. We're here,' a man bawled.

Sergeant MacGraw loomed in the doorway, a snarl on his face and a gun in his hand.

'One move and you get it!' he bellowed, glaring at me.

'Don't be dramatic,' I said, tapping ash on to the floor. 'She's kidding.'

'Yeah? She looks like it. Stand up and put your hands up!'

I stood up and put my hands up.

He came in cautiously.

'Well, well, a sex-maniac, huh? I always thought you were a screw.'

A uniform cop came in supporting Serena, who collapsed into a chair. Her scratches were bleeding now, and blood ran over her white brassière and on to her dress. She looked the part all right.

'Holy cow!' MacGraw gasped. 'It's Mrs. Dedrick! Here, you, put the cuffs on that punk.'

The cop came over and snapped handcuffs on my wrists. He gave me a light punch on the chest.

'It's going to be an awful long time before you see another woman, Bud,' he said in an undertone.

MacGraw was fussing over Serena. She was crying and trembling. He got her a drink and stood over her, his heavy face red and embarrassed, and every so often he kept muttering 'Holy cow!' and scratched his jaw.

'Give me my wrap,' she said suddenly. 'I'm all right now. I came here to talk to him about my husband. Without warning, he – he flew at me like an animal.'

'No animal would fly at you, baby,' I said gently. 'You'd be surprised how fussy animals are.'

MacGraw spun round and hit me across the mouth with the back of his hand.

'Wait till I get you to the station,' he snarled. 'I've been waiting years just for this moment.'

'Enjoy yourself,' I said. 'It's not going to last long.'

'Do you feel like coming down to Headquarters, ma'am?' MacGraw asked. 'You needn't if you don't feel like it.'

'Of course. I wish to see Captain Brandon. This man must be taught a lesson.'

'He will,' MacGraw said and showed his teeth. 'Well, if you're ready, ma'am, we'll go.'

The cop grabbed me by the arm and shoved me to the door.

'Bend your nightstick over his skull if he tries anything funny,' MacGraw said.

The cop and I got in the back of the police car; Serena and MacGraw got in the front.

Paula's small convertible flashed past us as we turned the bend into Orchid Boulevard.

v

Mifflin was going off duty as we all tramped into the charge-room. He had his hat and coat on, and was leaning up against the desk, giving the sergeant in charge his final instructions.

When he saw the handcuffs on my wrists, his eyes grew round. He looked from me to MacGraw.

'What's buzzing?' he demanded. 'What have you got this guy here for?'

MacGraw puffed himself out with righteous indignation.

'Charge of rape, Lieutenant,' he said. 'This rat assaulted Mrs. Dedrick. I got there just in time.'

Mifflin's face was a study. His eyes grew to the size of doorknobs.

'Is that right, ma'am?' he said, gaping at Serena. 'You're charging Malloy?'

'Yes,' she said curtly. 'Where is Captain Brandon?'

'He's off duty tonight,' Mifflin said, and there was a note of relief in his voice. 'Get Mrs. Dedrick a chair.'

As she sat down, she let her wrap fall open and both Mifflin and the desk sergeant had a view of the damage. Mifflin sucked in his breath and looked at me in reproachful horror.

'Did you do that?' he demanded.

I said I didn't do that.

MacGraw swung his fist at me, but Mifflin, moving much faster than I expected a man of his size to move, shoved MacGraw away, sending him reeling.

'Cut it out!' he said sharply. 'What do you think you're doing?'

MacGraw snarled at me.

'I want to get this rat downstairs.'

'Shut up!' Mifflin said. He turned to Serena. 'What happened?'

'I went to talk to him about finding my husband,' Serena told him, her voice level and hard. 'I hadn't been in his place more than five minutes, when he suddenly caught hold of me. There was a struggle. I managed to get to the 'phone and call for help. Then he tore my dress and scratched me. Fortunately this officer arrived as he was overpowering me.'

Mifflin pushed his hat to the back of his head and mopped his forehead with his handkerchief. He looked stricken.

'Don't get worked up,' I said smoothly. 'She's lying. I suggest we go somewhere private. She, you and me. This isn't anything she'll want the Press to get hold of.'

'I want the Press in here!' Serena said. 'I intend to ruin him. I want the widest publicity possible. He's to be charged and imprisoned and forced out of business!'

Paula came in at this moment, carrying a leather-bound box. She was breathing quickly, and for the first time in her life she looked dishevelled. Her hair was all over the place, the light overcoat she was wearing was wrongly buttoned up, and the legs of her trousers looked like twin concertinas.

'I couldn't get Francon,' she said, trying to get her breath. 'He wasn't in. They haven't charged you yet?'

MacGraw caught hold of her arm.

'You've no right in here. Get out!'

'Lay off!' Mifflin said. 'What do you want?' he went on to Paula as MacGraw reluctantly released her.

Paula put the box on a nearby table, opened it to reveal a small gramophone on which was a record.

'You may remember, Mrs. Dedrick,' I said quietly, 'that just before we had our interesting conversation I turned down a switch, telling you it was a telephone extension switch. Actually it set a recording machine into motion. When I entertain wealthy women alone and at night, I take care they don't bring an assault charge against me.'

Serena looked as if she could kill me.

'He's lying!' she said. 'Charge him! What are you waiting for.'

'Go ahead and play it,' I said to Paula.

Paula set the turn-table spinning and lowered the needle on the record.

Everyone was transfixed when my voice came out of the box with a clearness that was almost painful.

When Serena's voice said: *You can name your price*, she started out of her chair and made a dart at the gramophone, but Paula blocked her off.

'Stop it!' Serena cried. 'I don't want to hear any more! Stop it!'

I nodded to Paula, who lifted the needle.

'Better let it run through, Mrs. Dedrick,' Mifflin said gently. 'Or are you withdrawing the charge?'

She drew herself up. She made quite a regal figure. For a couple of seconds she stared right at me, her eyes glittering dangerously, then she walked to the door, opened it and went out, leaving the door open.

No one moved or said anything until her footfalls died away down the stone passage.

'Take the cuffs off,' Mifflin said shortly.

MacGraw took them off, looking like a tiger who had lost its dinner.

'Well, you certainly know how to take care of yourself,' Mifflin said with unconcealed admiration. 'That was quite a jam you were in.'

'Yeah,' I said, massaging my wrists. 'Let's go to your office. I want to talk to you.' I looked over to Paula, who was closing the lid of the gramophone. 'Nice, quick work. What did I do? Get you out of bed?'

'You got me out of a bath,' Paula said. 'If you're not going to get into any more trouble, I'd like to go back to it.'

'Go ahead, and thanks, Paula. You saved me from the tigers,' and I gave MacGraw a grin.

He walked out of the room, the back of his neck purple.

When Paula had gone, and Mifflin and I were seated in his overheated office, I said, 'If this case breaks the way I think it could break, there's going to be an awful stink in the Press, Tim.'

Mifflin groped hopelessly in his pocket for a cigarette, found none and raised eyebrows at me.

'Gimme a butt. What do you mean – stink?'

I gave him a cigarette, lit one for myself.

'The chances are Marshland's behind the kidnapping: Dedrick's a reefer-smuggler, working in with Barratt. He looks after the Paris end of the business. It's my bet Marshland found out about him and hired someone to get him out of the way. That's why Mrs. Dedrick wanted to buy me off.'

Mifflin looked startled.

'Then where the hell's Dedrick?'

'That's what I want to know. I have an idea Barratt could

tell us. There's a new character on the scene who knows as much about it as Barratt: a tall broad-shouldered fella who wears a fawn suit and a white felt hat.'

'We're looking for him. So it was you who phoned in that tip?'

'Yeah; I had a job to do, otherwise I would have hung around. Did you get the clue in the refuse bin?'

'He stayed the night there, huh?'

'Must have done.'

'Well, we're looking for him. What makes you think Marshland's hooked up with the kidnapping?'

I told him what I had found out at the Beach Hotel.

'According to Mrs. Dedrick, he's skipped to Europe, but I don't believe it.'

'Maybe I'd better go up there and see if I can talk to him,' Mifflin said.

'Look, will you hold back until tomorrow afternoon? Suppose you got evidence that Barratt's a reefer-smuggler. Think you could make him talk?'

Mifflin smiled grimly.

'We could try.'

'Know where I can get some reefers: about a couple of hundred of them?'

'The Narcotic Squad would have some. Why?'

'Let's have them. Barratt's not the only one who can plant evidence. You'll get a tip some time tomorrow where you'll find two hundred reefers in his room. You take him in, and bounce him around. He doesn't look as if he'd stand a great deal of toughing up. I think he'll squeal.'

Mifflin's eyes widened.

'I can't do that! If Brandon found out . . .'

'Who's going to tell him?'

He stared at me, scratched the back of his neck thoughtfully, shook his head.

'I don't like it, Vic.'

'Nor do I, but there's no other way to swing it. Let's have the stuff.'

'Well, all right. We're going to look pretty wet if he doesn't talk.'

'That's up to you. Turn MacGraw loose on him. He's feeling frustrated he didn't get his hands on me.'

Mifflin went out of the room. He was away for about twenty

minutes. He came back with a small wooden box.

'I had to tell the Narcotic Chief why I wanted these. He's been wanting to get his hands on Barratt for months. He welcomes the idea.' Mifflin looked shocked. 'Some cops just haven't any ethics.'

I took the box and stood up.

'Nor have I when I deal with a rat like Barratt.'

'Watch out, Vic. I didn't like the look that Dedrick woman gave you.'

'Nor did I. How's Perelli?'

'He's all right. Francon saw him this morning. You don't have to worry about him; anyway, just yet.'

'Any chance of seeing him?'

'Not a chance. Brandon's put a special guard on him. No one except Francon can go near him.'

'When you get your hands on Barratt, make him talk, Tim. I have a hunch he can blow the lid right off this case.'

'I'll get it out of him if he knows anything,' Mifflin promised.

I collected the gramophone from the charge-room, went into the street to call a taxi.

The time was ten minutes to eleven.

It had been quite a day.

CHAPTER SIX

I

THE next morning, I was kept busy with the routine work of the office until lunch-time. I missed Kerman, as there were many little jobs that had to be done, and which, now he was in Paris, I had to do myself. But by one o'clock I was through, and could give my attention once more to the Dedrick kidnapping.

'I'm going along to Barratt's place this afternoon,' I told Paula while we were eating a quick snack in the office. 'I have a little present I want to plant on him.'

I told her what I had cooked up with Mifflin.

'Once we get Barratt alone, and on a charge, we might be able to soften him. Tim thinks he can, anyway.'

Paula didn't approve of the idea, but then she never approved of anything that wasn't strictly dealt off the top of the deck.

'What do you plan to do – wait until he's out?' she asked.

'That's the idea. It'll cost money, but then I'm getting hardened to spending money. I'll bribe Maxie to give me the pass-key.'

'Be careful, Vic.'

I grinned at her.

'You're always telling me to be careful. What's the matter with you these days? You didn't talk like that two years ago.'

She gave me a quick, worried smile.

'I suppose I know you better. I wish you'd stick to our usual business, Vic, and cut out these dangerous jobs.'

'I'm not doing this for fun. If Perelli hadn't saved my skin, nothing would persuade me to stick my oar in this. He's not much of a guy to take risks for, but he took a risk for me. Barratt might easily have knifed me. I guess I have to go on until I square the score.'

It was half past one when I parked outside the apartment house in Jefferson Avenue.

Maxie was lolling against the counter of the reception desk as I walked across the lobby. There was no girl at the switchboard. The telephone harness was on the counter where he could reach it.

'Want some money?' I said briskly. 'I have some for you if you're going to be co-operative.'

He eyed me suspiciously.

'I never refuse money. What do you want?'

'Your pass-key.'

If I had let off a shotgun he wouldn't have been more startled.

'My – what?'

'Pass-key, and make it snappy. It's worth fifty dollars, cash on the nail.'

The small eyes blinked.

'Fifty bucks?' he said wistfully.

I spread five tens on the counter. If this spending jag kept up, I'd be ruined in a few more days.

He eyed the notes, licked his lips, scratched the side of his nose.

'I could get slung out,' he said, lowering his voice. 'I can't do it.'

I laid two more fives on the counter, bent over them and breathed on them gently.

'That's the limit,' I said, and smiled at him. 'Your pass-key for ten minutes.'

'Where do you want to go?'

'Barratt's room. Is he out?'

The small eyes grew round.

'Yeah; he went out about an hour ago.'

'What are you worrying about, then? It's not as if he's a friend of yours.'

'I'd lose my job,' he said thickly. 'Sixty bucks wouldn't keep me off the bread line for more than a week. It ain't worth it.'

'Well, all right, if that's how you feel about it.' I pushed the bills into a neat pile, folded them and put them in my hip pocket. 'I wouldn't want you to have a sleepless night.'

'Now, wait a minute,' he said, tilting his bowler hat to the back of his head and wiping a shiny forehead with his sleeve. 'I ain't fussy how I sleep. Make it another ten, and it's yours.'

'Sixty's my top. Take it or leave it.'

He struggled with his conscience, groaned, nodded his head. 'The key's hanging by the switchboard. Gimme the dough.'

I slid him the sixty and he hurriedly stuffed the notes into his pocket.

'Sure Barratt's out?' I asked.

'Yeah; I saw him go. No one's up there.' He looked furtively around the lobby. 'I'm going to draw myself a can of beer. Make it snappy, and for Gawd's sake don't let anyone see you go in.'

I gave him a second or so to get out of sight, then leaned over the counter and unhooked the key from behind the switchboard.

The elevator took me up to the fourth floor. I walked along the corridor to apartment 4B15. In the apartment opposite someone was playing the radio. Somewhere down the passage a woman laughed shrilly. I pressed my ear to the door panel of 4B15, but heard nothing. I rapped, listened, waited, but nothing happened. I looked to right and left. No one was watching me. Silently I slipped the pass-key into the lock, turned it gently and pushed open the door.

The man in the fawn suit was sitting in an armchair facing me. He held a .45 in his lap, the barrel pointing at my chest. He gave me a thin, cold smile.

'Come in,' he said. 'I thought it might be you.'

The moment I heard that deep baritone voice I knew who he was, and couldn't understand why I hadn't known it before.

'Hello, Dedrick,' I said, stepped inside the room and closed the door.

II

'Don't make any sudden moves, Malloy,' the man in the fawn suit said and lifted the gun. 'No one on this floor would bother about the sound of a gun, and I'm in the mood to make a mess of you. Sit down.' He waved his other hand to an armchair, facing his on the other side of the fireplace.

He couldn't have missed me at that range, and I had an idea he wasn't bluffing so I sat down.

'You're quite a puncher,' he went on, and his hand touched the back of his neck tenderly. 'I'll have a stiff neck for weeks, damn you!' His hard, black eyes roamed over my face. 'Bit of luck, you walking in like this. We'd made up our mind to get rid of you as soon as we could. You're getting a nuisance.'

'Oh, I don't know,' I said. 'The trouble is I'm full of theories and have no proof. Does Serena know you're here?'

He shook his head and grinned.

'No; she hasn't an idea. Make yourself at home. There're cigarettes by your elbow. We have a little time to kill before anything can happen. Barratt'll want to talk to you. Don't try anything funny unless you're tired of life, will you?'

I lit a cigarette while he watched me, his finger curled round the trigger of the .45, its barrel continuing to point at my face.

'Be careful with that gun,' I said. 'It looks very dangerous from this end.'

He laughed.

'You don't have to worry. It'll only go off if you don't behave yourself.' He stubbed out the cigarette he was smoking, reached for another and lit it. I sat still while he did so. The expression in the hard black eyes told me he would shoot if he had to.

'If I'd known you were going to be so damned interfering, I wouldn't have called you in the first place,' he went on. 'I thought it was smart at the time. I acted that little scene well on the phone, didn't I? And the untouched whisky, and the burning cigarette were nice touches, too.'

'Yeah, very pretty,' I said. 'But did you have to shoot Souki?'

'Oh, yes.' He frowned, as if he didn't like being reminded of Souki. 'He asked for trouble, and he got it.'

'And was it you who framed Perelli?' I asked.

'That was Barratt's effort. He has a way of settling debts. Perelli had it coming to him, anyway. It was a bright idea. At one time the heat was getting too fierce, but now they have Perelli in a cell, everything is fine and dandy.'

'Don't be too sure. The police are looking for you for the Gracie Lehmann killing.'

'You don't have to worry about me,' he said lightly. 'You worry about yourself.'

The door into the apartment opened and Barratt came in. For a second or so he stood rooted, staring at me, then he moved into the room, closing the door, his thin, handsome face lighting up.

'How did he get in here?' he asked.

'He had a key,' the man in the fawn suit said, and got to his feet. 'Better check to see if he's wearing a rod.'

'Get up!' Barratt said to me.

I stood up.

He came to me from behind and ran his hands over me. He

found the .38, jerked it out of the shoulder holster. Then he found the box of reefers.

He stood away while he opened the box, then gave me a sneering little smile.

'Very smart. Where were you going to plant them?'

'Oh, somewhere,' I said. 'You can't expect to hold the monopoly of planting evidence.'

He tossed the box on the table, came over to prod me with my gun.

'How did you get in?'

'Took the pass-key. It hangs by the switchboard downstairs. Didn't you know?'

He went through my pockets again, found the pass-key and tossed that on to the table.

He looked at Dedrick.

'He's lying, of course. Maxie must have given it to him. Well, all right; it's about time I fixed Maxie.' He took out a silver cigarette case, selected a cigarette, stuck it on his lower lip. As he lit it, his eyes browsed over my face. 'I owe you something, Malloy. You'll find I'm good at paying off old scores.'

'Can't imagine you'd be good at anything, but I'll take your word for it,' I said.

'What are we going to do with him?' Dedrick asked.

Barratt moved to the mirror over the fireplace and admired himself.

'The mine, of course,' he said. 'There's no better place for him. He'll take a nice long time to die.'

Dedrick grimaced.

'Why not put a slug through his head and leave him here? I don't want to go down there again. It gives me the horrors.'

'You'll do what I tell you,' Barratt said and ran his thumbnail along his thin moustache. 'Tie his hands.'

Dedrick went out of the room. He returned in a few seconds with a roll of two-inch-wide adhesive tape.

'One wrong move, and you'll get it,' Barratt warned me, raising the gun. 'Put your hands behind you.'

I put my hands behind me. There was nothing else I could do at the moment. Dedrick wound a length of tape around my wrists. He made a good job of it.

'Round his mouth too,' Barratt said.

Dedrick taped my mouth, crushing my upper lip against my teeth.

Barratt came over and stood before me, smiling viciously.

'I'm going to make you sorry you interfered with me,' he said, and hit me across the face with the gun-barrel. I staggered back. The back of my knees collided with the arm of the chair and I went over with a crash that shook the room.

'Take it easy!' Dedrick said, alarmed. 'We don't want anyone coming up here.'

Barratt snarled at him, came over to me and kicked me in the ribs. He kicked very hard, and I felt my ribs bend under the impact.

'How about Maxie?' Dedrick asked. 'We're wasting time, Jeff.'

'Get him up here,' Barratt said, and kicked me again.

Dedrick picked up the telephone receiver.

'Mr. Barratt is asking for you,' he said into the mouthpiece. 'Please come up.'

Barratt grabbed me by my coat front, hauled me to my feet and slammed me into the armchair.

'We'll fix Maxie, and then we'll blow,' he said. 'It's time I changed my address. Leave him to me.'

He stood against the wall by the door.

Dedrick faced the door.

There was perhaps a five-minute wait, then a rap came on the door.

'Come in,' Barratt said.

The door pushed open. Maxie came in. His round, fat face was sullen, and his lower lip was pushed out aggressively.

Dedrick kept the .45 down by his side, out of sight.

'Come in and shut the door,' he said.

Maxie gaped at me, changed colour, came into the room and shut the door.

'What goes on here?' he demanded.

Dedrick raised the gun and pointed it at Maxie's paunch.

'Did you give him the pass-key?'

Maxie glared at me.

'If he said that, he's lying. What are you pointing that gun at me for? Don't you know it's dangerous?'

'It'll probably be fatal,' Dedrick said, and smiled.

Barratt moved silently up to Maxie and tapped him on the shoulder.

'Hello, little brother,' he said.

Maxie nearly jumped out of his skin.

'Hey! What's the idea? Who's this guy with the gun?' He tried to make his voice sound tough, but his eyes showed his alarm. 'Guns ain't allowed in this building. I'll have to report it.'

'I'm afraid you won't have the time,' Barratt said. 'I'm a little sick of you, Maxie. Now Gracie's gone, I think we might get rid of you too.'

Maxie's mouth fell open. He looked with horror first at Dedrick and then at Barratt. Hurriedly he put up his hands.

'I won't make any trouble, Mr. Barratt,' he said. 'You can rely on me . . .'

He caught his breath in a strangled gasp when he saw the knife in Barratt's hand.

'Sorry, Maxie.' Barratt poked the knife into Maxie's side. 'You've seen too much, and you're too great a nuisance. Go into the bathroom.'

Maxie fell on his knees, his face turning green.

'Don't touch me, Mr. Barratt,' he said between locked teeth. 'I promise you . . .'

Barratt clubbed him over the head with the gun-butt, driving him to the floor.

Maxie fell forward on his hands, shaking his head, groaning.

'Give me a hand with him,' Barratt snarled.

Dedrick and he grabbed Maxie and hauled him across the room to a door that led into the bathroom.

As Dedrick released Maxie to open the door, Maxie suddenly stumbled to his feet, hit out at Barratt and made a staggering rush to the door of the apartment.

Barratt swung his gun and clubbed Maxie to his knees again. They dragged him into the bathroom. There was a struggle, and Maxie began to yell. The dull, heavy sound of a blow stopped the yelling. There came a rasping, choking gasp, and Dedrick backed out of the bathroom, his face white and set.

The gasping noise continued, making me feel sick. After a while the sound petered out.

Barratt appeared in the doorway. He looked at me and showed his teeth.

'It'll be your turn in a little while, my friend,' he said. 'But you won't get it the easy way.' He turned to Dedrick, who was watching him. 'All right, take him away. Careful how you go. If you run into trouble, shoot him.'

'You don't expect me to take him alone, do you?'

'Why not? I've got to get rid of Maxie. We'll have to move. What are you worrying about? Shoot him if he tries anything funny.'

'And get a load of law on my neck.'

'Shoot them too,' Barratt said and laughed.

Dedrick hesitated, then shrugged.

'Better lend me a coat to hide his hands. I'll bring it back when I've planted him.'

Barratt went into the bedroom, came out a moment later, carrying a light overcoat.

Dedrick hauled me to my feet.

'I'll be using your car,' he said. 'One false move, and I'll blast you.'

Barratt draped the coat over my shoulders, and wrapped a silk scarf around my mouth to hide the tape.

'We shan't meet again, Malloy,' he said to me. 'Maybe I'll see you, but you won't see me.' He shoved me towards Dedrick. 'Get going.'

Dedrick took my arm and led me into the passage.

There was no one to see us get into the elevator. When the elevator came to rest at the ground floor, Dedrick dug the gun into my side.

'Don't forget, one false move and you get it,' he said. I could see sweat running down his face.

We walked into the lobby. He shoved me across the stretch of carpet to the front entrance, down the steps to the Buick.

Two girls were walking up the drive. They glanced at us without interest, passed us and entered the lobby.

Dedrick opened the rear door.

'Get in!'

As I bent forward to get in the car, Dedrick smashed his gun butt down on my head.

III

My mind came fumbling out of a dark pit. Consciousness returned like a hangover on a foggy morning. First, I became aware of a throbbing pain in my head, then, as I opened my eyes, I found myself lying on my back, the beam of a flashlight playing on my face. I grunted, turned my head and tried to sit up. A hand on my chest shoved me back.

'Stay parked,' Dedrick growled. 'I'm just bedding you down.' His fingers picked the end of the tape loose that bound my mouth. When he had enough purchase, he gave it a quick hard pull, skinning it off my mouth. That hurt, and I grunted again.

The light was bothering me, but the dank, cold air and the darkness beyond the beam of the flashlight bothered me more.

'What's going on?' I growled.

'You'll find out.'

I felt something tight around my waist. Bending my head I could see Dedrick fastening a thick chain, looped round my middle, with a padlock. I looked beyond him at the rough-hewn walls, supported by blackened props of wood.

'Where's this – the mine?' I asked.

'Yeah; a hundred feet below ground.' He snapped the padlock shut and stood away. 'This isn't my idea, Malloy. You heard what he said. I've nothing against you. I'd put a slug through your head if it wasn't for him. He'll come and look at you tomorrow.'

'Is he going to leave me here to starve to death?' I asked, testing the tape that bound my hands. There was no give in it at all.

'You won't starve.' He paused while he lit a cigarette. I saw his hand was unsteady. 'You won't have time to starve.'

'What do you mean?'

'You'll find out. If you give me your word not to start anything until I've gone I'll undo your hands. At least, it'll give you a fighting chance.'

I was beginning to feel spooked.

'If I get my hands free, I'll probably strangle you,' I said. 'I scare easy, but not that easy.'

'Don't talk like a fool. You don't know what you're up against. Turn over. I'm going to free your hands.'

I turned over, and he shoved his knee in my back as he pulled the tape loose. He was out of range before I could grab him.

I pushed myself into a sitting position. I couldn't stand upright: the chain holding me was too short, but it was a nice feeling to have free hands again.

'I'll leave you a light,' Dedrick said. 'That's about the best I can do for you.'

'You have a bad dose of conscience.' As I rubbed my wrists, trying to restore the circulation, I stared up at him. 'What's going to happen?'

'I don't know.' He looked down the long tunnel, lifting his torch and throwing the powerful beam into the inky blackness. 'Take a look at that. Your guess is as good as mine.'

The beam of the torch rested on what looked like a heap of rags. I peered at it; saw bits and pieces of what once had been a lounge suit.

'There's a skeleton under those clothes,' Dedrick said, and I heard his breath whistle down his nostrils. 'We left him here for not more than twelve hours, and that's what he turned into: rags and bones, and not a damn' thing else.'

'Who is it?' My voice sounded hollow.

'Never mind who it is.'

I decided it couldn't be anyone else but Lute Ferris.

'It's Ferris, isn't it?'

'Just another guy who was a nuisance,' Dedrick said, and wiped his face with his handkerchief. 'Something's eaten him.' He looked uneasily into the darkness. 'There's some kind of animal down here: maybe a lynx.' He took another flashlight from his hip pocket and tossed it to me. 'That'll keep you company. If you hear Barratt coming, put it out of sight. He'd murder me if he knew I'd left you a light.'

'Well, thanks,' I said, and flung the beam of the torch he had given me on to his face. 'Why not go the whole way and let me free? You're hating this, Dedrick. Come on; you might still beat the rap, and if you get me out of this, I'll do what I can for you.'

'Not a chance,' he said. 'You don't know Barratt. He's the last man anyone in their right minds would cross. So long, Malloy. I hope it's quick.'

I sat still, watching the beam of his torch growing smaller and smaller as he walked down the long tunnel. And as the light grew fainter, the darkness around me came down with a choking thickness that brought me out into a cold sweat. I snapped on the torch. The white light sent the heavy, solid blackness back, almost as if it was alive. But it crouched just beyond the beam, waiting to pounce on me again.

My first move was to examine the chain locked around my middle. It was too strong to snap, and the padlock was solid and heavy. I traced the chain to the wall. It was fastened to a staple, embedded in solid rock. I caught hold of the chain in both hands, braced one foot against the wall and strained backwards. Nothing happened. I braced myself again and pulled until my sinews creaked. I might just as well have tried to pull over the Empire State Building.

I flopped back on the rock floor, panting, my heart going like a steam-hammer. If I was to get out of here, somehow or other, I had to work the staple loose. No one would ever think of looking for me here. Paula would go to the apartment house on Jefferson Avenue. She might find Maxie. But that wouldn't get her very far, or me either. She'd go to Mifflin. But what could Mifflin do? Why should anyone look for me in the shaft of a disused, ruined mine?

I was getting into a panic now. It was like being buried alive. My eyes kept going to the heap of tattered clothes lying about ten yards from me: all that remained of Ferris.

There's some kind of animal down here.

All right, I admit it. I was ready to run whimpering into a corner if I could have run. I was ready to yell for help at the top of my voice if it would have done any good. I've had the shakes more than once in my life, but nothing like the shakes I was getting now.

For about a minute I sat as still as death, getting hold of myself, telling myself not to dive off the deep end, calling myself every insulting name I could think of, while I fought off the panic that sat on my shoulder and leered into my face. I fought it off, but it left me sweating and cold and as limp as a length of boiled string.

I got out my cigarettes, split half of them before I could get my fingers round one of them. I got it alight, and lay back against the wall, drawing in smoke, and blowing it out again while I stared at the white light of the torch that stood between me and the darkness.

I had no idea how long I was going to be down here. The battery wouldn't last much longer than a couple of hours of continuous burning. I'd have to conserve it, even if it did mean sitting in the dark.

I counted my cigarettes. I had seventeen. Even that little red spark could be comforting, and while I smoked the torch would have to go out.

So I put it out.

Back came the choking, heavy darkness so thick I could feel it, and with it came my panic, nudging my elbow, making me sweat again.

I sat there in that awful dank darkness for what seemed an

hour, smoking the cigarette, watching the glowing end, concentrating on it and trying to forget the black walls that pressed in on me.

When I couldn't stand it any longer, I switched on the torch. I had sweated right through my clothes, and my watch told me I'd been sitting in the darkness for eight minutes.

I began to get worried then: really worried. If I was ready to walk up a wall after eight minutes of darkness, what would I be like in an hour, a day or even two days?

I put the torch on the floor by my side and laid hold of the chain again. I pulled and jerked at it in a mounting frenzy, until I heard myself yelling curses at it. I stopped that, and sat down again. I felt as if I'd run ten miles; even the muscles in my legs were fluttering.

Then I heard something.

Up to now the only sound in this old shaft, a hundred feet below ground, had been my breathing, the thump-thump-thump of my heart and the fainter tick of my watch. But now a new sound made me turn my head and look into the darkness.

I listened, holding my breath, my mouth half open, my heart hammering. Nothing. Slowly I reached for the torch, sent the beam down the long tunnel. Still nothing. I turned off the light and waited. Minutes ticked by. Then it came again: a gentle rustle, something moving cautiously, a pebble dislodged: sharp, violent sounds in the silence; sounds that wouldn't have been heard except for the quiet of this shaft where a feather settling on the ground would have been a disturbance.

I touched the button on the torch. The beam cut into the darkness like a razor cutting into flesh.

For a split second I saw something that looked like two glowing sparks: something that could have been the eyes of some animal; then they vanished, and I was struggling up on my knees, leaning forward, peering, trying to see.

You'll find I'm good at paying off old scores.

I gave him full marks. Those few seconds were, up to now, about the worst seconds I have ever lived through, and the thought that it wasn't over gave me a sick feeling in my belly.

I lit another cigarette, and kept the light on. I decided I'd keep it on until it went out, then I'd make the best of it, but so long as the light was on, I felt pretty sure whatever it was out there in the darkness would keep its distance.

I sat there smoking, listening to the thud of my heart and

trying to think how to get the staple out. But my brain felt as if it was wrapped up in cotton wool. My thoughts kept darting into the darkness; useless and frightened.

Then I saw the red embers again; just out of reach of the light of the torch. I didn't move, but kept my eyes on the two fiery beads that hung in the darkness, watching me.

More minutes ticked by. I couldn't make up my mind if they were coming closer or I was imagining it. So I waited, cold, stiff, scared, holding my breath for as long as I could, breathing silently through my open mouth when I had to.

They were coming closer: very cautiously and silently, and something was beginning to take shape. I could make out a ferret-shaped head and the outline of a sleek, round back. Still I didn't move. One of my legs had gone to sleep, but I scarcely noticed it. I wanted to see what I was up against. I hadn't long to wait. Into the beam of the torch moved a rat. Not an ordinary rat, but a monster: a nightmare of a rat, almost as big as a full-grown cat, measuring at a guess over two feet from nose to tail.

It came forward into the light, less cautiously now, looking towards me, its sleek, brown fur glistening in the hard light of the torch.

Close by my hand was a fair-sized stone. My fingers reached for it. The rat stopped moving. I snapped up the stone and threw it in one movement.

There was a rustle, a streak of brown, and the rat was gone, long before the stone hit the spot where it had been.

Well, I knew now. I knew what had turned Ferris into a heap of rags and bones. I knew too when that brute got hungry it wouldn't run away.

I looked around for more stones, and began making a little pile of them within easy reach. I examined the ground near me. Under dust and pebbles I discovered a short length of wood. It wasn't much of a weapon, but it was something. If I had to tackle this one rat, chained as I was, I felt I could lick it, but at the back of my mind I was beginning to wonder if there were more than one, and if so, how many. Again my eyes strayed to the heap of rags. A lot more than one rat had done that.

I held the club in my right hand, the torch in my left and leaned my back against the wall.

I waited; and somewhere in the darkness, not far away, the rat waited too.

The luminous hands of my wrist watch pointed to twenty minutes past four. I had been in the shaft a little over two hours. I had five cigarettes left, and the light of the torch was turning orange. I had been switching it on and off every five minutes for the past half-hour while I waited and listened, trying to make it last as long as possible.

I had heard no sound nor seen anything. The stale, dank air was making me feel sleepy. It was only by smoking and concentrating hard on the glowing tip of the cigarette that I managed to keep awake. I had tied my handkerchief round my throat to offer some resistance if the rat went for me. It gave me an optimistic feeling of safety.

I had got over my panic – or, rather, I had worn it out. There's a limit to fear, and after the first hour I had got on top of it. But I had given up all hope of getting out of this jam. My one thought was to kill the rat before it killed me. Beyond that I had no thoughts.

The two hours had dragged by like two months. There was nothing to do except smoke and watch and listen, and think of the rat. The hands of my watch crawled on.

Then the rustling sound began again. The sound of the hard rings around the rat's tail rubbing along the floor. I threw a stone in the direction of the sound and heard a little scurry. Well, he wasn't hungry yet. I threw another stone to drive him farther away.

The dying light of the torch worried me. I turned it off, sitting now in the darkness, breathing gently and listening. I sat there for perhaps ten minutes with my eyes closed, and I must have dozed off. Then something happened that drove the blood out of my heart and brought me wide awake: something touched my foot and moved along my leg.

I snapped on the torch, a cold prickle shooting up my spine, my left hand grabbing at the club. For one horrible moment I saw the rat within inches of me, creeping towards me, pressed flat on the ground, its red eyes gleaming viciously. As the yellowing beam of the torch hit it, it swerved away and was gone, moving like lightning, and leaving me gulping in the close air, petrified and sweating.

Then out of the darkness, beyond the feeble light, four

pairs of red sparks suddenly appeared, spaced about a foot apart and in a semicircle before me. Four now, not one.

I yelled at them: my voice harsh and off-key, but they didn't move. I grabbed a handful of stones and threw them. The red eyes vanished, but reappeared almost immediately, a little closer, if anything. I yelled again.

'Vic!'

I started up.

Had I imagined that faint call, somewhere in the darkness? I raised my voice and let out a yell that echoed like a thunder-clap down the tunnel.

'Vic! Where are you?'

'Here! Down the tunnel!'

I was so excited I forgot the rats. I was yelling now like a madman, and my yells changed to a yelp as a furry brown body suddenly streaked into the light and teeth snapped with a click into the folds of the handkerchief round my neck.

I felt the weight of its body on my chest, and smelt the dirt in its fur. Its wet nose was thrust under my chin as its teeth tried to cut through the folds of the handkerchief to get at my throat.

I nearly went crazy. Grabbing the sleek, horribly fat body, I tore it away from my throat. I felt it twist in my hand. The loathsome pointed head whipped round and razor-like teeth fastened into my wrist. In a kind of frenzy I dug my fingers into the fur, bent its back sideways, hearing its shrill squeal. The teeth came out of my wrist. Before it could strike again, I snapped its spine, feeling the bone go like a dry stick between my fingers. Shuddering with horror I threw the brute away from me.

'Vic!'

'Here!'

My voice croaked.

At the far end of the tunnel I saw a tiny pin-point of light.

'I'm coming.' Paula's voice: the sweetest sound I've ever heard.

'Down here. Mind how you come. There're rats.'

'I'm coming.'

The light moved steadily towards me, growing brighter. A minute or so later Paula dropped on her knees beside me, and caught hold of my hands.

'Oh, Vic!'

I drew in a deep, shuddering breath and tried to grin at her, but my face felt frozen.

'Paula! Jeepers! Am I glad to see you! How did you get here?'

Her hand touched my face.

'It'll wait. Are you hurt?'

I raised my hand. Blood welled from my wrist. If I hadn't had the handkerchief round my throat the brute would have nailed me.

'It's all right. A rat took a fancy to me.'

She took off her white silk scarf and tied it tightly round the wound.

'Really a rat?'

'Yeah. I killed it. It's behind you.'

She looked quickly over her shoulder. The beam of her torch fell on the brute. She caught her breath in a stifled scream.

'Uuugh! Are there any more like that?'

'One or two. He was particularly persistent. Do you wonder I sounded scared?'

She went closer and peered at the rat, then drew away with a shudder.

'It's enormous. Let's get out of here.'

'I'm chained to the wall. Barratt's idea of getting even.'

While she examined the chain, I told her briefly what had happened.

'I have a gun, Vic. Do you think you could shoot up one of these links?'

'We can try. Here, give it to me, and get out of the way. The slug may ricochet.'

She put a .25 into my hand and went a little way down the tunnel. The third slug cut the link. The noise of the shooting deafened me.

Slowly and painfully I crawled to my feet. She came back and supported me.

'I'll be all right in a moment. I'm stiff, that's all.' I began to hobble up and down, restoring my circulation. 'You haven't told me how you got here. How did you know I was down here?'

'A woman phoned. She wouldn't say who she was. "If you want to save Malloy, you'd better hurry," she said. "They've taken him to the Monte Verde Mine." She hung up before I could ask her who she was or how she knew. I just grabbed a torch and a gun and drove like mad to the mine.' Paula shook her head ruefully. 'I ought to have got Mifflin. I really lost my head, Vic. I don't know what I was thinking about.'

'That's all right. You're here and I'm free, so what does it matter?'

'But it does. I've been wandering about in this awful place for hours. If I hadn't heard you yell, I was going to yell myself. You don't know what it's like down here. Every tunnel looks alike.'

'I'll get you out. Come on, let's try.'

'What's that?'

She was peering at the heap of rags and bones.

'Lute Ferris,' I said, and moved stiffly over to the rags. I flashed my torch on them. Even the skull had been picked clean. In the centre of the forehead was a small hole. 'So they shot him. Now, I wonder why.' I examined what was left of his clothes, and discovered a leather wallet. Inside, was a car's registration tag made out to Lute Ferris, two five-dollar bills and a snapshot of a girl I recognized as Mrs. Ferris. I put the wallet back where I had found it and stood up.

'We'll have to bring Mifflin down here.'

Paula was staring at the heap of bones.

'Did the rats do that?' she asked in a low, horrified voice.

'Well, something did. Come on. Let's go.'

She looked a little fearfully into the darkness.

'You don't think they'll come after us, do you, Vic?'

'No. They won't bother us. Come on.'

We started off down the tunnel. I used my torch. The light was feeble, but if this was going to be a long job, we'd need Paula's torch later.

Half-way down we came to another tunnel that turned off to the left. I remembered Dedrick had gone that way.

'Round here,' I said.

'Why not straight on?'

'Dedrick went this way.'

We turned left and went on for about a hundred yards. At the end of the tunnel, another tunnel, intersecting it, went away into darkness both to the right and left.

'Now which way?'

'Toss for it. Your guess is as good as mine.'

'Let's go right.'

We went right. The ground was uneven and after walking

some minutes, I realized we were going downhill.

'Now, wait a minute. This goes down. We should be going up. We'd better go back and try the left-hand branch.'

'You see what I mean?' There was an edge to her voice I had never heard before. 'That's what's been happening to me. I've walked for hours.'

'Come on.'

We went back to the intersection and started off down the tunnel to the left. We walked for perhaps five minutes then suddenly we were confronted by solid rock.

'I – I don't think you're going to be much better at this than me,' Paula said breathlessly.

'Take it easy.' I was a little worried about her. She was usually so cool and unruffled. I had an idea she wasn't far off hysteria at this moment. 'Maybe that other way goes down and then up. We'll try it.'

'I was crazy to come down here alone!' She caught hold of my arm. 'Why didn't I get Mifflin? We're lost, Vic. We could go on like this for weeks.'

'Come on,' I said sharply. 'Don't waste time talking a lot of mush. We'll be out of this in ten minutes.'

She made an effort, and when she spoke again her voice was calmer.

'Sorry, Vic, I'm rattled. I'm terrified of being underground like this. I feel shut in and buried.'

'I know. Now, get hold of yourself. Once you start feeling sorry for yourself, you're sunk. Come on, kid.' I linked my arm in hers and we set off again.

The ground sloped steeply and we began to descend into what seemed a black pit.

Suddenly my torch went out.

Paula clung to my arm, stifling a scream.

'It's all right. Put yours on,' I said. 'Mine was due to fade. It's a wonder it's lasted so long.'

She gave me her torch.

'We'd better hurry, Vic. This won't last long.'

'It'll last all we want.'

Having someone to steady made it easier for me. But we increased our pace, both knowing we would be in a bad spot if the torch failed us before we could find a way out of the mine.

We kept going down, and the farther we went the more stifling the air became. Then to add to our troubles the roof of the tunnel became lower with every step we took.

Suddenly Paula stopped.

'This isn't the way!' Her voice was high-pitched. 'I know it isn't! Let's go back.'

'It must be the way. Dedrick turned left at the end of the tunnel. I watched him. Come on, let's look a little further.'

'Vic; I'm scared.'

She backed away from me. I could hear her rapid breathing, and I flashed the light on her face. She was white and her eyes were wild looking.

'I – I can't stand any more of this! I'm going back! I can't breathe!'

I was having trouble with my breathing too. There was a tight feeling around my chest and every lungful of air I took in had to be fought for.

'Another hundred yards. If it doesn't take us anywhere we'll go back.'

I caught hold of her arm and pulled her along. Fifty yards farther on, there was another intersection. The air was very bad now.

'There you are,' I said. 'I told you we'd come to something. We'll go right. If it goes down we'll turn back and try the other way.'

She went with me.

Every new tunnel we came to was exactly like the others. We might just as well be walking up and down the same tunnel for all the progress we seemed to be making. And as we went on into the darkness, walking became more difficult. My legs felt heavy, and I had to make a continuous effort to move them. Paula was gasping for breath, and I had to help her along.

But at least the floor of the tunnel wasn't going down. If anything, it was going up.

'I'm sure we're on the right road now,' I gasped. 'We're climbing.'

She leaned more heavily on me.

'The air's awful. I – I can't go much farther.'

I put my arm round her and helped her along. The roof of the tunnel was getting lower. We had to bend our heads. Another twenty yards and we were bent double.

We stopped, gasping for breath.

'We must go back, Vic!'

She pushed away from me and began to stagger back the

way we had come. I stumbled after her, jerked her round.

'Don't act the fool, Paula! Now, come on. You're getting into a panic.'

'I know.' She clung to me. 'I can't help it. It's this awful darkness.'

I could feel her trembling against me.

'Let's sit down for a moment. We're going to get out of this; only, you've got to keep calm.'

We sat down, and immediately discovered the air was a lot better near the floor of the tunnel. I pushed her flat and lay beside her.

After a few minutes the tightness around my chest and the weights around my limbs went away.

'This is better.'

'Yes.' She half sat up, pushing her hair off her face. 'I'm behaving awfully badly. I'm sorry. I'll try not to do it again.'

'Forget it,' I said and took her hand. 'You've got a touch of claustrophobia. You'll get over it. Feel like moving? We'll crawl some of the way. Keep your nose close to the ground. I'll go first.'

We crawled over the rough ground, bruising our hands and knees. After a while we had to stop again. I was sweating, and my breath rasped at the back of my throat. Paula flopped down beside me: all in.

'Do you really think we'll get out?' she asked in a small voice.

'Yeah; we'll get out,' but my voice carried no conviction. 'We'll take it easy for a few minutes; then we'll go on.'

I was beginning to realize that Dedrick couldn't have come this way. It looked as if we had taken a wrong turning somewhere. The thought of being in this mine much longer was beginning to get on my nerves.

Suddenly she gripped my arm.

'What's that?'

I listened.

Somewhere in the mine, I had no idea how far away or how near, there came the sound like rain falling and the soft rustle of dry leaves.

'What is it, Vic?'

'I don't know.'

'It sounds like rain.'

'Can't be. Keep still!'

We sat motionless, listening.

The pattering sound was nearer now: a sound of a thousand little leathery feet running over pebbly ground. I knew what the rustling sound was. I'd heard it before: only it wasn't one or four, but hundreds.

The rats were on the move!

V

I jumped to my feet.

'Come on. Let's see how fast you can run.'

'What is it?' Paula said, scrambling up.

I grabbed her hand.

'Rats! Now, come on. Don't be frightened. We'll lose them.'

Bent double, we ran down the tunnel. The pattering sound behind us grew louder. We blundered on, stumbling over stones, banging against the rough walls, but keeping up some sort of pace. The tunnel curved to the right; turning the corner, we found more head room. After a few yards it was possible to stand upright.

'Stretch your legs,' I said, and increased my speed, dragging her along with me.

The going was easier now. We kept on, gasping for breath, running blindly into the darkness. The tunnel seemed endless. Suddenly Paula lurched and would have fallen if I hadn't swung round and steadied her. She leaned against me, sobbing for breath.

'I'm done!' she gasped. 'I can't go any farther.'

'You can, and you're going to!'

I put my arm round her and forced her on, but we had gone only a few hundred yards when her knees buckled and she sprawled on the ground.

'Give me a minute. I'll be all right. Just give me a minute.'

I leaned limply against the wall, my ears cocked, while I struggled to control my laboured breathing. The pattering sound had died away, but I knew we wouldn't have more than a moment's respite.

'We've got to keep moving.'

Away in the distance, the pattering sound began again. Paula staggered unsteadily to her feet.

'Come on,' I said and, supporting her, went forward at a staggering jog-trot.

After a while she got her second wind, and we began to run again. The sound behind us had become ominously close. Somehow, probably spurred on by the squeaking and pattering behind us, we managed to increase our speed. We came to another intersection and without pausing to think, I swung right, dragging Paula with me. We pelted down a long, high tunnel.

Ahead of us the tunnel began to narrow. I flashed the beam of the torch to see where we were going. Before us was an archway, no more than a hole in the wall.

'In here,' I panted, pushed her through the archway and staggered in after her.

We found ourselves in a big, lofty cave. As I swung the beam around, lighting up the walls, I saw a great pile of wooden boxes standing in the middle of the cave.

Paula cried, 'There's no way out, Vic!'

She was right. We had blundered into a cul-de-sac. There was no escape now. We couldn't go back. The rats were already rushing down the outside tunnel.

'Quick! Block the entrance with those boxes! It's our only chance!'

We rushed to the pile of boxes, grabbed one apiece, staggered with them to the entrance, dumped them and jumped back for two more. We had the first row in place when we smelt the rats.

There was something blood-curdling and ghastly in the smell that drifted into the cave as the pattering feet came rushing down the long length of the tunnel.

'As fast as you can.'

I grabbed hold of two boxes, dragged them across the floor, swung them into place. As Paula ran back for another box, I turned the beam of the torch into the outside tunnel. The sight that met my eyes sent a chill up my spine.

The whole of the narrow floor of the tunnel was carpeted by a heaving mass of brown, furry bodies. The sound of their shrill squeaking, the rustling tails and pattering feet made a nightmare sound of horror.

I snatched out the .25 and fired twice into the seething mass. The crash of gunfire rolled down the tunnel, deafening me, and setting up echo upon echo.

The awful brown carpet swerved, but there was no room for them to retreat. Swarms of rats, stretching the length of the tunnel, prevented those in front from getting away.

The two bullets had brought down three of the monsters, and the rest of them flew at the bodies, piling one on the other, their razor-like teeth slashing and hacking while the air was filled with their horrible, piercing squeals.

I grabbed a box from Paula and set it in place, rushed back and dragged two more across the floor and heaved them up.

As Paula lifted hers into position, a rat sprang through the gap and knocked her over.

Her frantic screams brought me rushing to her. She was flat on her back, hitting out at the rat with both hands, while it snapped viciously, trying to get past her beating hands to her throat.

I smashed the gun butt down on its back, grabbed it and threw it over the wall of boxes in one movement.

There was no time to find out if she was hurt. I slung the box she had dropped into the gap and rushed back for more.

She was on her feet now, and came staggering over to help me. We had completed the second row, making a wall four feet high, but it wasn't enough. The entrance to the cave would have to be entirely blocked if we were going to be safe. Even then, with their numbers and weight, the rats might push over our improvised wall.

'Keep going,' I panted. 'A double row.'

We toiled on, dragging the boxes across the floor, slamming them into place, rushing back for others.

The noise outside was horrifying, and every so often the boxes swayed as the mass of struggling bodies thudded against them.

'There's another in!' Paula screamed.

She dropped her box and backed away, her hands protecting her throat.

I swung the beam of the torch, saw something streaking at me through the air, and threw up my arm.

The brute bit into my sleeve, just missing the flesh and hung, its feet scrabbling at my arm.

I dropped the torch, grabbed at its neck, missed, fumbled, and felt its teeth snap into my hand. As it snapped again, I got my grip and broke its back. I tossed it through the remaining gap in the wall and lifted the last box, pushed it into position, sealing the wall.

Paula picked up the torch and came over to me. We examined the wall of boxes. The rats were scrabbling at them, but they were holding.

'Come on,' I said. 'One more row and we'll be safe.'

'You're bleeding.'

'Never mind. Let's get one more row in place.'

We dragged more boxes across the floor and piled them into position. We were both practically out on our feet, but we kept on somehow until the third row was built up. Then we both flopped down on the floor, exhausted.

After a few moments, Paula made an effort and sat up.

'Give me your handkerchief and let me fix your hand.'

She bound up the wound, and then flopped down beside me again.

'What wouldn't I give for a bottle of Scotch?' I muttered, slid my arm round her and gave her a little hug. 'Well, you can't say we don't get some excitement, can you?'

'I'd rather not have it,' Paula said, her voice shaky. 'I've never been so scared in all my life. Do you think they'll go away?'

To judge by the hideous uproar going on outside, they were set for weeks.

'I don't know. Not for some time, anyway. But don't worry, they can't get in.'

'But, Vic, we can't get out. And if they do go away, we still haven't found how to get out of here, and the torch won't last much longer.'

While she was speaking, I examined the walls of the cave with the beam of the torch. Finally the beam rested on the remaining boxes in the middle of the floor.

'Let's see what's inside these boxes,' I said, getting stiffly to my feet. 'You take it easy while I look.'

I pulled down one of the boxes and found the lid nailed down. By dropping it on its corner I got it open. Inside, I found row upon row of neatly packed cigarettes.

'Reefers!' I exclaimed. 'This must be Barratt's storehouse. What a haul! There must be millions of them.'

Paula struggled to her feet and came over.

'He couldn't have carried all this stuff down that outside tunnel,' I said excitedly. 'Hunt around. There must be another way out of here.'

The walls were solid enough, so I turned my attention to the floor. It was Paula who found the cunningly concealed trap-door. By treading on one end, the other lifted sufficiently to get a purchase on it.

Together we lifted the trap. A blast of fresh air came surging into the cave.

'This is it,' I said, and flashed the torch into the darkness below. Rough stone steps led down into a passage. I went first. As we reached the bottom step, we could see sunlight coming into the far end of the tunnel.

We went forward down the passage until we reached the opening. The strong sunlight blinded us for a moment. Below us was a wilderness of scrub bushes and sand. We seemed to have come out on the side of a deep quarry. A zigzag path led from the opening of the tunnel down into the quarry.

I was standing in the sunlight, with Paula behind me, when I heard a distant shout.

It was only then that I saw, far below me, two big trucks, half hidden in the scrub and half a dozen or so men staring up at me, and pointing. As I stepped hastily back into the darkness, they began to run towards us.

CHAPTER SEVEN

'THEY'RE Barratt's men!' I said, pushing Paula back into the tunnel. 'They can't have seen you. I'm going out there to draw them off. The moment you think they're out of the way, make a dash for it. Grab one of their trucks if you can. Get to a telephone and call Mifflin. Bring him out here in a hurry. Okay?'

In an emergency, Paula never argued. She squeezed my arm, nodded to show she understood, and I left her, running out into the sunlight again.

Below me, the men were coming up the zigzag path. They were moving as fast as they could, but the angle of climb was steep, and they hadn't made much progress. They yelled at me, as I looked hastily above me, getting the line of country.

The path continued past the opening of the tunnel and led, a few yards farther on, to the top of the quarry. I ran up the path, now in full sight.

I reached the head of the quarry. Before me stretched sand dunes, scrub and rising ground of the desert which lies at the back of Monte Verde Mine. To my left lay the San Diego Highway: my way of escape, but Paula's way of escape too. If I went that way, she would come up behind the pursuing men. I had to draw them away from her. If I was to help her, I had to go to the right: into the heart of the vast track of sand and waste – ground which afforded plenty of cover.

I ran easily over the loose sand, zigzagging a little to keep the various bushes between me and the men behind.

After I had covered a couple of hundred yards or so, I paused to look back over my shoulder. They hadn't reached the top of the quarry yet, and for a moment I wondered if they had found Paula. But I could hear them shouting, and judged they'd appear in a minute or so. I ducked behind a thick bush and waited.

Almost immediately the first head appeared above the edge of the quarry. Then four men appeared. They stopped and looked to right and left. Three other men joined them.

They were big, tough-looking birds: four of them in red-and-white striped sweat shirts, the kind worn by the fishermen who lounge along the waterfront of Coral Gables. The other three were city characters, in ill-fitting sports clothes, typical street-corner loafers.

One of them, a short, square-shouldered man, seemed to be in charge. He was giving directions. Four of the fishermen ran off to the left. The remaining men spread out in a half-circle and began to move towards me.

Keeping behind the shelter of the bushes, I ran, bent double over the sand, to another line of scrub. Again I paused to look back. The line of men had stopped. They couldn't make up their minds which way I had gone.

I decided if I wasn't careful they might go back to the tunnel and catch Paula, so I moved out into the open.

A yell behind me told me I had been seen, and I broke into a run. The evening sun was setting fast now, and threw a red glow over the desert; but it was still hot, and running over the hot sand was hard work.

I kept glancing behind me. The four fishermen had joined in the chase. They were now strung out in a wide arc, driving me farther into the desert, and cutting me off from the Highway. But they weren't making much progress. The heat seemed to be bothering them more than it did me. If I could keep the distance between us, until the sun dropped below the horizon, I stood a good chance of giving them the slip.

The idea seemed to have occurred to them, for there came a crack of a gun behind me and a slug zipped past my head.

I didn't worry a great deal about being shot at so long as I kept moving. You had to be a pretty good shot with a revolver to hit a moving target, but I kept swerving every now and then to be on the safe side.

Again I glanced behind me. The figures were falling back now. They kept coming, but I had greatly increased the distance between them and me, and I slowed down, panting a little, and feeling as if I were in a steam-bath.

I was worrying about Paula. If someone had been left to guard the trucks, she might be caught. But there was nothing I could do but keep on. There was no hope of doubling back. The line of men were too spread out, cutting off all retreat to the Highway. They knew, so long as they could keep me penned up in this half-circle, sooner or later they would come up on me.

The set-up reminded me of the game of fox and geese. At the moment the line behind me was unbroken. In a little while I would have to turn and see if I could pierce it. But I couldn't do that until it was dark.

I went on, no longer running, but moving at a jog-trot. The men behind me had also slowed down, and the distance between us remained the same.

Away to my right, I could see the first of the foothills. This worried me. Before long, they would make a barrier, and would allow the line of men to swing in on my left. If I didn't look out I could be trapped.

I decided to make the attempt to break their line before I got into the foothill country.

Breaking into a run, I sprinted ahead, then began to wheel sharply to my left.

There was an immediate shout behind me.

Glancing round I saw three men pounding across the sand to cut me off. I increased my speed, but I had a lot more ground to cover. I was panting now, and every now and then I stumbled in the loose sand.

One of the fishermen, a big, powerful guy, could run. His long legs flew over the ground as he headed me off.

We raced for the gap between the first of the foothills. If I could beat him I would be out in the open country again. If he beat me, I'd be bottled up in a narrowing strip of desert where, sooner or later, I would be trapped.

I judged the distance and saw he was gaining on me. Gritting my teeth, I increased my speed. I pulled ahead. The other men, all running now, were hopelessly outpaced, but this one guy stuck to me. The gap loomed nearer. I could see him now: see the red, hard face, the sweat running down from under his cap, the fixed grin. He swerved towards me, came at me like a charging bull.

I tried to dodge, but he was ready for that. He closed in on me, his hands grabbing my coat.

I swung at him, but he ducked, his arms encircling me in a bear-like hug. We stumbled, wrestled and went down in the sand.

I slugged him on the side of his head, but it was only a half-arm blow and didn't carry much steam. He raised himself off me and clubbed down at my upturned face with his fist. I just managed to get my face out of the way and belted him in the chest, a good, solid punch that sent him over on his back.

I scrambled to my feet in time to stop his rush with a jab to his face. His head went back, and I sailed in, punching with both hands. I caught him on the side of his jaw and his knees buckled. A long, looping right-hand punch sent him to the sand.

The way was open now, but my breath had gone, and I could scarcely move one leg after the other.

'Hold it!'

The menace in the voice made me turn.

The short, square-shouldered character had come pounding up. In his right fist he held a .45, pointing at me.

I stopped.

'Reach up and clasp some cloud!'

My hands went up. It was a relief just to stand there and get my breath. With any luck at all, Paula would be well out of the way by now.

The fisherman I had knocked down got to his feet. He came across to me, a sheepish grin on his face.

'Frisk him, Mac,' the broad-shouldered character said.

Mac ran his hands over me, found the .25 and tossed it to his companion.

'That's the lot, Joe,' he said and stepped back.

Joe came closer; his small eyes probed my face.

'Who are you? Ain't seen you before,' he said, puzzled.

'Malloy's the name.'

'That's the guy she was telling you about,' Mac said, showing interest.

Joe scowled.

'Yeah; that's right. Poking your snout in Barratt's affairs, were you?' he demanded, pushing the gun at me.

'Well, yes; put it that way if you like,' I said. 'Didn't he tell you?'

Joe grinned.

'You got us wrong. We ain't Barratt's boys. We're a little private party all on our own.'

The five other men came pounding up, panting and gasping for breath. They closed round me threateningly, but Joe waved them back.

'Mac, take these guys and finish the job. I'm taking him to the cabin. When you're through, come on back.'

Mac nodded, motioned to the other five men and set off across the sand towards the mine, leaving me alone with Joe.

'Look, pally,' Joe said, making a stabbing movement with his gun, 'just do what you're told, and you'll be all right. I don't want to make a hole in you, but if you tempt me, I'll do it.'

I was now calm enough to study him. He was about forty, with a round, fleshy face, small eyes, thin lips and the heaviest five o'clock shadow I've ever seen. Although he was short, I could tell by the build of his shoulders, by the short neck and the size of his hands, that he was as powerful as a gorilla.

'Go ahead,' he said, 'and keep moving. I'll tell you when to stop.' He waved vaguely towards the foothills. 'You've got quite a nice little walk, so stretch your legs. If you even look over your shoulder, I'll plug you. Understand?'

I said I understood.

'Get going, then.'

I started off, not knowing where I was heading, hearing him behind me, too far away to make a grab at him, but close enough for him to hit me if he squeezed the trigger.

I was asking myself who this mob was. Where did they spring from? What was the job they had gone back to finish? I thought with satisfaction that the chances were they'd run into Mifflin and his boys.

That's the guy she was telling you about.

Who was *she?*

We were in the foothills now, and the going was hard. We were climbing. Every now and then Joe would grunt, 'Take the right-hand path,' or 'Bear to your left,' but he didn't close the gap between us, and there was nothing I could do but keep walking.

By now the sun had dropped below the horizon, and the light was fading. Before very long it would be dark. That might give me an opportunity, but I knew I had to be careful. Joe looked as if he had been born with a gun in his hand, and it would have to get very dark before I took any chances with him.

'Okay, pally,' he said suddenly. 'Park yourself. We're going to have a breather. Turn around and sit down.'

I faced him.

He was about four yards away from me, and sweating like a pig. The uphill climb in this heat didn't agree with him.

He waved me to a rock while he picked one for himself. I sat down stiffly, glad of the rest.

'Have a butt, pally,' he went on taking out a pack of Lucky Strike. He took one and tossed the pack to me. 'What's it like – in that mine?' he asked, lighting his cigarette and blowing a stream of smoke down his short thick nose.

'Not the kind of place you'd pick for a vacation,' I said, lighting a cigarette and tossing the pack back to him. 'It's full of man-eating rats.'

His small eyes bugged out.

'Rats? I heard there were rats, but I didn't believe it.' He squinted down at his cigarette. 'See any reefers while you were in there?'

'About a couple of million of them. I didn't stop to count them, but that's a conservative guess.'

He grinned, showing small, broken teeth.

'Jeepers! As many as that, huh? I told her that's where he kept the stuff, but she wouldn't have it. How are they packed?'

'In boxes. Who is she?'

He scowled at me.

'I'm the guy who asks the questions, pally. You answer them.'

I had a sudden idea.

'What's your racket?' I asked. 'Hi-jacking Barratt?'

'You guessed it, pally. We're taking that stock of reefers. We have our own little organization now.' He stood up. 'Okay, let's go. Straight up the hill, and keep right. Get going.'

We went on up the hill. It was almost too dark now to see where I was going, but Joe seemed to have eyes like a cat, He kept jerking out directions, warning me away from rocks and shrubs, as if he could see as easily now as in the sunlight.

Suddenly he said, 'Hold it.'

I stopped and waited.

He gave a shrill whistle. A moment later a light flashed on a few yards in front of us, and I could see, carefully hidden behind a screen of trees and bushes, a cleverly concealed log cabin, built into the side of the hill.

'Neat, huh?' Joe said. 'We built it ourselves. You'd have to walk right on it before you knew it was there, and by that time you'd be as full of lead as a church roof. Go ahead. Walk right in.'

I went ahead.

The door stood open and I walked into a large, roughly furnished room. Standing before a log fire, her hands behind her back, a cigarette in her full red lips was Mary Jerome.

A white moth fluttered around the storm lantern hanging from a beam in the centre of the room, and cast an enormous shadow on the floor. It zoomed away from the light, fluttered rather helplessly round the room, and, as it passed Joe, he reached out, slapped it to the floor and put his foot on it.

I didn't pay any attention to what he was doing. I was looking at Mary Jerome; the last person I expected to find in this cabin.

She was wearing a red-and-yellow cowboy shirt, a pair of canary-coloured corduroy slacks, and her dark hair was hidden under a red silk bandana. She was paler and more fine-drawn since last I saw her, but she was still lovely to look at.

'Hello,' I said. 'You may not believe it, but I've been hunting all over for you.'

'Pipe down, pally,' Joe said. 'No one asked you for a speech. Sit over there and keep quiet.'

He poked the gun into my spine, pushed me over to an armchair facing the fire.

I sat down.

'Where did you find him?' Mary Jerome asked.

Joe grinned at her, obviously very pleased with himself.

'He was in the mine. We spotted him coming out of the upper tunnel. He bolted into the desert, but we caught up with him.'

'Was he alone?'

'Why, sure.'

'Then why did he run into the desert?'

Joe frowned at her, ran his fingers through his short, crinkly hair.

'What do you mean?'

'If he wanted to get away, he would have run towards the Highway, wouldn't he?' she asked patiently.

Joe's face lost its animated expression. He turned to snarl at me.

'What's cooking, fella? Weren't you alone?'

'Why, no. I had a girl with me,' I told him. 'She's gone for the Law.'

Mary lifted her shoulders in a resigned shrug.

'I give up, Joe,' she said in disgust. 'You make a mess of everything you handle.'

'For crying out aloud!' Joe said, his face turning red, 'How was I to know?'

'Never mind; but you better do something about it.'

'Yeah.' He pulled a face, glared at me. 'Jeepers! It means walking back to that damned mine again. Can you look after this fella?'

She nodded.

'I'll take care of him. You'd better hurry, Joe.'

'Want my gun?'

She took the heavy .45 and balanced it in her hand.

'Get going, Joe.'

He looked over at me.

'Don't kid yourself she can't use that rod. She can.'

He went out of the cabin.

I listened to him crashing through the bushes on his way down the hillside. It would take him the best part of half an hour to reach the mine.

By that time Mifflin would have arrived.

Mary Jerome moved away from the fire and sat in an armchair facing me, but on the far side of the room. She dropped the gun into her lap and leaned back, resting her head against the padded back of the chair.

I considered the possibility of diving across the room, but decided there would be nothing in it for me except a slug through the head.

'It seems a long time since we met,' I said. 'Was it you who told Paula I was in the mine?'

'Yes. Don't ask me why. I guess I'm going soft.' Her voice sounded weary.

'Who's this guy, Joe? A pal of yours?'

'Not exactly.' She raised her head and stared at me. 'You're bursting to ask questions, aren't you? Well, go ahead and ask them. I'm through with being smart. I'm pulling out of here. I thought I could handle Joe, but I can't.'

'Let's pull out together.'

She shook her head.

'Nothing like that. Joe wouldn't like it, and I can't afford to get on his wrong side. We'll wait a while. If he doesn't come back, you can go.'

'But suppose he does come back?' I said and moved cautiously to the edge of my chair. 'What'll happen to me?'

She shrugged.

'He won't harm you. Joe's not like that. He'll keep you here until he's ready to pull out himself. You don't have to worry.' She lifted the gun and pointed it at me. 'Sit back and relax. You're staying here until Joe gets back.'

That didn't worry me a great deal, as I felt pretty certain Joe wouldn't come back.

'Just where do you fit in this set-up?'

She give a bitter little smile.

'Can't you guess? I'm Lee's wife.'

I sat forward again and stared at her.

'Dedrick's wife?'

'That's what I said.'

'But he's married to Serena Marshland.'

'He married me first.' She reached for a box of cigarettes, lit one and frowned into the fire. 'Lee can take a little thing like bigamy in his stride.'

'You mean Serena's marriage was a fake?'

'Yes. Of course, she didn't know at the time. She knows now,' and again she smiled bitterly.

'Did you tell her?'

'I told her father.'

'Was that why he went to see you at the Beach Hotel?'

She raised her eyebrows at me.

'You found that out? Yes, that's when I told him. I had to have money. I was cleaned right out. He gave me a thousand dollars to keep out of sight.'

'Now don't rush this. Suppose you begin at the beginning. When did you marry Dedrick?'

'Oh, about four years ago, I forget the exact date. It isn't anything I cherish. Being married to Lee isn't a romantic dream. I met him in Paris, and fell for him. He's the kind of heel most women would fall for. I don't know why he married me, but he did. He always had plenty of money, and never seemed to do any work. I guess his money attracted me. Well,

I got what I deserved.' She flicked the cigarette into the fire, and reached for another. 'I found out he was smuggling dope into Paris. Joe worked with him. He persuaded me to help him too.' She smiled at me. 'You don't know how persuasive he can be. Then he met the Marshland woman. I hadn't an idea what was cooking. He was often away for weeks at a time, and I thought he was handling a consignment. Then without warning, he disappeared. Joe and I were left holding the baby. Joe tried to carry on, but he just hadn't what it takes. The police nearly caught us. We managed to get out of France, and came here. That was when I found out he had married Serena Marshland. I went to Barratt. You know about Barratt?'

I said I knew about Barratt.

'He wants watching,' she said, her face hardening. 'He fooled me all right. He said Lee had married Serena Marshland to get her money, and as soon as he had it, he would return to me. He asked me to co-operate; to keep away from Lee and give him a free hand. Like a fool, I believed him. I was staying at the Chandos Hotel, and on my way back from seeing Barratt I was shot at. I knew then that Barratt was going to get rid of me, and I moved to the Beach Hotel.' She glanced at me, asked, 'Are you enjoying this?'

'More or less,' I said. 'It's not what I was hoping to hear, but never mind. Go on.'

'What were you hoping to hear?'

'Finish what you've got to say. I'll tell you later.'

She shrugged.

'There's not much more. I thought if I could only see Lee I might persuade him to come back to me. I found out he was going to Ocean End, and I went there to see him. That's when I met you, and heard he was supposed to have been kidnapped. He hasn't been kidnapped, has he?'

'No. But by faking his own kidnapping he collected five hundred thousand dollars off Serena, and that ain't hay. The last time I saw him he was staying with Barratt.'

'I've read about that. It's just the kind of thing he would get away with. Well, that's about all. I knew Barratt kept his main supply of reefers in the mine. Joe and I hooked up together. I wanted to get even with Barratt. My idea was to burn the stock: it's worth thousands, but Joe has other ideas. He's planned to hi-jack the stuff and start an organization of his own. Dope smuggling's too dirty for me. I've had enough of it. Joe won't get anywhere. He hasn't the brain for the work. I'm quitting. He's getting ideas about me.' Her mouth curled. 'A woman can't live under the same roof with a man for long. Sooner or later, he makes a pest of himself.'

'Some women can,' I said and grinned at her.

Then suddenly, without warning, the distant sound of gun-fire brought us both to our feet.

'What's that?' Mary asked sharply, running to the window.

'Maybe the cops are chasing Joe,' I said hopefully, 'but just to be on the safe side, I'll put out the light.'

As I turned down the wick of the storm lantern more shots rang out, much closer now, and I hastily lifted the lantern from its hook and blew out the flickering flame.

'It's Joe and Mac!' Mary said, and threw open the door.

The flash of gunfire lit up the darkness outside. Away in the valley came answering flashes and bullets smacked into the wooden roof.

Joe and Mac, breathing heavily, charged into the room, and slammed the door.

III

For a moment or so neither of them could say anything. They leaned against the wall, panting for breath, while slugs slapped into the solid walls of the cabin and gunfire rolled in the valley.

'Get the rifles,' Joe gasped. 'It's Barratt!'

Mary stumbled across the room. I heard her open a cup-board. She came back with two rifles and gave them to Joe and Mac.

'Are you in this?' she asked, as calm as if she was sitting down to a cup of tea.

'Yeah; if it's Barratt, I am,' I said.

She went back to the cupboard and produced two more rifles and a sack of ammunition.

'What happened, Joe?' she asked as we loaded the clips.

'Jeepers! The boys walked right into them. There are about ten of them and Barratt. I guess he'd come to shift the stuff. They must have spotted our trucks and came down on us.'

'Where do you get this us stuff from?' Mac growled. 'You weren't even there.' He was kneeling in front of the window, and turned his head to look at Mary. 'They were at the top of the quarry. We were at the bottom. It was like shooting rabbits. They got Harry, Lu and George with their first volley. The rest of us got behind the trucks. They kept crawling around the edge of the quarry, picking us off, until I was the only one left. I just lay there and waited. Finally, they decided they'd picked us all off and came down to investigate. Harry and George were still alive. They were badly hurt, but they were still breathing. Barratt shot them both through the head. I managed to sneak away while they were checking up on the others. I got to the top of the quarry, when Joe turned up. They spotted Joe. The chump was smoking. You could see him a mile away, and they came after us. I told Joe not to shoot, but he kept letting his rod off, and of course, they just kept coming. I was hoping to get away in the dark, but not with Joe lighting up the countryside for miles. So here we are, and right out there, they are, and it's going to be some picnic.'

Joe said, 'I got two of them. You don't think I was going to let that mob shoot at me without shooting back?'

While they were talking, I was examining the valley below the cabin. There wasn't much cover until you started to climb the hill. Once they got a foothold on the hill, they could get up to the door of the cabin without being seen.

I edged the rifle over the window sill, sighted into the darkness and pressed the trigger. Almost immediately flashes lit up the shrubs on the far side of the valley and slugs whammed against the walls of the cabin.

'They're over on the far side,' I said. 'If they can get across the floor of the valley, we'll be cooked.'

'The moon will be up in a few minutes,' Mac said. 'It's just below the peak of the hill as we came along. Then we'll have plenty of light.'

I thought I saw some movement below, shifted the sights of the rifle and fired.

A tiny, shadowy form darted back under cover again. Both Joe and Mac fired at the same time. A faint yell followed the crash of gunfire. These two might not be very strong in the brain department, but they could shoot.

'That's another of the punks,' Joe said with satisfaction.

I put my hand on Mary's arm and pulled her close to me.

'Is there any way out of here besides the door?' I asked in a whisper.

She shook her head.

'How about the roof?'

'There's a ladder that takes you up to the roof, but once up there, there's no way to escape.'

'Sure?'

'You might with a rope, but it wouldn't be easy.'

'I guess I'll take a look,' I said. 'Got a rope?'

'There's one in the kitchen.'

Joe suddenly fired again.

'Look out!' he bawled. 'They're coming.'

We could make out six or seven moving figures, running across the floor of the valley. We all fired as fast as we could pull our bolts. Two of the figures fell. The others drifted back again under cover of the opposite bank.

'Get the rope,' I said to Mary. 'And get that trap open. We may have to leave in a hurry.'

'What are you two whispering about?' Joe demanded suspiciously.

'We're preparing a get-away,' I told him. 'By way of the roof.'

'Fat chance you have,' he snorted. 'They'd pick you off like a sitting rabbit when the moon's up.'

'We may have to,' I said, seeing the first rays of the moon appearing over the hill top. 'Here it comes.'

Two or three minutes later the floor of the valley was flooded with white light.

'Well, at least, it's as bad for them,' Mac said, sitting back on his heels. 'We can't miss them from here.'

'What do you think they're playing at?' Joe said, uneasily. 'They haven't let off a heater for the past five minutes.'

'Why should they?' I said. 'They're waiting for the moon to pick this joint out, and it will. They'll be able to see in through the windows.'

'I have the rope,' Mary called from an adjoining room.

'I'm going up on the roof,' I said. 'Keep an eye on them.'

'You better keep an eye on yourself,' Joe said sarcastically. 'Don't expect flowers for your funeral.'

I went into the inner room.

Mary held a flashlight in her hand, and as I came in she swung the beam to a short ladder that led to a trap door in the roof.

'You'd better not go up there,' she said. 'They're certain to see you.'

167

'Hey, you two; give me some covering fire,' I called into the outer room. 'I'm going up on the roof.'

'Hope it keeps fine for you,' Mac said and laughed.

They began firing down into the valley. I waited, listening, but there was no answering fire.

'I wonder what they're playing at,' I muttered. 'Well, here goes. Let's see what's up there.'

I mounted the ladder and very cautiously lifted the trap-door. I slid it to one side and peered around the flat roof that spread out before me.

Moonlight fell directly on it, and it was nearly as light as day up there.

Above me the hill went up steeply, offering little foothold, and not much cover. To try and scale the hill from the roof in this light would be asking for trouble. The only chance would be to wait until the moon moved round and the hill face was in the shadow. I didn't know if we had the time to wait.

I slid down the ladder again.

'Not much good. A rope won't help. It's too light. In another hour it might be done, but not now.'

'In another hour we'll be pushing up the daisies,' Joe said cheerfully from the other room.

'How about some coffee?' I suggested to Mary. 'We might be stuck here for some time. I'll go back and keep watch while you get it.'

I returned to the outer room.

Mac was chewing an unlit cigarette, staring down into the valley. Joe sat on the edge of a chair, and peered around the window-frame.

'You didn't see a girl in the quarry, did you?' I asked Mac.

'No – why?'

'I had a girl with me when you spotted me. I sent her for the cops.'

'That's not going to help us. You'd never hear gunfire out of the valley. I don't know how it is, but it's a fact. Unless they come here to look for us, they won't know a battle's going on,' Joe said. 'Besides, it would hurt my pride to be rescued by a cop.'

'I reckon I could sink my pride,' Mac said and laughed. 'I'd sooner be pinched by a cop then fall into Barratt's hands.'

'Think it's safe to smoke?' Joe asked.

'Go and sit on the floor if you must smoke,' I said. 'I'll take your place.'

'You're a pal, pally. I'm glad I didn't shoot you.'

'So am I.'

He lit a cigarette while he sat on the floor.

'These punks don't show much initiative, do they?' Mac said. 'Maybe they've scrammed.'

'Go out there and find out,' Joe said. 'I bet they're cooking up something.'

I had an idea they were, too. So long as the floor of the valley lay in the moonlight, I could understand them not showing themselves, but, once the light had shifted, they would probably make a rush.

Mary came in with cups of coffee. Joe laced his from a pint flask he hauled out of his pocket.

'Anyone want rum?' he asked, waving the flask.

Mac helped himself, handed the flask to me, but I shook my head.

'Just coffee for me.'

'Fancy your chances getting out of here?' Joe asked as he sucked up the rum and coffee noisily.

'I don't see why not.'

'Shut up, Joe,' Mac said curtly. 'You're creating despair and depression. No one would miss you if you were shot.'

'That's a lie!' Joe said hotly. 'My old mother would.' He got to his feet to cross the room for another cup of coffee. 'I've a flock of judies too. They'd all miss me.'

There was a sudden, steady rattle of gunfire. One of the distant bushes seemed to burst into flame as a Thompson-gun chattered its song of death.

'Down!' I bawled, and flung myself flat.

Joe took two lurching steps to the door, turned slowly on his heels and dropped.

No one moved. The Thompson continued to rattle. Slugs whined through the windows, cut across the door, hammered into the opposite wall. Then the Thompson stopped as suddenly as it began.

'Watch out,' I said to Mac, and crawled over to Joe. The burst of gunfire had caught him across the chest. It had ripped him open the way you rip open a can with a can opener.

'Is he dead?' Mary asked, and by the shake in her voice I knew she was badly shocked.

'Yeah.'

'Well, I hope I'll get out of this so I can tell his Ma,' Mac said. 'I bet she'll hang out flags. She always hated the punk.'

'Don't show yourselves in front of the windows and keep down,' I said, crawling over to where Mary knelt by one of the windows.

'You bet,' Mac said. 'I thought that son of a bitch was up to something.'

Then the Thompson started grinding again. Slugs zipped through the room.

'Look out! They're coming!' Mac bawled.

I could see figures running into the moonlight. They swerved to right and left, making it impossible to hold the rifle sights on them. Mac brought one down, but the other five got across the floor of the valley and disappeared into the bushes.

'Not so good,' I said, ducking down as slugs sent splinters from the window frame. 'They're over now. They can get right up to the door without us seeing them.'

'They can't get in,' Mac said, 'without getting shot up. Where's Joe's rum? I feel like anothe swig.'

He crawled over to Joe, turned him over and fetched out the flask from Joe's hip pocket.

As the Thompson stopped grinding, I raised my rifle and fired three quick shots into the bushes where the gun flashes had been.

There was a sudden movement. A man sprang out, holding the Thompson and went crashing down on his face.

'Nice shooting,' Mac said, who had returned to the window. 'Now if any of those rats want that Tommy they'll have to come out into the open for it.'

Gunfire banged right by us, making us start back. Slugs smashed through the door.

'They're right outside,' I whispered to Mary. 'Go into the other room.'

'Why?' She peered at me, her eyes large in her white face.

'Get in there and don't ask questions.'

She went, crawling on hands and knees.

'Got an automatic on you?' I asked Mac, my lips close to his ear.

He nodded.

'So's Joe.'

I crawled over to Joe, found the .38 automatic, pushed down the front of his trousers, and crawled back to Mac.

'Listen: I'm going up on the roof. The moment I start firing, open the door. With any luck, they won't see you until it's too late. You've got to shoot quick and you've got to hit them. There're five, remember.'

'They'll get you the moment you show on the roof.'

'I'll chance it.'

A voice bawled from out of the darkness, 'Come on out, or we'll come and get you.'

I crawled across the floor into the inner room.

Mary was waiting for me.

'I'm going up,' I said. 'They're right outside, and we might surprise them. Stick around down here and keep your eyes open. There may be trouble.'

And as I climbed up the ladder, I thought that last utterance was a nice example of the understatement.

Gently I pushed back the trap, waited, listening. Then slowly I raised myself so that my head and shoulders appeared above the opening of the trap. Nothing happened. I wondered if those left on the far side of the valley were watching the roof. I hoped they weren't. Moving out into the brilliant moonlight gave me a sinking feeling, but I moved out.

Lying flat, I edged across the roof, taking my time, careful not to make a sound, expecting any moment to be shot at from the other side of the valley.

It seemed a long way across the roof. As I drew near the edge, I moved more slowly, edging forward inch by inch.

More shots crashed out, startling me, but they were shooting at the door and not at me. Under cover of the noise, I pulled myself forward until I could see over the edge of the roof.

I looked down on the shrubs and bushes that sloped away steeply into the valley. For a moment or so I couldn't see any movement. Then I spotted a man, crouched behind a rock, about twenty yards from the cabin. Keeping as still as death, I searched the ground before me. I spotted the others, spread out in a half-circle before the cabin. None of them were taking any chances. All of them were partly protected by rocks or shrubs. I reckoned I would pick off two, but the other three would get me unless Mac got them first. I decided it would be safer and wiser to tell Mac where they were hiding before trying to pick them off.

As I began to edge backwards, one of the men glanced up and saw me. He gave a yell and fired at the same time. The slug fanned past my face. I took a snap-shot at him, saw him fall, swung around and fired at the second man in the half-circle, saw him start to his feet, and then I wriggled back as a crash of gunfire broke out below me and bullets struck splinters from the guttering where my head had been.

Bent double, I made a bolt for the trap-door, as gunfire broke out from the other side of the valley. I heard slugs zip past me as I half fell, half scrambled down the ladder.

'Are you hurt?' Mary asked breathlessly.

'No.'

I didn't pause, but ran into the outer room in time to see Mac standing in the open doorway, blazing away into the darkness like General Custer in his last stand.

As I joined him, he stopped firing and stepped back into the shelter of the doorway.

'We got 'em, pal!' he exclaimed. 'The whole damn five of them. How about a quick rush into the bushes before the rest of them get over here?'

Mary joined us.

'Come on,' I said. 'This is our chance. Mac'll go first. Then you. I'll be behind you. Jump for the bushes. Ready?'

She nodded.

'Go ahead.'

Mac took a flying leap through the doorway into the thick undergrowth below.

IV

We lay in the darkness and thick scrub, well away from the cabin and stared across the floor of the valley. There was no movement on the opposite hillside, no gunfire, no voices.

Mac rubbed his face with his hand and hunched his shoulders. The desert was cold now, and the wind, coming off the hills, had a nip in it.

'They're keeping quiet, aren't they?' he said in an undertone.

'Yeah.' I took the half-empty flask of rum from him and offered it to Mary. 'Have some before this guy drinks the lot.'

She shook her head.

'I'm all right.'

I tilted the flask and let some of the raw spirit trickle down my throat. It wasn't my idea of a drink, but it was the right stuff to keep out the cold.

'I think we can go on,' I said. 'No point in lying here if they're not coming over.'

'Do you think they've gone back to the mine?' she asked.

'Maybe. Let's go and see. He may have decided to go back there and shift the reefers rather than lose any more men. With any luck, the cops will be there to meet him.'

'Unless he spotted your girl,' Mac said, getting to his feet.

'Come on. Let's get over there.'

I led the way, moving fast, but keeping under cover, taking no risks. The way was downhill. Ahead of us the bushes and shrubs began to thin out, and the face of the hill gradated slowly to the floor of the valley. We had only another fifty yards ahead of us before we reached the flat, open plain of the desert.

We paused and examined the ground before us. The moonlight reflected on the sand. You could have seen any movement a half a mile away.

'If they're still in the hills, this is where we get shot in the back,' Mac muttered. 'Going to chance it?'

'Yeah. You two stay here. If nothing happens to me, come on after me.'

'You're a sucker for trouble, aren't you?' Mac said and gave me a slap on the back.

Mary said in her calm, matter-of-fact voice, 'I don't think they're up there. I think they've gone on to the mine.'

I hoped she was right as I slid down the little slope on to the sand. I began to run, zigzagging a little my shoulders hunched, and covering the ground rapidly. Nothing happened. I ran on for a couple of hundred yards, then stopped and turned. Mac and Mary were running after me. I waited for them to catch me up.

'They're at the mine,' I said. 'Spread out and keep moving. Drop flat if there's any shooting.'

We began to run over the undulating sand towards the mine. Every now and then we paused to get our breath, but I kept them at it. I was worried, thinking of Paula, wondering if she had got through. The silence worried me. If Mifflin had arrived, there should have been shooting.

After a while, the sloping edge of the quarry came into sight.

I signalled to the other two to stop, waved them to me.

'We crawl the rest of the way,' I said. 'Barratt may have left a look-out, and we don't want to run into him. You keep in the rear,' I went on to Mary. 'Leave this to Mac and me.'

We set off again, moving slowly now, using every scrap of cover, making no noise.

Mac suddenly pointed, and I followed the direction of his finger. I could just make out a man's head, outlined against the horizon, as he knelt in the scrub, looking our way.

Mac put his mouth close to my ear.

'I'll take him,' he said. 'I was a Ranger once. This is right up my alley.'

I nodded and watched him crawl in a circling movement towards the watcher.

Mary slid over the sand and lay by me. She too had seen the head against the horizon.

We waited. Nothing happened, and I began to wonder what Mac was playing at.

The watcher suddenly half stood up, looking our way. He made a beautiful target against the sand and the moonlight. Then he gave a sharp cough and dropped face downwards in the sand.

Mac waved and disappeared once more behind the sand ridge. I crawled, on, motioning Mary to keep in the rear.

'He didn't know anything about it,' Mac whispered when I joined him. 'I'm beginning to enjoy this.'

We crawled to the edge of the quarry and looked down.

The blazing headlights of the two trucks lit up a scene of tremendous activity. Men were loading the wooden boxes on to the trucks, while others came staggering down the steep path from the tunnel, carrying more boxes. One of the trucks was already loaded and the other was half filled.

Standing in the entrance of the tunnel, waving his men on, and shouting at them to hurry was Barratt.

Mac's hand lifted and the sight of the .38 grew steady on Barratt's chest, but I grabbed his wrist.

'No! My girl must be down there. She couldn't have got through. I'm going to look for her. If they spot me, start shooting, and get Barratt first.'

He nodded, and I began the slow, dangerous climb down into the quarry. Every now and then I dislodged a shower of stones, and I ducked behind a bush, holding my breath. But the men working below me were far too busy getting the boxes into the truck to be on their guard.

Keeping in the shadow, I reached the bottom of the quarry. There was plenty of cover, and I worked my way silently over the ground towards the trucks.

I could hear Barratt's voice as he cursed the sweating men, telling them to hurry. I kept on until I reached the loaded truck. On its blind side, I stood up and looked inside the cabin.

Paula was in there, tied hand and foot and gagged. She turned her head and we looked at each other. I opened the cabin door and swung myself up inside.

She looked pale and a little scared, but as soon as I got the gag off she smiled at me.

'Am I glad to see you,' she said huskily.

'That makes two of us,' I said, cutting the cord that tied her wrists. 'What happened? Did you walk right into them?'

She nodded, rubbing her wrists while I freed her ankles.

'He still thinks you're in the mine,' she told me. 'He hasn't an idea that I've been in there. He thought I was trying to find a way in. As soon as they have finished loading, he intends to take me in there and leave me there.'

'That's what he thinks. Come on; let's get up to the top of the quarry. We have friends up there.'

Keeping on the blind side of the truck, we began to edge silently back the way I had come. When we were half-way up the side of the quarry there came a sudden yell behind us that froze us to a standstill. We looked back. Barratt was staring into the tunnel. The three men working by the truck also stared towards the tunnel. The frantic, blood-curdling yell came again. Barratt suddenly fired into the tunnel, shouted and began to run frantically down the path towards the trucks.

'The rats!' I said and grabbed Paula's arm. 'Up as fast as you can.'

Both Mary and Mac began firing into the quarry as we scrambled up the steep slope. We heard shots and yells below us, but we didn't look back nor pause until we flung ourselves, sobbing for breath, into the scrub overhanging the edge of the quarry.

Mac came charging round to join us.

'Rats!' He was pointing, his fleshy, red face tight with horror. 'Look at them! Those guys down there haven't a chance.'

I looked down into the quarry. It was alive with rats. They swarmed round the five men, who had come together and were shooting at them. I could see Barratt waving his arms and screaming. Three enormous brutes sprang at him and he disappeared beneath a heaving sea of sleek, brown bodies. The other men were dragged down as more rats came rushing down the path from the tunnel, squealing and fighting to get at them.

I caught hold of Paula.

'Let's get out of here.'

The four of us ran across the sand towards the Highway.

CHAPTER EIGHT

I

IT was just after midnight when Mary Jerome, Francon, Paula and myself filed into Brandon's office. Mifflin, red-faced and thoughtful, brought up the rear.

Brandon sat behind his desk and glared at us as we came in. He wasn't looking his usual immaculate self. Mifflin had hauled him out of bed to hear me repeat my story.

'Well, sit down,' Brandon growled, waving his hand to the half-circle of chairs lined up before his desk. He swung around to glare at Mifflin. 'What did you get?'

'Two truck loads of reefers and sixteen corpses,' Mifflin told him. 'Barratt's dead. Only one member of the gang was alive when we got there, and he's talked. But it's Malloy's story. Do you want him to tell it?'

Brandon favoured me with a heavy scowl as he opened a drawer and took out a cigar box. He selected a cigar without offering the box to anyone and sat back.

'That's what he's here for,' he said, pointed a fat finger at Mary Jerome and asked, 'Who's this?'

'Lee Dedrick's wife,' I told him.

He started, stared at me.

'Who?'

'Lee Dedrick's wife.'

He swung round on Mary Jerome.

'That right?'

'Yes,' she said in her cold, flat voice.

'When did you marry him?'

'About four years ago.'

He put the cigar down, ran well-manicured fingers through his thick white hair.

'Does that make the Marshland marriage bigamous?' he asked in a strangled voice.

'It does,' I said, enjoying his consternation. 'Do you want me to begin at the beginning or do you want to ask questions?'

He picked up the cigar again, pierced it savagely with the end of a match.

'Does Mrs. Dedrick – Serena Marshland know about this?'

'She does now.'

He drew down the corners of his mouth, lifted his fat shoulders in a shrug of resignation and waved his hand.

'Go ahead, but don't expect me to believe it.'

'A lot of this is guess-work,' I said, shifting forward to the edge of my chair. 'Some of it can be proved; most of it can't. We do know for certain that Barratt was the boss of a smuggling ring. Lee Dedrick and Lute Ferris were his aides. Dedrick took care of the Paris end and Ferris smuggled the stuff in from Mexico. We have proof of that. We also know Dedrick was married to this girl here' – I waved to Mary Jerome – 'who had no idea what his racket was. He deserted her, married Serena Marshland and returned to New York. All he wanted was Serena's money. Now this is where I start guessing. Souki found out who Dedrick was. Maybe he tried to blackmail. I don't know. It seems possible he threatened Dedrick, who saw his plans to get hold of Serena's fortune blowing up in his face. He murdered Souki to shut his mouth. To cover the murder and to get as much money out of Serena as he could, he faked his own kidnapping. The idea worked. No one suspected he had killed Souki, and no one suspected he hadn't been kidnapped. Barratt helped him. He kept under cover in Barratt's apartment while Barratt collected the ransom and framed Perelli for the kidnapping. It was easy enough. Perelli had an apartment opposite Barratt's. Barratt hated Perelli. He hid the fishing-rod, some of the ransom money and the gun in Perrelli's room and tipped the police. They moved in and grabbed Perelli.'

Brandon glanced over at Mifflin and snorted.

'Know what this sounds like to me?' He thumped the desk as he glared at me. 'A typical Malloy pipe-dream. You're trying to get Perelli out of a jam. Nothing you've said yet convinces me he didn't snatch Dedrick. What else have you got?'

'A reception clerk named Grace Lehmann who works in Barratt's apartment house saw him with the fishing-rod. She tried to blackmail him. Dedrick went to see her and murdered her.'

Brandon gave a scoffing laugh.

'Who did you say killed her?'

'Dedrick, the man in the fawn suit. The man Joy Dreadron saw with Grace Lehmann.'

'That's a pretty tale. The Lehmann woman committed suicide. Your only witness is a street-walker. Do you think I'd take her word? None of your witnesses are worth a damn, anyway.'

I lifted my shoulders.

'How do you know the man in the fawn suit is Dedrick?' he demanded.

'I recognized his voice. He spoke to me over the phone, if you remember, when he staged the faked kidnapping. He has a voice you don't forget.'

'Tell that to the jury and see where you get,' Brandon sneered. 'All you've got is that Barratt ran a smuggling ring. I'll give you that, but nothing else. The rest of the stuff is a pipe-dream.'

I looked across at Francon, who shook his head.

'Well, all right, then I guess we can all go to bed,' I said to Brandon. 'I didn't ask to come here, and if you don't want to believe the story, it's okay with me.'

'We'll go over it again,' Brandon said, beginning to enjoy himself, 'and we'll have it down in writing.' He nodded to Mifflin, who opened the door and bawled for Sergeant Mac-Graw.

After a while MacGraw came in, a placid expression on his white, flabby face. He sat down at a table, a pad of paper in front of him and waited.

I went through the story again, covering everything that had happened to date. It took some time. Then Brandon tried to shake me, tried to shake Mary Jerome, and even Paula. He got nowhere.

'There's not a scrap of evidence in any of this,' he said at last. 'Bring that yarn into court and see what the D.A. does to it.' He turned to Francon. 'So far as I'm concerned, Perelli snatched Dedrick. Nothing this parlour detective has found out makes any difference to me. Any witness he claims to have is either dead or unreliable. If you think Perelli's alibi with this Lola woman will stand up in court, you're crazy. Now, get out, the lot of you! You've wasted enough of my time already. Bring Dedrick here, and I might believe you, and that's my final word!'

Outside in the passage the four of us looked at each other.

'That's the way it is,' Francon said. 'He's right, Vic. It makes a nice story, but it gets us exactly nowhere in court. We've got to find Dedrick.'

Mifflin joined us at the end of the passage.

'Well, come on,' he growled. 'Haven't you people got any beds?'

'Are you looking for Dedrick?' I asked.

'We're looking for this guy in the fawn suit,' Mifflin said carefully. 'We've been looking for him since Lehmann's killing. You don't have to pay any attention to Brandon. He knows Grace Lehmann was murdered. He was just sounding off.'

'If you're looking for him, why haven't you found him?'

Mifflin's red face turned purple.

'If he's to be found, we'll find him. Don't start making cute remarks. If he was still in town, we would have had him by now.'

'Not if he's holed up. You haven't searched every house in town,' I said. 'And that's the only way you will find him.'

Francon was getting bored with this.

'Well, I guess I'm going to bed. I have a busy day in front of me,' he said. 'You have a week before they bring Perelli to trial. Two more days before I quit. I'm not going into court with nothing in my hands, Vic. I warned you; and I mean it.'

He went off before I could argue with him.

Depressed and tired, Paula, Mary and I went down the steps to the street.

'Shall I take Mrs. Dedrick to my apartment?' Paula asked.

'If you will. We'll meet tomorrow at the office. Maybe I'll have an idea by then.'

I got them a taxi and saw them off, then, as I was walking over to the Buick, Mifflin joined me.

'Sorry about this, Vic,' he said. 'There's nothing I can do about it.'

'I know.' I leaned against the car and groped for a cigarette. 'Do you think Dedrick has managed to leave town?'

Mifflin shrugged.

'I don't know. We have men watching the roads, the airport and the station. He was lucky if he did. He's either got through the cordon or he's found a hide-out where no one would think of looking for him. Something like that.'

I nodded.

'We've checked every likely spot,' Mifflin went on. 'If he has found a hide-out, it's a good one.'

I had a sudden idea.

'Yeah,' I said. 'It's my bet he's still in town. Stick around, Tim. I believe I've got something. Don't go to bed yet. Maybe I'll give you a call. Will you be at your home?'

'That's where I'm going now,' Mifflin said. 'What's the idea? Where do you think he is?'

I climbed into the Buick and started the engine.

'Where you wouldn't dare look for him,' I said out of the window. 'Ocean End, brother.'

I engaged gear and drove away fast as he yelled after me.

II

I turned off the car headlights as I swung the nose of the Buick into the private road leading to Ocean End.

The most unlikely place, and yet the most obvious for Dedrick to hide out would be Ocean End. If Marshland had left the estate, and Serena was there alone, Dedrick might not have much trouble to persuade her to give him sanctuary, depending on the story he told her.

It was no more than an idea, but although I was aching for my bed, I knew I couldn't rest until I had put it to a test.

Half-way up the drive, I stopped the car and got out. I reluctantly decided it would be safer to walk the rest of the way.

The main gates were closed. I had heard stories about the various burglar alarms fitted throughout the estate, so I kept away from them. I walked beside the high wall until I came upon a creeper that looked strong enough to take my weight. With a little effort, I reached the top of the wall and surveyed the moonlit garden spread out before me.

I dropped quietly from the wall, landing in the soft soil of a rose bed.

In the distance I could see the house, and I moved cautiously towards it, keeping in the shadows, using every scrap of cover I could find until I reached the terrace.

The ground floor was in darkness, but two of the upper windows showed lights. The time was twenty minutes past two: late enough for anyone to be up.

My rubber-soled shoes made no sound as I mounted the steps that led to the terrace. Above me the light from one of the windows fell directly on the terrace, making a sharp, bright pattern on the white stone. The climb up to the window wasn't difficult. The window led out on to a balcony, and by standing on the terrace balustrade I swung myself up on to the upper balcony. I hung on with both hands, drew myself up and peered into the uncurtained window.

I could scarcely believe my luck. The man in the fawn suit lay flat on his back on the bed. He had a glass of whisky in one hand and a magazine in the other. A cigarette burned evenly from his thin lips, and he read with frowning concentration.

I had played a hunch, and it had come off. Yet, come to think of it, it wasn't so much luck as good reasoning. Where else would he have been so safe?

I wasn't going to tackle him on my own. I wanted witnesses. Regretfully, I climbed down from the balcony and reached the terrace.

I tried to remember where the nearest phone-box was: too far away, anyway. Now I knew he was there I wasn't going to lose sight of him. If he had been in bed and asleep, I might have risked leaving the estate in search of a telephone, but not when he might suddenly take it into his head to bolt.

I remembered there was a telephone in the lounge.

I walked silently along the terrace to the casement windows that led into the lounge. In the bright light of the moon, I examined the doors for any sign of wiring or alarms, but failed to find any. But before attempting to break in, I decided to walk around the house in the hope of finding a window left open.

It was my lucky night. At the back of the house I found an unlatched window. I eased it open, put my head into darkness and listened. I heard nothing. I groped in my hip pocket and pulled out Paula's flashlight. The battery was on the blink, but the light was strong enough for me to see I was looking into the passage, leading to the hall.

Very carefully I hoisted myself up, climbed through the window, closed it and soft-footed down the passage to the hall.

The house was very still and silent. I stood listening for a few moments before going into the lounge. I shut the door.

The telephone stood on a table by the settee. I sat down, lifted the receiver off its cradle and dialled Mifflin's home number.

I sat listening to the burr-burr-burr on the line, listening also for any sound upstairs.

There came a click on the line and Mifflin's voice growled 'Hello.'

'I've found him,' I said, my mouth close to the mouthpiece. 'He's at Ocean End. How soon can you get over here?'

'You're sure?' Mifflin's voice shot up with excitement.

'Yeah; I'm sure. I've seen him. Now listen, Tim. Collect Paula and Mrs. Dedrick. I want them as witnesses. Park your car before you reach the house. You'll have to get over the wall. Don't touch the gates. Come up to the terrace, and don't show yourselves until I call you. Tell Paula to get everything he says. Okay?'

'You're really sure he's there?' Mifflin asked. 'I'll lose my badge if I break into that woman's house . . .'

'Forget your badge! Get moving. I'll have the two girls ready for you by the time you reach Paula's apartment. I expect you in twenty minutes,' and I hung up before he could protest.

Next I dialled Paula's number.

'Throw your clothes on,' I said when she answered the phone. 'Get Mrs. Dedrick up too. Mifflin's calling for you in about ten minutes. I want you over at Ocean End. I've found Dedrick.'

Paula said she would be ready. She didn't waste time asking questions.

I hung up and lit a cigarette. I was sweating with excitement.

Somewhere in the silent room a clock ticked busily. I swung my legs up on the settee and tried to keep calm. With any luck, this would be the end of the case. By tomorrow, if it worked out the way I hoped it would, Perelli would be free.

I closed my eyes. It seemed a long time since I had any sleep. A lot had happened since Maxie had given me the pass-key to Barratt's apartment. It seemed almost too good to be true that within an hour the thing would be finished.

Then suddenly from somewhere upstairs there came a single choked bang of a gun.

I was off the settee across the room and had the door open before the echo of the shot had ceased to roll through the silent house.

I stood in the hall, staring into the darkness, listening. A door opened. A light flashed up. Someone ran along the gallery above me, past the head of the stairs. I caught a fleeting glimpse of a woman in a blue silk wrap. Another door opened; then a wild, horrified scream rang out.

I sprang forward, mounted the stairs three at the time, reached the gallery as another scream sounded from a lighted doorway at the end of the gallery.

I ran down the gallery, paused outside the door and looked into the room: Dedrick's room.

Serena was bending over the bed, frantically shaking his shoulder as he lay still and silent on the bed.

'Lee!' she was screaming. 'What have you done? Lee! My darling! Speak to me!'

I went quickly into the room. One brief look at the man on the bed told me he was dead. The side of his head was smashed in, and blood ran down his face on to his white shirt.

I caught hold of Serena's arm.

'All right,' I said sharply. 'You can't do anything.'

She spun round, her face white and her eyes glazed with horror, to stare at me. She started to scream, raised her hands as if to push me away, then her eyes rolled back and she fell into my arms in a faint.

I lowered her gently to the floor, bent over the dead man.

A .38 Colt automatic lay on the bed by his right hand. Smoke still drifted from the barrel. There was a fixed, grinning look of terror on his face, and I could see the powder burns on his skin.

'What's happened?'

I turned.

Wadlock, in a faded red dressing-gown, his hair standing on ends, stood in the doorway.

'He's shot himself,' I said curtly. 'Let's get Mrs. Dedrick out of here.'

I bent over her, lifted her and carried her out of the room.

Wadlock stood aside, his old grey face twitching.

I carried Serena down the stairs and into the lounge and laid her on the settee.

'Open the casement doors and let's get some air in here,' I said as Wadlock switched on the lights.

While he was opening the doors leading on to the terrace I poured a stiff whisky into a glass and returned to Serena. As I knelt beside her, she opened her eyes.

'Take it easy,' I said. 'Here, have some of this.'

She pushed my hand away and half sat up.

'Lee.'

'Now, look, you can't help him. No one can help him. Just take it easy.'

She dropped back on the pillow and hid her face in her hands.

'Lee, why did you do it?' she moaned, half to herself. 'My darling, why did you do it?'

Wadlock came over and looked at her helplessly.

'Get the police,' I said. 'Tell them what's happened, and keep out of this.'

'I don't understand,' he said, bewildered. 'What are you doing here?'

'Never mind. Get the police.'

He started to say something, changed his mind and went slowly from the room. I heard him mounting the stairs.

'Drink this,' I said, turning back to Serena. 'You'll need it. Come on. The cops are going to get tough when they find out you've been hiding him.'

She took the whisky, gulped some of it, shuddered and put the glass down.

'Why should they? He made me promise not to tell them. He came back two days ago. He escaped from his kidnappers. He said they would kill him if they found out where he was. He wouldn't let me tell even Wadlock.'

'Did he tell you who kidnapped him?'

'Barratt and Perelli,' she said breathlessly. 'He said Barratt hired Perelli because Lee wanted to give up his past life.'

That was exactly what I didn't want to hear.

'Are you sure he said Perelli?'

I spotted a slight movement out on the terrace, and guessed Mifflin had arrived.

She turned away from me.

'Why should I make it up?'

I moved over to the casement doors. Mifflin, Paula and Mary Jerome were out there. I beckoned to Mifflin, motioning to Paula and Mary to remain where they were.

Mifflin came into the lounge like a cat on a hot stove.

Serena turned swiftly and stared at him.

'Dedrick's upstairs,' I told Mifflin. 'He's dead. Suicide.'

Mifflin grunted, walked quickly across the room to the door. I watched him mount the stairs.

'How – how did he get here?' Serena asked, her hand going to her throat.

'I guessed Dedrick would be here. I spotted him through the window and called Mifflin.'

'You – you used this phone?'

I nodded.

'Then Lee must have heard you and listened in. That's why he – he shot himself.'

I stared at her.

'Why should he shoot himself?'

She looked away.

'The police want him on a – a murder charge, don't they?'

'Yeah; so they do. I don't think it could have happened that way. I looked for a telephone extension in his room. There isn't one.'

She didn't say anything.

Then I had another idea: I was full of them tonight.

'You know he was married before he married you?' I said quietly.

She spun round; her face hardening.

'I don't wish to discuss that.'

'I thought you'd like to meet her. She's just outside.'

She started to her feet.

'I won't have her here! She's not to come in!'

'But she'll have to identify Dedrick. I'm afraid she'll have to come in.'

'No! I forbid her to come into my house!'

Her face had turned ashen, and her big, glittering eyes seemed to sink into her head.

'I loved him!' she went on wildly. 'I won't have that woman go near him!'

I went to the casement door.

'Come in,' I said to Mary Jerome. 'I want you to go upstairs and look at Dedrick. Don't pay any attention to her. I'll see she doesn't . . .'

I stopped short.

Serena had moved swiftly to a drawer in the writing desk at the other end of the room, pulled it open and swung around. She had a small automatic in her hand.

'She stays where she is!'

Mary stood quietly in the doorway, looking at Serena. Her eyes were cold and contemptuous.

'What are you afraid of?' I asked, moving slowly towards Serena.

'Stay where you are!'

I saw her knuckle tighten on the trigger and I stopped.

'Be careful,' I warned.

'Get that woman out of my sight! She's not going near him!'

'What's going on?'

Mifflin came in.

Outside, there came a squeal of brakes, and a pounding of feet on the terrace. Sergeant MacGraw and two uniformed cops burst into the room.

Serena took a quick step back. I was watching her. I saw her lift the gun, turning it on herself. There was a look of sick terror in her eyes as she pressed the barrel into her side. I was waiting for that move. I threw myself forward, knocking her to the floor as the gun went off.

Mifflin dashed forward, dropped on his knees and wrenched the gun out of her hand.

I rolled away from her.

She lay on her side, her head cradled on her arm, sobbing.

'Is she hurt?' Mifflin panted.

I shook my head, pointed to the bullet scar on the floor near her.

'What the hell goes on?' MacGraw barked. 'What is all this?'

'Take her upstairs and let her look at Dedrick,' I said, waving my hand to Mary Jerome. 'She has the answer to this, although she doesn't know it.'

'But what . . .' Mifflin began.

'Take her up. It's better to hear it from her than me.'

He shrugged, jerked his thumb to the door.

'Go ahead,' I said to Mary. 'It's all right. There's nothing to be scared of.'

She followed Mifflin, and as they climbed the stairs together, I lifted Serena and carried her to the settee. She lay on her side, her face hidden, her body racked with sobs.

MacGraw showed his teeth at me.

'So you're still solving them, Bright Boy,' he sneered. 'Right in there at the finish to tell us how it was done.'

'Well, someone's got to do it for you,' I said, and crossed the room to Paula.

'What is it, Vic?' she asked.

'Cross your fingers. This may be Perelli's out.'

We waited.

After a few minutes, Mary came down the stairs, followed by Mifflin.

'What do you know?' Mifflin said, breathing hard. 'That's not Dedrick up there. She says it's Lute Ferris.' He looked over at MacGraw. 'You know Ferris. Go up there and look at him.'

MacGraw ran up the stairs.

Mifflin said to me, 'Didn't she say he was Dedrick?' He nodded to Serena, who still lay on the settee, hiding her face.

I nodded.

MacGraw leaned over the banisters.

'It's Ferris all right,' he called.

'Then where the hell is Dedrick?' Mifflin demanded.

'Ask her. She'll tell you,' I said, pointing to Serena. 'It's my bet he's the heap of rags and bones in the mine.'

Serena suddenly sat up, her face white and her eyes glittering.

'I shot him,' she said in a voice scarcely above a whisper. 'And I shot Ferris too. Do what you like with me. I don't care. Do what you like with me.'

III

It was around five o'clock the next afternoon when the office door pushed open and Mifflin tramped in.

I was lolling in my desk chair. Paula was standing over Jack Kerman, who lay on the office couch. He had just returned from Paris, and at this moment was endeavouring to justify an expense sheet that looked like Danny Kaye's income-tax assessment.

'Twenty dollars a night for champagne,' Paula was saying, waving the expense sheet in Kerman's face. 'And nothing to show for it. Nothing at all.'

Kerman grinned feebly.

'Don't drive it into the ground,' he pleaded. 'A guy's got to live . . .'

'Come right in, Tim,' I said, taking my feet off the desk. 'I was hoping you'd look us up. Sit down. Hey, Jack, quit lying, and get the Lieutenant a whisky.'

'That's about all he's any good at,' Paula said tartly.

'Nice to hear I've even that to my credit,' Kerman said bitterly. He rolled off the couch and busied himself with glasses, while Mifflin lowered his bulk into a chair opposite my desk.

'Thought you'd want to know how it worked out,' he said. 'It's been some day. Brandon's having fits.' He blew out his cheeks. 'We had no trouble with Serena. She talked. It's a funny thing: once a woman really lets herself go, can she talk!'

'Men aren't exactly backward in that line either,' Paula reminded him gently.

He winked at me as he stretched out his hand for the whisky Kerman had poured him.

'This is going to do me a lot of good' he said, sipped and sighed appreciatively. 'Yeah, very nice, and I certainly need it. Francon has taken over Serena's defence. He had a lucky break. He was with Perelli when I brought her in. The way he switched from Perelli to her made me dizzy. Perelli was released about an hour ago. Brandon hated letting him out, but there was nothing else he could do after he'd listened to Serena. Perelli tells me he's coming round to see you as soon as he's located his girl friend. He said something about a celebration.'

'Hot dog!' Kerman said enthusiastically. 'We'll throw them a party!'

'And you can finance it,' Paula said.

'Do you want to hear the story the way Serena told it to Brandon?' Mifflin asked me.

'You bet.'

'Well, you weren't far off the beam. Souki started the trouble. He hated Dedrick at sight, and when Dedrick was staying with Marshland, Souki went through his baggage. He found evidence of Dedrick's smuggling activities as well as his marriage to Mary Jerome. Before he could report his discovery to Serena, he had to leave with Dedrick for Orchid City. He left the evidence in Serena's room. She promptly charted a plane and came after Dedrick. They met at Ocean End. Souki had returned to the Orchid Hotel, and was coming out to fetch Dedrick at ten. Serena accused Dedrick of marrying her bigamously. He laughed at her, admitting he had married her for what he could get out of her. Apparently you don't talk like that to a Marshland. She shot him.

'Dedrick had arranged to meet Barratt and Ferris at Ocean End. They walked in a few seconds after the shooting, and caught Serena red-handed. Barratt saw his chance, and took it. So long as the shooting wasn't discovered, he had Serena in his power. He offered to cover up the murder if she paid and continued to pay. There was no out for her.

'Ferris took Dedrick's body in his car and hid it in the mine while Barratt drove Serena back to the airport. He and Ferris returned to Ocean End and waited for Souki to return. They shot him and Ferris phoned you, making out he was Dedrick. By shooting Souki and phoning you they established the faked kidnapping had taken place at ten, whereas, of course, Dedrick had been murdered at eight; giving Serena an alibi.

'You know the rest of it. When Ferris heard Barratt was dead, he went to Ocean End and forced Serena to hide him. She heard you when you telephoned me, and listened in on her extension. She knew Ferris would talk if he was caught. She decided to silence him, hoping we would believe he was Dedrick. It was a gamble that might have come off. She went into Ferris's room, shot him and staged the suicide scene. If it hadn't been for Mary Jerome, she might have got away with it.'

I shook my head.

'I don't think so. I think Wadlock would have given her away. He knew Dedrick; and besides she slipped up when she said Ferris had listened in to my conversation with you. He hadn't a phone in his room. That made me wonder why he had shot himself so conveniently and suddenly. It crossed my mind then that maybe he wasn't Dedrick. What'll happen to her, Tim?'

Mifflin shrugged.

'With Francon looking after her, anything can happen. It's a wonderful thing what money can do.'

'I don't think even Francon can save her: not when the whole story comes out. What's happened to Mary?'

'She's in the clear. She'll be our chief witness, but we have nothing on her.' Mifflin heaved himself out of his chair. 'I guess I'll blow. Perelli doesn't seem to like coppers. I wouldn't want to spoil his celebration.'

When he had gone, Kerman asked casually, 'What's Perelli's girl like – nice?'

'Never mind what she's like,' Paula said briskly. 'You have other things to worry about just now,' and she reached for his expense sheet again. 'What's this item – fifty dollars for perfume?'

I settled down again to enjoy his feverish and unconvincing explanations.

NO ORCHIDS FOR MISS BLANDISH
BY JAMES HADLEY CHASE

When Dave Fenner was hired to solve the Blandish kidnapping, he knew the odds were against him – the cops were still looking for the girl three months after the ransom had been paid. And the kidnappers, Riley and his gang had disappeared into thin air. But what none of them knew was that Riley had been wiped out by a rival gang – and the heiress was now in the hands of Ma Grisson and her son Slim, a vicious killer who couldn't stay away from women . . . especially his beautiful new captive. By the time Fenner began to close in on them, some terrible things had happened to Miss Blandish . . .

0 552 10522 8   60p

THE SUCKER PUNCH BY JAMES HADLEY CHASE

Chad Winters was a small-time bank clerk – until he was put in charge of the Shelley account. Vestal Shelley was plain, a bitch . . . and worth over seventy million dollars. No one had ever dared stand up to her before – but Chad determined to get his hands on her money, found the perfect way to treat her . . . and ended up as her husband. But he hadn't reckoned on falling violently in love with Vestal's secretary – a ruthless woman who also wanted her share of the fortune . . . and who cunningly turned Chad's thoughts to murder . . .

0 552 10575 9   65p

A SELECTED LIST OF CRIME STORIES THAT APPEAR IN CORGI

WHILE EVERY EFFORT IS MADE TO KEEP PRICES LOW, IT IS SOME-
TIMES NECESSARY TO INCREASE PRICES AT SHORT NOTICE.
CORGI BOOKS RESERVE THE RIGHT TO SHOW AND CHARGE NEW
RETAIL PRICES ON COVERS WHICH MAY DIFFER FROM THOSE
ADVERTISED IN THE TEXT OR ELSEWHERE.

THE PRICES SHOWN BELOW WERE CORRECT AT THE TIME OF
GOING TO PRESS (FEB '78)

All these books are available at your bookshop or newsagent, or can be ordered direct from the publisher. Just tick the titles you want and fill in the form below.

....

CORGI BOOKS, Cash Sales Department, P.O. Box 11, Falmouth, Cornwall.

Please send cheque or postal order, no currency.

U.K. send 19p for first book plus 9p per copy for each additional book ordered to a maximum charge of 73p to cover the cost of postage and packing.

B.F.P.O. and Eire allow 19p for first book plus 9p per copy for the next 6 books, thereafter 3p per book.

Overseas Customers. Please allow 20p for the first book and 10p per copy for each additional book.

NAME (Block letters) ....

ADDRESS...

....